Transcending Love

Louise Jelley

Junonia Publications
www.junoniapublications.com

A CIP catalogue record of this book is available at the British Library.
This book is a work of fiction. Although some settings are real, the people depicted, businesses, organisations, places and events described are fictitious. Any resemblance to real persons, live or dead is purely coincidental.

ISBN 978-1-8382402-0-2

Louise Jelley lives in Warwickshire with her husband and two children. As well as writing, she works for a local charity. Transcending Love is her debut novel, but she is already working on her next; Glitch.

You can find Louise online at
www.louisejelley.com
Twitter - @LLJelley
Facebook - @AuthorLLJelley
#TranscendingLove

For Martin, Luke and Madelaine, thank you for your patience.
X

You're only ever supposed to die once in reality. Over the years I recall dying at least twice and yet I still have blood coursing through my veins and breath in my lungs and a waking consciousness. When it happens – death, that is – darkness descends, the cold becomes your new friend and paralysis engulfs you. But a new dawn brings light, warmth, and a desire to live, breathe and experience once again.

L.L. Jelley

Chapter One

Elise

'Elise, we've missed the alarm – the snooze just went off,' says Joel. The weight of Joel's arm momentarily pins me down, followed by the inevitable pull on the duvet to stir me from my slumber.

'No.'

'It's gone six thirty,' says Joel.

'No, leave me alone. I want to finish.'

'Finish what? Although I probably needn't ask,' says Joel.

'Nothing, only flying,' I reply.

'You'll have plenty of time to pick up where you left off tonight, when I'm not here,' says Joel.

'Oh great, Joel, thanks for reminding me. Where are you going again?' I ask, already knowing the answer to my question.

'Istanbul today; nowhere exotic. You can read all about my adventures on Thursday.'

'Oh, you're so annoying when you do that. I'm calling in sick, and I'm going to disappear into the depths and abyss of this duvet and all its togs.'

'You can't, we have to get up. Look, I'll be back on Friday and we've got Amanda and Henry coming over for dinner.'

Joel caresses my forehead with one hand, his other slipping under the duvet, his tenderness so comforting and his lips so soft. *This is where we should always be – together as one.*

'No. You're right, we must get up,' I say, easing Joel's hand away from my inner thigh, kissing him tenderly one more time, and pulling my lips apart from his. I take a moment to stare into his slate-grey eyes and then sit up. 'You're right, time to get up.' Joel's expression crumples, his eyes dropping and widening. 'You set the alarm, now I've decided I'm up. Don't flash those eyes at me. You have a plane to catch.' It's Joel who is now sinking back under the duvet pulling the pillow over his head, muffling his groans.

Our three-bed Victorian terrace is far from modernised and its heating system is something of a relic. On a cold frosty morning in March your breath can still be seen to rise in the air, and this morning is just that kind of morning. Spring has yet to be sprung. The single-glazed sash windows keep little heat in and little cold out, and what is not already frozen will run down the panes, pooling on the sill. The solution, or should I say our solution, for tackling this annual occurrence comes in the form of layers, for me multiple. Joel has got used to me layering up to survive the morning shudder until the warmth finally permeates the rooms. Sexy it isn't. My winter night-time wardrobe comprises brushed cotton pyjamas, hiking fleeces, ski tubes and a fluffy dressing gown. The only warm place is under the duvet with Joel, but sometimes a girl has to get up.

Grabbing my robe and my fluffy mules, I head for the bathroom. Joel, whilst having been the first to declare the need to rise, still lies across the bed hoping that my initial reluctance to stir was my way of inviting him to stay in bed for a little bit of love. How wrong is he? No, I wanted to dream, and as I have been awakened, my sleep having been broken, it's time to rise.

By the time I exit the bathroom, Joel is up and has brought me a mug of tea. He sits poised on the end of the bed, watching me dry and dress, his eyes looking me up and down.

‘Fine specimen,’ he declares.

Throwing my damp towel at him in response, I tell him, ‘Get a move on.’

Catching the towel, Joel stands up, tall and solid, my man. Moving past me towards the bathroom, flicking the towel towards my bottom, his cheeky smile broadens before he disappears behind the door.

We take only forty minutes to wash, dress and grab a bite. By ten past seven we head out to Reading Station; I want to catch the 7.27 a.m. train direct to Paddington, and Joel one a few minutes later that would go on to Heathrow.

We live a ten-minute brisk walk from the station, which is long enough for Joel and me to stride side by side, and even after a decade together we still hold hands.

‘What time on Friday do you think you’ll land?’ I ask.

‘Um, not sure yet; I’ll be back, promise. What’s on the agenda with you this week?’

‘Well, as you know, that is governed by the post bag. It can’t be as bad as last week though – “Poodle Parlour Antics” and “Spy Planes over London”.’

As usual, the foot traffic heading towards the station becomes denser, peak times being the worst.

When we bought here, so did everyone else. Our journeys to and from work now resemble those of ant workers, in one orderly line, no deviation from path, answering to the beck and call of the city.

On entering the station, Joel's hand tightens around mine. The last couple of minutes of our walk have been in silence, pondering the inevitability of goodbyes. Joel, having been away a lot recently, knows I worry about him and the places they send him on assignment. In my heart I know that Joel is just following his dream.

At the entrance to the platform, Joel lets the bag slip from his shoulder and then wraps his arms around me, encasing me in his body and his warmth. Releasing me a little, he takes hold of my chin and lifts it to his mouth where our lips slowly and softly touch. I pull away from him for the second time in no more than an hour; Joel is whispering, 'I'll call you Friday en route home; love you always.'

Puckering my lips, I blow him a kiss, then turn and walk towards the barriers leading to my platform.

It's the start of another beautiful day; to be precise, March 12th 2012, the 4,165th beautiful day since I had met Joel Hamilton.

Chapter Two

Joel

Once seated with the train underway, I pull out my tablet from my duffle bag and open the digital newspaper I downloaded earlier.

An elderly gentleman sits down in the vacant seat opposite and removes a tabloid from a carrier bag and turns the first page. We both catch each other's eye line, smile simultaneously, and then resume our respective reads. The rules of our journey having been set, we can both selfishly ignore one another without offence.

Scrolling through the headlines, the conflict in Syria dominates and overshadows the domestic news stories and economic turbulence. My focus wanes even at eight am, the prospect of twelve hours of travelling leaves me feeling woozy.

My mind scrolls to Elise. I hate goodbyes. At the station, as Elise turned to depart for her platform, a pressure pushed on the notch of my throat. The feeling lasted momentarily, as selfishly I'm excited to be off on assignment. Elise on the other hand wears her emotions like some wear a chain of office. She cannot disguise the glazing which brightens her eyes nor the slight quiver to the left side of her lip as she forces a smile. She worries, I know she does and I've seen those expressions before many times.

I said goodbye to my dad lots growing up and watched my mum's anxieties pour out at the thought of not knowing if he would return. When you're a kid growing up on a military base, you sort of understand what's happening, but for me my dad returned so life was good. For others, that was not always the case. By the time my dad retired from active duty and we moved to Sanibel Island, I had experienced more exposure and awareness of conflict than most of the other kids at my school. My work, whilst not in the military, takes me away often. So far, I always return.

Chapter Three

Elise

By eight forty-five, having survived a bracing walk from Oxford Circus to Broadwick Street, I breeze through the entrance to my office. *True Life* magazine is currently my life. I work in the Alternative Lives section producing copy for their monthly editorial. My office is on the third floor and overlooks the hubbub of Carnaby Street. A swift ride in the lift signals the start of another week.

'Morning guys – is anyone else cold or is it just me?' I ask whilst unbundling from my winter coat and making for my desk.

'It's you, Elise, most of the time, but you can have credit today as it is nippy,' Jo replies.

'I'm honoured, thank you for the credit. Pleasant weekend, Jo?' I ask.

'Yes, great thanks. Met a new man on Friday night; you missed a good evening.'

'Ooh, you must fill me in on all the juicy details. I want to know everything.'

'Well, first things first, ladies,' says Philip. 'We have an enormous post bag to go through this morning. There's quite a lot of celebrity gossip which needs reviewing, so Jo's sex life must wait for now.'

'Spoilsport,' I say. 'For all we know, Jo's sex life might be ten times more exciting than anything else in that post bag.'

'You may well be right, darling, but we need to find three more articles for the June cover, so unless Jo wants to do an exposé on Friday night's antics, we need to get reading,' replies Philip.

'Yes, boss,' Jo and I reply in unison.

Philip is Sub-Editor, I'm Lead Writer and Jo is Junior Writer having joined us six months ago. We're the small and beautifully formed team responsible for the weird and wacky: those stories that breach reality, border fiction, and defy belief. We manage the articles about the celebrities falling from fame rather than finding it. Writing for a magazine, especially writing such nonsense, is not what I thought I'd be doing ten years on from leaving university. Reminding myself that it pays the bills eases my underlying frustrations.

With the kettle on and the biscuit tin open, we arm ourselves with a pile of mail and set about the Monday morning routine. Seated in our oversized throne-like chairs, which we purchased for the office specifically for our break-out times, we scan the letters hoping to find a golden nugget for an article. When the mailbag is empty, we review the papers looking for small insignificant stories which can be developed. The stories about political intrigue, the economy, the state of the euro are all put to one side; instead, we focus on the sexual indiscretions or the demise of a local celebrity.

One article catches my eye, and is titled 'Dreams – What Do They Mean?' The article is by the magazine's resident agony aunt Jade Johnson. It's brief and was definitely a filler. Whilst the title is succinct enough to lure you in, the content is fleeting and comprises the statement that 'Dreams are part of your subconscious', followed by a list of types of dreams and their meanings. It's far from exhaustive with only eight dream themes covered, including water, sex and flying. That's it; the article ends with no real conclusion.

'What do you think of this one?' I ask Jo and Philip.

They both peer above their respective reads.

'"Dreams – What Do They Mean?"' I say.

'Oh yes, Elise,' Jo replies. 'That's right up your street – you could feature in the article.'

'Me, what do you mean?' I reply, trying to feign ignorance and offence in good measure.

'Well, you're the one who constantly tells us how much you dream, and how great they are,' says Philip.

'Yes. But this article is not about frequency, but meanings, and the story seems incomplete; it's barely an article in its current form. I believe it worthy of research.'

Jo nods, which is positive. Philip, raising his eyes above his glasses, says, 'Give it a whirl, but I must have a draft by the end of the week if it's to make June's cut.'

'Great.'

'Oh, and don't forget your backup story,' says Philip.

My backup story is one about a talking dog. I've been avoiding using it for ages. The talking dog – or to be precise, growling, snarling, yapping terrier – article is complete, but lacks some originality.

'You're lucky, Elise,' says Jo. 'Your imagination being what it is, that story will take you on a ride.'

'She's always on a ride,' says Philip. 'She doesn't need encouraging any more. I bet whatever you dreamt of last night was wild and exotic.'

'Yes,' I reply. 'But all too steamy to share with you.'

'No flying then?' asks Philip.

'There's always time for flying, Philip.'

'We should place you in a no-fly zone, Elise – you're a danger in the skies,' says Jo.

'Joel should pin you down at home more, keep you grounded,' Philip says with a wink and a smile.

The reddening and warming of my cheeks signals it's time to get to work and back to my desk. 'Joel's away now till Friday, so anything can happen.'

Seated, I re-read the article and focus on the brief meanings that are given for water, et cetera. 'Flying – you are suffering sexual frustration and need more freedom in the bedroom'.

'An explanation at last. Listen guys, according to Jade Johnson's article I must be sexually frustrated, as apparently that's what flying in dreams represents.'

'Oh good,' says Jo. 'It's not just me then.'

'But I'm not. It couldn't be further from the truth.'

'OK, thank you for that, Miss "I've got a good lay". Some of us are just happy with an old episode of *Sex in the City* to cuddle up to,' says Philip.

Philip is a gay guy who in the past five years has gone through many partners, all fleeting, none of whom could be considered relationship worthy. He's, in his own words, a male slut but is now taking a sabbatical from dating and is 'finding himself'. From this last comment, he's 'finding himself' in front of a box set of *Sex and the City* with Sarah Jessica-Parker; or would it be that character Stanford Blatch, Carrie's gay male best friend, who's the pull?

Anyway, research is what's needed to develop this dream story further. It has to be more than a list of possible meanings.

The internet – the portal to the global library and knowledge bank, an infinite sea of information – is great, but my first search of 'dreams' throws back 3,920,000,000 results. The top result being for a bed and mattress company which, whilst appropriate, is not what I'm looking for. Scrolling down, I find the definition of a dream: a series of thoughts, images and sensations occurring in a person's mind during sleep.

Information relating to research is widely available and there's definitely a divide between experts on the true purpose of dreams, so I must dig deep and find an angle.

After ignoring the results relating to aspirational dreams, I focus more on the subconscious ones. Dreams have been the topic of scientific, philosophical and religious speculation throughout history;

theorists appear to agree and disagree on their true purpose.

I have my own dream history, and I can't ignore it – the past, that is, and the present. I long to find meaning, and maybe this article will finally open my eyes. I refine my search parameters to 'subconscious dreams' which reduces the result to a mere 11,800,000. With so much information available it's difficult to know where to start, but results on the first page relate to scientific study as opposed to theories, so maybe science holds the key.

Chapter Four

Joel

With the first stretch of my journey by plane - London to Istanbul, Turkey, having departed on time, I drop down my seat tray and pull out my Arabic phrase book. My choice of phrases to learn is somewhat random. I want to be able to show respect to those that I'm interviewing, even if my interpreter has to do the rest.

The plane is full with couples and families casually dressed, seemingly travelling for pleasure, and businessmen and women in suits and blazers dressed for impending meetings on their arrival. Having surveyed the company I'm in, I relax, stretching out my legs under the seat in front and close my eyes. My mind drifts to Elise. She always marvels at how I manage to sleep anywhere, even standing up on a tube on one occasion, she said. Elise on the other hand is more of a fitful sleeper. Even last night I could sense her shuffling and turning in bed; dreaming.

I'm awoken by a rumbling which is intermittently accompanied by a female voice saying 'lunch madam, lunch sir.' The kind faced air hostess is stood to attention behind the rough-looking metal trolley. With a fixed smile, she passes me a plastic tray containing an empty cup, and a roll filled with something resembling egg.

'Coffee Sir,' she asks.

'Yes,' I reply, holding forward my plastic tray for her to fill my cup an inch.

'Milk Sir.'

'No.' I reply. 'Strong and black is what I need right now.'

The egg roll evaporates in seconds and with nothing else to eat I carefully position the plastic coffee cup towards the corner of the tray and open my pocket guide to Arabic in the vain hope of learning some more phrases.

'Swotting are we?' says the man to my left.

'Urgh, yes I suppose I am,' I reply.

'That's an Arabic phrase book if I'm not mistaken,' he says.

'Yes, I'm heading eastwards to Gaziantep to visit the Mosaic Museum hence the Arabic. I thought it might come in handy as the cultures change the further east you go. What about you, business or pleasure?'

'Business: a couple of meetings in Istanbul then back home again. I wouldn't want to be you going eastwards, you've heard the latest I assume. They've started bombing near the border now, near Aleppo,' he says.

'Yes, I've heard the news, but I won't be anywhere near there. Like you, my trip is short, as I said, just some museums.'

Not wanting to explain the whole journalism thing, a little lie is better than the truth. I don't want to become a target on what should be a fact finding humanitarian mission, although the Foreign Office has warned news agencies of the very real risks posed to journalists.

I return my focus to my Arabic guide and pick up my coffee cup delicately as dictated by the size of the handle and take a long sip, the coffee now cold is bitter and unpleasant.

When the Air Hostess returns to collect the tray, she asks once again if we want refills, this time I say 'No.'

Chapter Five

Elise

'Anyone coming out for lunch?' I ask.

Jo pops her head up from behind a newspaper and says, 'No, but can you grab me a wrap please? I'll give you the money when you get back.'

'Yes, OK. What about you Philip? Do you want to stretch your legs, or can I get you anything?'

'Yes, wait up, I'll come with you darling. I've been meaning to check out the new salad bar, you know, the one that has been shoehorned in between the estate agent's and the tapas bar. I saw a rather lovely chap there last week unloading lettuces, so I think salad for lunch is the order of the day. I'm sure they'll do a wrap to suit Jo's taste too.'

I button my coat and encircle my neck and shoulders with my oversized scarf before linking arms with Philip, heading for the elevator and exiting the building. The salad bar is located only a short stroll along Broadwick Street away from the tourists and mad shoppers. The fresh air is welcoming having been cocooned since before nine and the cacophony of horns, drills and voices provide a distraction from my morning's research. Every third building is undergoing some form of construction and is either draped in netting or shored up with scaffolding. The scaffolding provides a temporary resting place for dozens of pigeons, two of which are fighting over discarded chips which lie abandoned on the block weave paving that endlessly wears my heels away.

'Philip, before we get lunch I want to nip inside the newsagent's on the corner and grab a paper.'

'Don't you think we have enough papers back in the office?'

'Yes, but this one is for my personal use. It's a copy of Joel's paper. He's in Istanbul, you know.'

'Hasn't told you then, what he's covering?' says Philip in a rather superior all-knowing fashion.

'Yes, and no. Istanbul is where he's flying to. I do understand the reasons for him not telling me exactly what story he's covering, but not knowing sometimes feels worse. I worry; you know me. The world is unsettled, Philip, nowhere more so than in the Middle East, and whilst Joel might not spell it out to me, Istanbul in Turkey is Europe's doorway to the Middle East.'

'So, you're spying on him, then?'

‘It’s not spying, Philip, it’s research. I trust him; I just fear for him, that is all. Something sits uncomfortably with me when he’s away. Anyway, his actual article will not be published for a couple of days.’

On reaching the corner of Broadwick with Dufour’s Place I nip into the newsagent’s, grab a *Standard* and shoot out again into the cold. Crossing the road towards the salad bar, Philip pulls on my arm, pausing momentarily. The large plate-glass window, immaculately cleaned and shiny, provides a clear unobstructed view of all the deli delights. The words ‘compact and bijou’ come to mind. There isn’t a lot of room for customers inside, with a couple of high tables and chairs at the back, but the main pull appears to be the contents of the refrigerated counter full of salads and fillers. A brightly painted delivery bicycle stands propped up against a nearby railing, clearly signed ‘Wick’s Deli-ghts’.

‘Come on, I’m hungry. I can’t believe you’ve got me eating salad in March. What is the world coming to? All this for an introduction.’

Philip goes first and I follow, stepping over the threshold of the eatery and joining the queue.

‘Next.’

'Philip, you're up,' I say.

'Me,' Philip replies, putting his hand up like a naughty schoolboy.

'Yes, what can I get you?' the server asks.

'Falafel and feta wrap please, and I'll have a large mixed salad with warm peppers and chicken to take away, thank you. Elise, what would you like?' asks Philip.

'I'm not ready – too much choice. You get those; I need a minute.' I stand to the side of Philip giving him space, making sure that it's clear we're not a couple, despite us having linked arms earlier. That said, it wouldn't take a fool long to work out Philip was gay.

Stepping forward I order a salad, smile at the server – spending a moment to take in his looks and appeal – and then exit back out onto the pavement. 'Well, was that him? Was that lettuce guy? He's cute, I'll give you that.'

'Yes it was, thank you, and oh my lord he's cute, isn't he? Did you clock his jawline and frame? Just so lovely,' replies Philip. Linking arms once more I can feel Philip's excitement, the judders reverberating through my elbow.

'Well, do you think he's gay – did you get a vibe?'

‘Not sure just yet; I’ll have to eat salad a lot this week. I may get a better idea tomorrow. He looks good though, doesn’t he?’

‘They do deliveries Philip, you could always have him come to you.’

‘Give it time darling, give it time.’

Philip’s excitement at the prospect of some new eye candy on the street is evident, and it does not surprise me that his sworn oath of celibacy may already be coming to an end.

Once back in the office, I briefly fill Jo in on the salad bar and its potential, and then attach myself back to my desk. With a plastic fork in one hand and a mouse in the other, it’s time to continue my research, with realisation dawning that it’s a much bigger subject than I imagined.

Page after page, various experts would appear to claim that dreams cannot be controlled, but from my own experiences I know that not to be true. I’ve had awareness of my dreams for years and more recently definitely have control, especially when flying. If I want to go somewhere, or climb to escape, I can. I force myself to fly, to rise. It requires focus, but I can determine my destiny.

Opening up some of the entries links me to history websites with articles claiming that dreams are recorded as far back as 5,000 years ago, or 3,000 BC, during the Mesopotamian era. The Mesopotamians believed a person's soul leaves the body during a dream and visits the places the dreamer sees in their sleep. Romans believed dreams were messages from the gods. With ancient history now being quoted, it actually looks like I've some sound basis on which to explore. The whole 'soul leaving the body' idea does resonate with me and definitely warrants further exploration.

Websites and individual records detail extracts from documents produced by experts and theorists, with Sigmund Freud and Jung both believing sexual tension was at play and 'unconscious repressed emotions'. *Why does it have to come down to sex? And what are 'unconscious repressed emotions' anyway?* Even after 5,000 years, there appears to be no tangible proof of what happens during a dream.

'I'm off, are you nearly finished Elise?' says Jo.

'I don't think I've even scratched the surface, but I'll wind up soon. Has Philip gone already?' I ask.

'Yes,' replies Jo. 'He snuck out a few minutes ago. He said he'd enjoyed his salad so much he wanted one for tea, so wanted to catch the deli before they closed.'

'It'll only end in tears – our tears of laughter when we listen to his tales. I think I'll give him an Elise chat tomorrow and remind him of his celibacy vow. If he gets too hyped up over this one, he'll only have further to fall.'

'Yes, one of your agony aunt chats should do the trick. You know, you really have missed your vocation there. See you tomorrow, don't stay too late.'

'I won't, I'll finish and be out the door soon. Have a good evening. Bye.'

Needing to work on the specific meaning of dreams, I enter a search query and wait for the results. 75,000,000 entries. *No way, not tonight; I barely got past page three on my last search.* That's my cue. Time to go. I can pick it up again tomorrow, and if all else fails there's always the talking dog article.

Chapter Six

Joel

Twelve hours' travelling on a combination of trains and planes and I finally arrive at my destination; for tonight anyway.

Oğuzeli Airport, Gaziantep in Turkey is deserted as I clear security and make my way to the exit. As expected, I'm greeted in the arrivals hall by a man holding a board with my name handwritten in black marker pen: Mr Hamilton. The unassuming man is casually dressed in trousers, not jeans, an open-necked checked shirt, a heavy jumper and a scarf. Having only spoken to Emin, my interpreter, on the telephone I decide to take a leap of faith and assume he's my welcoming party.

Stretching out my hand towards him, I say, 'Emin, *as-salaam alaykum,*' meaning 'peace be upon you'.

'*Ahlan was sahlan,* welcome, Mr Hamilton,' he replies with a broad smile. Reassuringly Emin then carries on in English.

'Long journey, Mr Hamilton?' says Emin.

'Yes, just a bit, but I'm here now.'

'You have been practising your Arabic, Mr Hamilton.'

'You could say that, but poorly, as you'll soon find out. I'll try, but I need you to do most of the translating for me.'

'No problem, Mr Hamilton. Let me get you to the hotel; I have a car waiting. Are you hungry?'

'Not really, I just need sleep and a wash.' With no bags to collect, we exit the airport into the fresh night air and to a waiting car. Emin rides shotgun with the driver and I take to the back seat with my duffle bag.

'What time do we leave in the morning?' I ask.

'Early, I am afraid; we have a car collecting us at eight. We go to Reyhanli Camp first and then on to Yayladagi, but they will not allow us to stay after four. We can return on Wednesday if necessary.'

'That's good. Let's see how tomorrow goes. What we find will determine if we need to return.'

'Very good; we are nearly there – your hotel is just a couple more minutes away.'

Driving through Gaziantep seems so normal considering the potential carnage being unleashed over the border in Syria. Gaziantep is, at first sight, a bustling city even at night, illuminated, vibrant and modern.

On arrival at my hotel, I quickly exit the vehicle and bid Emin farewell until the morning.

My hotel is several stories high with clean architectural lines. The interior is cool and calming with lime green and grey cube seating placed throughout the lobby, bar and lounge area. It's functional, albeit a little soulless, and the extensive marble flooring, whilst light and shiny, feels like a cold slab underfoot. Travelling over the years as a journalist accustoms you to all sorts of accommodation, but here I expected, well, less. Maybe because the refugee camp is close by it seems wrong to be indulging in relative luxury compared to their situation, the sum of which I will find out tomorrow; but for now a bed and shower beckon. Emin will soon return for what promises to be an eventful day.

Chapter Seven

Elise

I find the air fresh and welcoming, having been cooped up on the train coming out of London. The walk home, whilst taking just ten minutes, is in darkness, my breath lingering in the air, unable to keep up with me. Walking briskly brings me to the doorstep.

The glow from the timer light in the front room floods through the bay window, but the rest of the house is black, reminding me once again that Joel is away – not for one night but four. Turning the key and pushing the door open, I feel warmth emanating from within, inviting me in.

Once inside, door locked and chain secured, I unfasten my coat and leave it bundled on the hall bench with my bag. Walking through to the kitchen, I flick a switch, which illuminates and brightens, and the house comes alive. A plate of leftover omelette in the fridge will make a satisfying meal once covered in baked beans, and a glass of wine will wash it down. If Joel were home I wouldn't be eating leftovers for tea.

No, he would create something out of nothing, fresh and hot.

Leaving the microwave to hum away, I run upstairs to get changed, putting on yoga pants and one of Joel's sweaters. Once I'm back downstairs, the distinctive ping chimes in the kitchen. The sweet comforting smell suggests I've cooked myself a masterpiece. Taking a sip of wine, armed with cutlery, I make my way through to the front room, placing the plate down on the coffee table.

Slumping onto the sofa, grabbing the remote, I awaken the TV with one click and an evening of channel-hopping begins. With a programme running in the background, fork in hand, I combine eating with flicking through the newspaper I'd purchased at lunch.

The continuing conflict in Syria and the refugees descending on the Turkey and Jordan border areas dominate. Knowing full well that Joel would really want to be covering the frontline itself makes my heart start to trot. He hasn't gone away for long enough to be thrown into the fight, so with any luck it'll be the refugee crisis he covers on this occasion.

With my tea soon devoured, I pop back to the kitchen and grab a packet of crisps and a chocolate bar. As I'm walking back through to the sitting room, a robotic tone chirps from my mobile.

'Hello.'

'Hi, Elise.'

'Oh, hi, Amanda, how are you?'

'Great, thanks, I just wanted to check the arrangements for Friday,' says Amanda.

'Friday's good; Joel promises he'll be home, we're looking forward to it. It seems like it's been ages.'

'Great, we are too. What can we bring apart from the usual bottles?'

Pausing momentarily, I clear my throat before continuing. 'I don't know, Amanda, I've no idea what Joel's cooking. He'll probably decide on his way home. Look just bring a bottle, that's all. You're staying over, aren't you?'

'Yes, if we can. How are you coping with Joel away?'

'Fine. First night is always the worst, you know, but I've just done myself tea and am about to tuck into dessert.'

'What you mean is you microwaved a ready meal and are having a chocolate bar for pudding. I'm right, aren't I, Elise?' I might not be able to see Amanda but

I can visualise her forehead pinching at the mere thought of microwaved food and multipacks.

'Yes, you're right, but it's all good. The food needed eating. "Waste not, want not", they say. I'll pop to the shops tomorrow and cook myself something fresh.' *Even when I'm home alone the food police are checking up on me.*

'Look after yourself, Elise. You don't want Joel coming back home to a heffa that's lived on takeaways all week.'

'I get the message. I'll have you know I plan to get some running in this week, and you can't talk. When was the last time you entered your kitchen?'

'OK, deuce. Right, we can carry on abusing each other on Friday. What time should we arrive? I'm sure you will want Joel to yourself for a bit – you know what I mean.' Amanda's voice trailing off suggestively.

'How about we say any time after seven, if that's OK with you?'

'Yes, great, can't wait. Look after yourself and we'll see you Friday. Bye, lovely.'

'Bye.'

*

Big Ben's bongs followed by the blaring sound of the *News at Ten* bring me round from a momentary doze. It's time for the comfort of a proper bed rather than a sofa. Having drifted off already downstairs, it'll not take me long to fall asleep.

*

The air feels cool, chilled by the night sky, but not pure. It's heavy, laden almost. Thrusting forward, I race towards a cluster of shapes on the ground which, from a distance, look like mounds too large to be made by an insect. Nearing them, dropping low enough to make out what they are, I feel the weight of the air increase; my eyes sting – I must not rub them, I must not lose focus. Wherever I am it's rural, no high-rise buildings or modern structures, just vast swathes of land. The land is arid with very little greenery. Flying lower, I skim the ground, and the surface ripples. This is a desert.

Gaining height, with the view ahead clearer, I see the clusters are domed-shaped constructions. Some sit isolated, others linked in pairs, all varying sizes. Illumination from the moon emphasises their curvature; they are sparsely spread, separated by walls, reminiscent of beehives. A village, or maybe a town? A new discovery from my aerial perspective – a gathering of people in front of one of the larger conical towers. Ten, fifteen people maybe, dressed in ankle-length robes, turbans, and all sporting beards; men all together. Hovering above, observing, I'm intruding. They kneel in lines and start swaying in unison. They're praying. This is private.

Swooping, covering an infinite distance in the blink of an eye, I'm being drawn towards a much larger conurbation – a city, a long way off and yet still visible on the landscape. Approaching fast, I pull up above what appears to be a crater, large and circular. Descending lower, the view becomes clearer. The crater is ruins; not ruins caused by modern-day warfare, but historic and aged. This is a landmark for a city or region, one that was prominent many years ago and now sits within its heart.

Gaining height, thrusting to keep momentum, I circle this city that's illuminated orange. Its expansive network covers vast distances. It's alive and vibrating, and the faint but distinctive amplified wailing in Arabic signals a call to Morning Prayer.

Dawn breaks, the world is waking.

The city light diminishes, and uniform parallel lines appear: rows upon rows of tents, identical, white with sloping tops. People are milling around as small as ants below, babies, children crying, hidden in the shadows. These are not homes, and this is no holiday camp. A fire lit in a far corner of the enclosure keeps the company of men. Detached from society, they have a temporary existence, clinging to life.

The sun is rising; the warmth turning cold, the light to dark…

Chapter Eight

Joel

Whilst a few degrees warmer than home, it's nevertheless still cool, but the day looks promising. Parked outside the hotel foyer an old style Toyota hums away idly. *My ride?*

Emin stands expectantly, adjacent to the rear passenger door.

'Morning, Emin.'

'Morning, Mr Hamilton, how are you today? Did you sleep well?' Emin patiently stands with his hands loosely crossed in front of him waiting for my response.

'Yes, Emin, very well thank you; just not long enough. So how far have we to travel today?'

'Quite a way, Mr Hamilton. Reyhanli is nearly three hours by car and then it's at least another hour onto Yayladagi.'

'Well, I'd better do a thorough job today, then, as I'm not sure I want to make the journey twice. Did you say we're starting in Reyhanli?'

Even at eight in the morning the road outside my hotel is busy and the noise from the stream of traffic obliterates some of Emin's words. 'Yes, Mr Hamilton. They are expecting us at eleven. We can leave straight away if you are ready.'

'Yes, I'm ready. I take it this is our ride?' Emin pulls open the rear passenger door and gestures for me to get in.

'Yes, it is. It is best not to hire a vehicle or use a new one. An old car like this attracts less attention. This is Ata; he will be our driver today and tomorrow and he is very safe, I assure you, Mr Hamilton.' I duck and step sideways into the car and onto the rear seat, placing my rucksack to one side. Emin then firmly shuts the door before climbing into the front passenger seat in front of me.

'Sounds good to me. Morning, Ata, thank you for driving today; are you clear on where you're going?'

'Yes, Mr Hamilton – Emin has given me the details.'

'Mr Hamilton, Ata has explained to me the timings for travelling today and we will have only two hours in each camp. Also, Mr Hamilton, Ata does not speak much English, just Turkish.'

'Thanks, Emin. Two hours is not a lot.'

As we clear the city swell of Gaziantep the roads open up, as does the countryside, with a vast barren landscape interspersed between the towns and villages. I close my eyes and for once in my life feel unable to sleep. My mind turns over the questions I need to ask. Softly Emin and Ata chat away in Turkish, oblivious to the turmoil unravelling in my mind, and my stomach. Even with my eyes closed, the swerving and jolting paint a picture of the unseen landscape.

'Mr Hamilton, are you awake? We are nearing Reyhanli,' says Emin twisting towards me his tone soft.

'Yes, yes I am.' Opening my eyes and squinting, filtering the harsh sunlight now streaming in through the dusty windows, I see the approach to Reyhanli now within view. Reyhanli as a town has so far been untouched by the neighbouring troubles in Syria, but it's not as modern as Gaziantep and the buildings look tired and run down. The camp itself is just outside the main town, a large area separated from the rest of society, surrounded by wire and barbed fencing.

Prominent in the distance, the bright red Turkish flag with its star and crescent dominates the peak of the border guards' tower. Pausing at the entrance,

Emin engages one of the guards in conversation whilst another checks our papers. A steady stream of people – men, women and children – file in. They're laden with bags, their sole possessions limited to what they can wear and carry.

Once inside, the sheer size of the camp is apparent; rows upon rows of stark white tents are neatly aligned with only three feet separating them. A makeshift road has formed down the centre, strewn with litter and covered stalls for traders. Washing hangs on the outside of the tents and smoke is billowing from within.

At first glance, the tent city seems quiet and orderly, with no immediate signs that the residents have just fled a conflict zone. What strikes me are the children. Groups of them, mixed in age from as young as two to maybe fifteen, are running around, playing, entertaining themselves, smiling and happy.

'Mr Hamilton, I have arranged for you to talk with several families who were amongst the first to arrive. The Turkish authorities insist that they have a representative present during your interviews.'

'OK, Emin. That's fine with me. What about the people who are just arriving or those that have recently come across? Would I be able to speak with them? After all they might tell me something about the conflict and what they have escaped from, you know, I could get some current perspective on the problems they're facing. No one expected refugees to still be flooding in.'

'I will ask, Mr Hamilton. Ata is to stay with the car. If you are ready, we can start.'

We are welcomed into a couple of tents. They are compact and yet house entire families, regardless of size. The authorities provide them with communal washing facilities for bathing and also to wash clothes, but they rely on the weather to get clothes dry. Possessions are limited and some of those who had arrived a few months ago wearing winter clothing don't have clothes suitable for the oncoming summer. Those who came by vehicle across the border talk of selling off possessions to get cash to buy basic food supplies, although they all, without exception, praise the generosity of the locals who provide bread daily.

The horrors endured are etched on their faces. Young men appear old, aged by the conflict and the responsibilities they now have as heads of households. Some boys, maybe only fifteen years of age, are responsible for the family, their fathers and brothers having been killed. Seemingly, the women take on the domestic chores and are not encouraged to speak.

'Emin, ask them if they still have faith?'

I listen intently to Emin engaging with the families, empathising with their plight; he's a humble man who, whilst of Turkish origin, has previously worked in Syria and knows of many of the towns and cities that the refugees have fled from.

'They believe they will be saved. They have faith,' says Emin.

'What do they mean, Emin?'

'Several of the family elders maintain that balance will return to the region. A bright light, not a star, was sighted over the camp last night and they have taken this as a sign. They are deeply religious, Mr Hamilton, and this news, it would appear, is spreading amongst the refugees. Personally, I am not sure. Logic would suggest that if it wasn't a star then maybe it was a helicopter or plane, nothing more, but whatever it was it has given them hope and that is what they need right now.'

'OK. Shall we move on and see if we can chat to some recent arrivals? Please thank them for their time and wish them well.'

'Yes, of course.'

A group of new arrivals sit on benches either side of a large wooden refectory-style table and are all tucking into some fresh bread. For some, this is their first meal in days. Children are clinging to their parents, their faces sad and unwashed. Whatever they've escaped from, the images are still raw in their minds.

Emin greets all the men in the group and explains to them why we are here. They are keen to share their stories and answer Emin's questions. Their overly exaggerated hand movements and chatter signal their excitement at being invited to recall tales.

Fighting, escaping, bombing and shelling are themes. They don't know each other. They're not related but have formed friendships along the route and across the border. One man explains that he has lost his son within the past few days – a small boy who fell asleep one cold night and didn't wake up again. He had no time to grieve as he needed to carry on moving, to keep the rest of his family alive.

'They have hope too,' says Emin. 'They believe that they will be saved and able to return to their homeland. Two of the men report seeing a bright light flashing through the sky near Aleppo. They describe it as a moving star but believe it to be a deity, a god or a sign from God.'

'When was this, Emin?'

'Last night, Mr Hamilton. It sounds like the same light being sighted, but in two different places. It could still be a plane or helicopter.'

'Emin, Mr Hamilton, it is time for us to go,' says Ata.

'Thank you, Ata. I'm glad someone is watching the clock. Let's get on the road to Yayladagi. Emin, once again please thank these men and their families for their time and wish them well.'

The journey to Yayladagi provides me with an opportunity to review my notes. The humanitarian aspects are all covered well, the photographs speak volumes; I just need a second perspective. Intriguing as it is, the flashing white light mentioned by several men is probably nothing, no more than a plane, although most of those that we spoke to have taken it as a religious sign.

I can't dismiss this sighting, this potential story, out of hand, but at the same time it can easily be explained away and, after all, the reports are from people who are clinging to hope, traumatised, and suffering from starvation and exposure to the elements. Your mind can play tricks on you when you are under pressure, and when you are looking for a positive out of a negative, you will grasp at anything.

On arrival at Yayladagi, Emin ingratiates himself with the elders at the camp who are more than happy to give us an audience. Children happily play and pose for photographs, showing us their makeshift soccer pitch and their prized ball. It's a ball which is no longer black and white, the hexagonal patterning now faded, worn and peeling, but it still rolls. A loudspeaker booms messages around the camp in Turkish and Arabic; according to Emin, it announces the arrival of food supplies and medical aid.

'Emin, I would like you to ask them specifically about their faith, but don't lead them.'

Emin crafts a question which, once delivered, is met with silence. Not one reply. The men instead look at each other. Their expressions and raised eyebrows signify disbelief, as if a secret has been leaked. One by one they nod until an elderly gentleman, maybe the oldest in the group, with an impressive-looking beard, answers. It isn't a frantic, urgent answer like the ones Emin had received in Reyhanli. The man is not anxious and desperate to tell a tale. Instead, he proffers a slow and thoughtful, measured response, the other men nodding as if agreeing with the tale being told.

Whatever he is saying pricks Emin's attention. Emin looks across at me twice whilst the elderly gentleman recounts the tale. Emin says nothing, but I can tell from his expression that he too is a little concerned, maybe even perplexed by what he's hearing. Emin is definitely not dismissive, though.

'Well?' I say impatiently.

'Mr Hamilton, I will have to transcribe the recording for you. The reply was very long but in essence he said that several people had seen a sign from Allah, possibly an angel sent to save them, and that they have fresh hope for the future, a renewed faith.'

'How would they describe it, Emin?'

'A white light moving in the sky, but with the form of a person, not a machine.' 'Can you ask them if anyone has a picture, you know, evidence?'

Emin delivers his next carefully crafted question and waits. Silence. The men look to the elderly man with the beard once more to respond.

My impatience is getting the better of me. Calming myself, I hold my pencil and note pad firm.

Emin turns to me and says, 'Yes there is a picture, just one, but it shows just a white light, nothing more.'

'Can we see? Ask them if they have it, or if not, who does?' Feeling bad for barking orders, I make a mental note to apologise. The tent is silent. They say nothing. One of the younger men instead places his hand in his trouser pocket and pulls out a phone. Having accessed it, he passes it to Emin.

Emin stares at the photo for a few seconds before passing it to me. There, as clear as day, is a white flash in the night sky. The flash is accompanying the very faint outline of a person. *What am I looking at? What is this? What does it mean? And most of all, how can I get a copy?*

'Emin, I would like a copy of this image. Please can you ask the man if he would be happy to send me the photo by text?'

'Emin and Mr Hamilton,' says Ata, stood rigidly at the tent entrance.

'Yes, Ata?' I look at Emin and without speaking Emin knows what I'm thinking: it would need to be him who asks Ata what the issue is, not me, as I'm the sad English-speaking person who has no clue what's being said.

‘Mr Hamilton, Ata said that the guards would like us to leave now. It is ten past four and we must go.’

‘OK. Emin, will he text me the image?’

‘No, he will not, Mr Hamilton. He is afraid of what will happen.’

‘OK, right, well can I have one more look at it? Maybe I can photograph the image from the phone.’

‘I will ask,’ says Emin. ‘They are happy for you to look at it again, but not for a copy to be made; here is the phone.’

As I hold the phone and absorb the image once more, Ata pokes his head through the entrance to the tent, this time accompanied by a Turkish guard. The elders stand immediately and are briefly distracted by the guard and what he’s saying. We’re outstaying our welcome, but I seize the opportunity and snap a picture of the image on my phone.

‘There you go, Emin, please thank them for their time and wish them well for the future. I think it’s time for us to go.’

‘Yes, Mr Hamilton, I think it is. Are we finished here, or do you need to stay another day?’

‘No, we’re finished. Let’s head back to Gaziantep and tomorrow we can review and transcribe the tapes.’

'Very well. Ata, please head to Gaziantep.'

Tomorrow has potential. First I'll review my notes, then the transcriptions and photographs, and then research. I'll be researching if any other flashing lights have been sighted near the border. The captured image might just be the only evidence available of this reported phenomenon. It could be a star or even the burning tail of a meteor, and it could also be a hoax.

Chapter Nine

Elise

With no comfort blanket keeping me tied up in bed, I head into work early, on a mission. Mission research.

Picking up where I left off the night before is easy. With a long list of key questions to check out, there's a need to be selective with the data, as it's endless.

Dream dictionaries. I've never seen one on the shelf of the local bookshop, but online they're everywhere either as dictionaries or interpretative guides. There's *DreamWorks, Dream Cloud, Dream Moods, Body and Soul* and, yes, *Dream Dictionary,* all promoted by websites. They contain meanings and interpretations for everything. You name it, it's there, from emotions – sadness, happiness, love, hate – to animals, including turtles and snakes, objects, actions and activities. Defining dreams is seemingly big business and yet the question remains, why? Who, after all, are these people behind the businesses, promoting these alleged meanings?

Is it all pretence? There's no tangible evidence whatsoever that a given meaning of a dream is correct. There are historical resources indicating that interpretations were often prophetic. For centuries kings and leaders looked to those who had vivid dreams to interpret them and guide them, even for use in war. The Bible also appears to have dozens of references to dreams. Everything I read suggests that only in the last 100 years have more rudimental interpretations been applied.

'Morning, Elise, you're in early; no Joel to keep you warm?' says Jo.

'How perceptive of you, Jo.' Bouncing through the door following Jo is a rather smiley Philip.

'Morning, Jo, morning, Elise,' says Philip.

'Morning, Philip – you seem chipper. Pray tell,' I say.

'Well, darling, it started with me getting salad for tea last night and ended with a name and telephone number.'

'Well done you, although Jo and I were only saying yesterday that maybe, just maybe, you should steer clear of the salad bar and stick to your resolution. We wouldn't want it to end in tears – our tears, of course.'

'I know, I'm a wicked boy and I'm pleased that my personal life keeps you entertained, but I couldn't help myself. Anyway, whilst I have his number I haven't called him yet. No, I'm waiting. I think I'll get salad for lunch today and see what he says, if anything.'

'*Sex in the City* on box set will not break your heart, whereas...'

'I get the drift. Anyway, talking of hearts, you're in early this morning; couldn't sleep?' says Philip.

'No. I slept, I dreamt and I'm still quite tired, if you must know, but I thought I would crack into some research. Not that it's looking like an article at all yet,' I say, stretching to awaken my crumpled torso.

'Friday, remember, Elise, I need your drafts and a backup,' says Philip with a wag of finger.

'Oh yes, task master, I'm on course for Friday but maybe not the dream one.'

'Why not, Elise?' asks Jo. 'I thought it would've been right up your street.'

'It is, but it's far more complex and I'm not sure of an angle. Coupled with the fact that the *True Life* readership might not have the collective grey matter to comprehend it.'

'Ooh, we are uppity this morning; not only was it an empty bed but you got out the wrong side,' says Philip with a tight lipped disapproving expression.

'That came out wrong,' I say apologetically. 'Dream interpretation is complex. I've read loads in the last twenty-four hours, but it's such a vast subject. Unless I've a specific angle to work with, I'll not be doing the story justice. Whatever happens, Philip, on Friday you'll have plenty of material to choose from; I've never let you down – well not yet, anyway.'

'Drink anyone?' says Jo as she grabs the tray and collects up yesterday's mugs.

'If I say gin you would probably get me one, but I need a clear head so tea please. Thanks, Jo.'

Dropping my head down towards the keyboard, inhaling deeply, the enormity of the subject weighs heavily. The research intrigues me and potentially might answer questions I've asked all my life. I still have questions, personal ones that I want answered, but it'll not be the June article Philip wants it to be, that's for sure.

It's time to look up the Mesopotamian era and their history of dreams. Several websites talk of the Mesopotamians believing that the soul left the body during sleep and visited other places. That's also supported by Chinese historians. The flying I experience could be explained as my soul leaving my body. After all, I feel as if I go to lots of places and the rush and whoosh that accompanies each experience may well be the wrenching of the soul from my physical being. *I know what Joel would say.*

Joel's never quite understood my flying experiences. The day that I demonstrated it to him just had us rolling around in fits of laughter as I thrust my chest forward as if a superhero. It's fair to say I did not look like a superhero. There was no cape, no arm stretching forward, pointing where I wanted to go. No, my thrusting and thrashing around looked more like a beached whale in distress and had us both in stitches. Whilst I tried in vain to demonstrate the physical feeling of flying I was unable to convey the intensity and pull that accompanies the experience. It's a propulsion forward as if everything from your chest upwards has an engine powering it. *No wonder he's never taken my dreams seriously.*

'What are you laughing about, Elise?' says Jo.

'Nothing really, just flying and Joel, that's all.'

'You miss him a lot, don't you?'

'Yes, I do. I worry too, which is why I think I'm dreaming a lot, and feeling tired, but that's love, Jo. You'll find your man one day.'

'You never know, I may well have already; after all, the chap I met on Friday is quite nice. How did you know Joel was the one for you?'

'I just did. We met at university and fell in love.'

'There has to be more to it than that.'

'Are you two working?' asks Philip.

'Yes, Philip, it's research. Elise is about to tell me how she met Joel and fell in love,' replies Jo.

'I'm definitely not research.' Leaning forward my elbows perched in front of my keyboard I proceed to share my secret of finding and falling in love.

'Joel and I met at Birmingham University during what was my second year. I didn't really meet him, but more bumped into him, literally. I blame one of my mates – Jules, actually. We had drunk a cocktail concoction of vodka, gin and vermouth and then Jules and I cycled from the campus heading for one of the student hangouts. As I said, I literally bumped into Joel as he was stepping off the pavement – I virtually cycled over him.'

'Did you know straight away he was the one?' asks Jo leaning forward on the heel of her palms staring straight at me.

'I would like to say it was love at first sight, and I believe it was, but first sight was really through an alcohol-fuelled haze with a slightly concussed twinkle. I do actually recall seeing stars when our heads hit. Joel blamed himself for jaywalking and wanted to make it up to me. Buying me a drink was not the best idea, so instead I took a leap of faith and left the girls and walked back with Joel to his place. Joel was very chivalrous pushing my bicycle; it was, it turned out, all of about 500 metres back to one of the university student halls. Not the same one that I was in, but one which was not a million miles away.

'We talked endlessly on the way to his room. Looking back, it was nerves and the alcohol, but I never once felt awkward. You would have been proud of me, I was able to keep a steady pace in a straight line walking beside Joel, close but not touching. In those few early moments of the birth of our relationship, just like the creation of the earth, we were connected. The warm and fuzzy tingling feeling was firing the very atoms which formed us. The urge of being unconditionally drawn to him overwhelmed me.'

'That all sounds so yummy,' says Jo.

'By the time I had entered Joel's room, my head had cleared. Joel offered me a coffee and went off to the communal kitchen to make it, leaving me alone in his room. The room was adorned with newspaper articles and magazine extracts, and as it transpired, his ambition was to be a journalist – figures, right? There was nowhere really for me to sit and I wasn't going to sit on the bed, so I stood and waited. I can remember him returning and as he walked through the door, I jumped a little as if I'd relaxed too much and had been caught off guard. I'd done nothing wrong, but Joel was, after all, a stranger, a good-looking one at that, and I was in his room. God, I remember it as if it was yesterday.

'Joel pulled out two bean bags from under his bed and we slumped in unison to the floor and continued chatting for hours. He formally introduced himself, 'I'm Joel George Hamilton, nice to meet you.' It was so formal it made me instantly smile, and I felt compelled to reply in the same way, 'I'm Elise Williams, no middle name, nice to meet you too.' We talked about his folks in America, mine in Warwickshire; him being born to an American dad, George, and English mum, Violet; his gap year before Birmingham and his dad having been in the military. We shared our life stories in those first few hours. I think it was past four when our night came to an end.'

'Is that it?' says Jo.

'No. I can remember the noise of the other students returning from their evening out, and their fun and games seemed to continue in their rooms and in the kitchen. The walls were thin and nothing, including privacy, was sacred. It was one of Joel's mates that first burst into the room, obviously not expecting to see me sat there on the floor. As quickly as he entered, he left, but it was enough to break our conversation and brought us back to the reality of the time, place and situation.

'Standing up from the beanbag, feeling sluggish and tired, I was met at head height by an equally tired Joel. Whilst as you know he is taller than me, our faces were parallel to each other. The depth of his eyes looked into mine, his breath warm. We weren't touching, but I tingled, there was an obvious tension between us. I could feel it and I knew he could too. We stood transfixed, glued to the spot, millimetres apart. The first touch I felt of his lips on mine was warm, soft and sweet. He kissed me, taking control, leading the way that our lips would move into each other. My hands were instinctively grabbing the back of his jeans and I was pulling myself close into him, feeling his warmth and tone. He cupped my face with his hands soft, not rough, and focussed just on my mouth, lingering after each movement. My body was melting, and ours were warming up together, the heat was rising, then most rudely the door burst open again. This time I remember I jumped back, away from Joel, releasing my grip, my hand now touching my lips, holding onto that last kiss. God, just talking about it again makes me want him.' I feel lost in the moment as I hug myself, oblivious to my audience.

I start again, 'I can remember feeling embarrassed all of a sudden, with the intruder once again vanishing as quickly as he had appeared, but the moment had now paused. A button had been pressed which would allow us both time to breathe and consider what was happening.'

Jo sits transfixed, her gaze hanging on my every word.

'I recall looking up at Joel, his eyes wide. The urge to rush was overwhelming, and we moved closer, but this time I recall nestling my head into his broad chest, into an embrace which I've felt so many times over the years since that first night, but one which, on that occasion, signified that the pause button would remain pressed.

'Nothing was said. Joel put his arm around my shoulder and we walked out of his hall back to mine;

a mere hop in the scheme of things. He didn't come inside. We said goodbye at the main entrance. There was a long lingering kiss which stirred and aroused but which was left open to tease. I'd met Joel Hamilton, fallen in love, and Day One of my beautiful life had begun.'

'And so it continues, Elise,' says Philip.

'You're just jealous, Philip; that's not a nice character trait.'

'Have you heard that story before Philip?' asks Jo straightening and sitting back in her chair.

'Maybe once, maybe twice,' says Philip shrugging his shoulders nonchalantly.

'That's so lovely; maybe that's where I'm going wrong. I have the kiss and more, and before I know it, the relationship has ended and I haven't learnt half what you did on that first night. You're so lucky, Elise, to have that dating business out of the way,' says Jo.

'Dating is fun, remember,' pipes Philip.

'Don't take Philip's word either, Jo. Just take your time and enjoy what's in front of you, and when it's over, maybe, just maybe, the next one will be Mr Right. You'll know because by then you'll have kissed plenty of frogs.'

'Do you dream about Joel when he's away?' asks Jo.

'Sometimes. There's a fine line between a dream and a fantasy, and if I'm being honest, I fantasise about Joel a lot. My dreams do relate to him sometimes though, even the bad ones, I feel somehow connected to him all the time.'

'The dream article should be an autobiographical account of you and your night-time activities,' says Jo.

'No, I don't think so. That's what worries me about this subject – it's too close to home. No, if I write it, and that's a big if at the moment, then I'll find an angle which will be as far detached as possible from Elise Hamilton. I'm not featuring in one of *True Life* magazine's editorials.'

'Friday. As long as I have them by Friday, that's all I ask,' says Philip standing from behind his desk as if to assert his presence and authority.

'I think that's our cue to get back to work, Jo.'

Chapter Ten

Elise

Fifty-one minutes, not bad for ten kilometres. That should've earned me a chocolate bar or two.

'Evening, Elise,' says Edgar. 'Looking good.'

'Thanks, Edgar, in truth I'm probably glowing more like a ripe and ready tomato, but good I'll accept. All well with you?' I ask.

'Can't complain. Just off for a walk with my daughter's dog. I'm dog sitting whilst she's away,' says Edgar.

'Company and exercise all rolled into one. It's a lovely evening for it, stay safe,' I reply. Edgar next door lost his wife Vera last year and has been a bit of a recluse, so it's nice to see him getting out for a walk and having the company of his daughter's dog.

Unlocking the door and entering the house, once more solely lit by the timer light, is yet another reminder of Joel's absence. After a quick shower and TV dinner, the evening is mine once more to research and channel hop. Bringing work home with me is not something I make a habit of, but the dream article is going nowhere slowly so I need to put in the extra time. No harm will come from a little after-hours reading, after all. Slumping down on the sofa with my laptop and a glass of wine doesn't seem like work, anyway.

Because of unnecessary distractions earlier thinking about Joel, I'm yet to focus on my flying experiences properly. If flying in dreams actually represents the soul leaving the body, that could explain several things. I've travelled to, and seen, cities and countries during my dreams I've never been to in my waking life, and when I think back, the images were vivid and felt real.

Standing up and pushing my laptop to one side momentarily, I head for the stairs and my bedroom to fetch my dream diary, or diaries to be precise. I've accumulated six over the years. They're not annual diaries with daily sections but notebooks full of scribblings I've made, sometimes on waking or later in the day, depending on what I can remember.

I first started writing them whilst at university. A friend suggested it after one particularly fretful night's sleep. Since moving in with Joel some years ago, I've kept my diaries close to hand in the bedside cabinet. The full ones are tied neatly with a lovely piece of ribbon. The current one is always on top, accompanied by a pen so I can make notes whilst the memories are still vivid and strong. To aid my research, though, I will need all of them.

Back downstairs snuggled on the sofa again, I start at the beginning with the very first diary I started. This one is rather messy and has no particular order to it. I made those first notes in the order the dreams occurred and then backdated some information. There's a section also written whilst at university, but which relates to my early and late teens.

These notes, though, still make me shudder. The recurring dream of a wolf in a rocking chair – more like a nightmare. The eighteenth-century cobbled streets, with me as a young girl running yet again from something or someone unknown, and opening a small door, entering, and then nothing, black and empty. There's also one where I'm a man, fighting in a war in the 1950s in Asia somewhere:

> *I'm shot in the legs after a spray of gunfire. I fall to the ground and freeze. I pretend to be dead, lying as still as I can and not breathing. I'm not sure I could move even if I wanted to. A*

presence is approaching and moving to stand above me. I'm frozen in time. An object, maybe the butt of a gun, is pressed to the back of my head instantly followed by an excruciatingly loud bang. Still frozen, unable to move or respond, I can't feel pain but have the sensation of liquid running down my neck and pooling around my head. I can't move, yet there's a spark in me telling me to get up, get up and wake up.

Flicking through page after page and moving through the books, what's apparent is that over time my dreams became more vivid, clearer, and my recordings more concise, my ability to remember details, colours and places vastly improving. The nature of them continually develops with more focus on confrontation and resolution.

According to one diary, I was maybe twenty-two or twenty-three when I first realised I was lucid dreaming and that I could alter the direction of the dream and the outcome. There's a note with a sunny face saying:

> *Lucid dreams are great.*

On the page also is a cut-out from a magazine article describing 'Lucid Dreaming: the ability to control your dreams.'

The entries after this are different, with frequent comments like:

> *I'm no longer scared. It was a dream.*

Back then, the realisation that I had control over my dream state, as long as I stayed focussed, gave me power. With this power and control I had more freedom and the intensity of the dreams increased exponentially. The sheer exhilaration I feel during a dream is hypnotic, addictive. Sometimes I don't want to wake, I want to remain in the dream world, and whilst I know they're dreams, they feel real. It's the closest I can be to living two lives, three lives, unlimited lives.

In some I'm alone, either just flying or running, in effect exploring, soaring for hours anywhere in the world visiting city after city, and continents that feel a million miles away. Time and distance are no object, my arrival is often instantaneous. In others I engage with strangers, but they seem real, and my running and flying help me escape some conflict and fighting, but not all. There are entries relating to dreams I've long forgotten, snapshots of my alternative existence. There's no mention of me ever having killed anyone but a catalogue of entries where I'm fleeing and being hunted.

There's a note in one margin:

> *Must put ability to run fast into practice in my everyday life, need to move beyond plodding.*

An aspirational dream come true, maybe?

Looking back through all of my diaries, I can see lots of my life reflected. My judo and taekwondo as a child and even my boxercise has been put to excellent use. When I've needed to fight it comes to me naturally, instinctively. My running is also evident. Flying is the one thing that I cannot physically do. It's the one aspect that cannot be explained unless, and that brings me back around to the research, it's my soul. I don't physically fly, but maybe my soul does.

Tonight, if I've learnt one thing from my diaries, it's that flying holds the key. My diaries tell me lots more than the internet could ever do, but there's still the question of what flying truly represents.

To move this on, I need to continue the research. A quick query in the search engine relating to 'soul leaving the body' brings back 'astral projection', the top result by far. Astral projection is interpreted as an 'out-of-body experience with the soul travelling on an astral plane.' Another theory, maybe just like all the others. What's frustrating though, is there's no scientific basis to this idea. Even if I attribute my flying experiences to astral projection, who is going to believe me. I'm the only witness.

Closing my laptop down for the night and taking a sip of what's now warm white wine, I feel this subject matter is not article worthy for *True Life*, it's too close to home and it would become an autobiographical account. No, whilst I believe there's more to research for my personal benefit, I have to put it to bed and move on at work. It's time to fine-tune the 'Talking Dog' article and visit the cat lady in Islington.

Chapter Eleven

Elise

Thursday morning comes around quicker than expected. Today is the day I learn of Joel's exact location – confirmation, maybe, of what I already suspect. Feeling strangely nervous as I enter the corner shop, I quickly locate Joel's broadsheet and make for the counter.

'Morning, just this, thanks.'

Handing over the money is easy, but as I wait for the change, I feel anxious. The trotting in my chest having returned. This is something I do regularly when Joel's away. I'll wait until I believe they'll print his article, buy the paper and then learn where he is, or was, as often he's moved on. Maybe it's just excitement at the prospect of reading the article, or more likely it's because it will confirm my suspicions, that either he's in Syria or somewhere very close.

'Morning Philip, morning Jo, all well?' I say breezing into office.

'Yes, you?' replies Jo.

'Yes, OK thanks.'

'Morning darling,' says Philip. 'Got it then?'

'Yes, and I will take a few minutes to read it with my morning drink; can I make anyone else one?'

'Please,' say Jo and Philip simultaneously.

Having performed my tea making duties, I ready myself with the broadsheet front and centre on my desk. Flicking through, I find 'Refugees' Plight' by Joel Hamilton on page three.

'So where is he?' asks Jo.

'Syrian border, reporting on the refugee crisis,' I reply

'Is that safe?' says Jo.

'Yes, it's not like they've sent him into a conflict zone.' *Not sure who I'm trying to convince more, me or Jo.*

'Got him then,' says Philip.

'I haven't "got" him Philip, I'm reading his article which, if printed today, means job done, home tomorrow. Can I get back to it now?'

Joel's story is an excellent read, as always, and it focusses on the humanitarian aspects. Joel will be happy, I know he will, although having got that close to Syria he may be more than a little frustrated.

'Philip, just to keep you appraised of what I'm working on, I've boxed off the dream article. It wasn't going anywhere and I couldn't see an appropriate angle to work with for the June edition.'

'What about later in the year?' asks Philip.

'No, I don't think so. I can't see how I can make it any more original than Jade Johnson's version, and that was barely worth the paper they printed it on. No, I have for you instead a fine-tuned piece about a terrier that talks, and I'm now off to pay a visit to an elderly lady in Islington to work up a story relating to her cats. It'll be great, I promise.'

'So, are you off then, all day?' says Philip.

'Yes, you don't mind, do you? I'll be out most of the day and what I don't finish today I'll polish off tomorrow. Why?'

'Nothing, but Jo's never up for doing lunch and I was hoping you would be about when I pay a visit to the salad bar later on, you know, for moral support.'

'Why, Philip, what have you done?'

'Nothing, I'll have you know – not yet anyway – but we have a drink date set up and I'm a little nervous. It's tomorrow night, and yet I feel compelled to see him today rather than wait.'

'He might think you're stalking him, Philip, or are desperate, of which you're neither, but just saying. Look, I'm sure I'll be back by three, so wait until then and I'll be your chaperone; not that you need one – you seem to have done all right so far on your own.'

'You're a darling; I would miss you if you were to ever leave.'

'Leave? Are we not permanently rooted in this office? Have we not waved goodbye to life beyond *True Life*?'

'Come on, Elise, you're sounding a little disaffected. This conversation should end now, before you ponder the idea of life beyond any further. I'll hold you to three – no later though.'

'I'll be back.' *I'm not sure I can promise to be here forever, though.*

*

A tube ride to Islington makes for a refreshing change. Whilst cool, the freedom from the office gives me a chance to clear my head. I don't want to think about Joel, where he is and what he might be doing. I need to focus on me and the here and now and my impending interview.

Mrs Crabtree lives in a Georgian mid-terrace property set within the conservation area at the heart of Islington, only minutes from the Angel tube station.

Approaching the door, I feel it's hard not to be envious of the property. It's very tidy looking and somewhat grand in appearance – four storeys. I love period houses and this one's in a great location, but sadly way out of our price range. Three thuds of the heavy brass knocker on the door should do it, and then I stand back and wait. Minutes pass. Mrs Crabtree told me to be patient. She said she would take her time getting to the door, commenting that she wasn't as mobile as she used to be.

As the door opens, a stream of cats and kittens run out into the road and disperse in all directions. A detectable odour lingers in the air, which intensifies the nearer I am.

'Morning, I'm Elise Hamilton from *True Life* magazine; here's my ID card.'

'Hello, come on in, no need to stand on ceremony letting the chilly air in, dear. Follow me through to the front room. I've boiled the kettle already – tea?' she says.

'Yes please. Have you anything herbal? I don't drink milk.'

'You're a strange one. Let me have a look. I got a lovely caddy of mixed tea from someone at Christmas.

I'll see what's in there. Do you have sugar, or do you avoid that as well?' she asks.

'No sugar, thank you, sorry to be a pain.'

Mrs Crabtree totters off and soon the kettle bubbles to a boil, followed by the chinking of china. I sit patiently in what is a lovely homely sitting room, light and airy but filled with old well-worn furniture and pictures. There are family photographs, but these are overshadowed and outnumbered by portraits of cats.

'Here we go, please move that paper, will you, and take the tray, thank you. I hope you're OK with lemon tea. Now, you're here to talk about my cats. I'm not sure what all the fuss is about,' says Mrs Crabtree.

Mrs Crabtree sits down in a single upright chair. Her personal throne is next to a small side table littered with reading glasses, papers, hand cream, various pill packets and pens.

'That's perfect, thank you. Well, Mrs Crabtree, your local branch of Cats Protection has contacted us. They say that you've been fostering cats for over twenty years and should get some recognition for all that you do for the charity, and of course your feline friends.'

'Oh, how wonderful, but there's no need for recognition; I love them. I have no one else, you see,' replies Mrs Crabtree. As if called to order, two gleaming white kittens dart into the room and under Mrs Crabtree's throne.

'Let me introduce you to Snow and White, they are my most recent acquisitions. Their poor mother did not survive delivery, and Snow and White were the only kittens she delivered alive. All very tragic, really. They are so adorable, don't you agree?' says Mrs Crabtree.

'They're gorgeous, and very lucky to have you looking after them. How many do you think you've fostered over the years?' I ask.

'I believe, Snow and White, take me to 109 over what has got to be seventeen years now.'

'Wow, that's amazing. Have you always looked after them on your own or do you have family supporting you?'

'I have family, my dear, but they are not supportive. To be honest, I think they wanted me to pass soon after my late husband, so they could get their hands on this house. I have plans now though and my cats will be coming first.'

I continue to ask Mrs Crabtree a host of questions, to which she gives rather succinct replies whilst taking me on a tour of the house. Two thirds of this magnificent building having been given over to cat beds, feeding bowls and litter trays. Mrs Crabtree herself, a lady of mature years remains fit and lithe from climbing the three flights of stairs daily to clean and feed all of her feline friends.

Seated back downstairs I review my notes and set about finishing my second cup of tea.

'What a wonderful thing you've done for all these cats,' I say.

'Do you have cats, or any pets for that matter, my dear?' she asks.

'No.' Placing my teacup to one side, a smooth tickling sensation brushes across my ankles – Snow and White now deciding that I'm their new best friend.

'Children?' She asks.

'No.'

'Well, one day you'll find out that people let you down, whereas animals don't. It's in their eyes, you see; they stay true. The eyes are a portal to the soul – were you aware of that?' says Mrs Crabtree.

'No, I can't say I was. Interesting.'

After an interview lasting two hours, I escape back out into the welcoming fresh air, having taken copious notes, drank far too much tea and photographed what seems like a hundred cats. Mrs

Crabtree's house, whilst seemingly idyllic on the outside, is largely given over to cats on the inside, and it's fair to say it's not my cup of tea after all.

I have enough material to complete a suitable story to satisfy Philip. It doesn't have a weird and wacky edge to it, but enough depth to satisfy readers' needs. Riding the tube back to the office gives me time to reflect. Mrs Crabtree is a fiercely independent and somewhat spikey old lady. Quite obviously she has been let down by family, and therefore has bequeathed time, love and money in her feline friends, who she believes will not let her down. Her comment about "eyes being a portal to the soul", intrigues me. I hadn't thought of it before, but when I'm dreaming my eyes are physically closed and yet I see. On the day that I shelve my dream article I find myself interviewing a lady whose wisdom might just have opened my eyes.

*

On arrival back at the office, my focus is on Philip and his flirtations.

'Right Philip, I'm back, are you ready?' I say on entering.

'He's already been,' says Jo looking up from her computer.

'Really, Philip, I didn't think you had the courage on your own.'

'I couldn't wait; I know it was impetuous of me but I couldn't help myself,' says Philip.

'Well, what happened?' I ask as I slump onto my swivel chair.

'Disappointingly zilch. He smiled and acknowledged me. But that was it.'

'What did you expect him to do, leap over the counter and embrace you over the char-grilled chicken?' I reply.

'No – well, that would've been nice – but you're right, I need to relax and wait. I can't wait though,' says Philip.

'You need to step back, remind yourself it's just a drink and not be too hasty. If you like him, and he likes you and you want it to last for more than twelve hours, then less is definitely more. Keep reminding yourself "stay for a drink and then I'll go".'

'But—'

'No buts, Philip, you've been here so many times. If you want to move on to experience a fresh kind of relationship then slow down and leave him wanting a second date. If you put it all out there, it'll end in tears.'

'I've heard enough. I'm not a pubescent teen, you know. Anyway, Friday – articles please, ladies,' replies Philip as he repositions his glasses and then fixes his stare back on his computer screen.

Philip might not be a pubescent teen, but he's acting like a petulant child.

Facing forward, I poke a key and my screen brightens once more. I erase Philip's relationship woes from my mind and crack on with typing up my notes.

*

Coming home again to a cold house doesn't really inspire me to be creative in the kitchen. My diet will change the minute Joel walks through the door and my metabolism can cope with one more night of beans on toast.

By eight I'm ready to assume my favourite position on the sofa. Popping on the TV but keeping the volume low, I crank open the laptop.

With confirmation of Joel being near to the Syrian border, I want to research elements of my dream from

Monday night. I'd flown over an area which I was convinced was a desert and saw buildings, maybe houses, that I've never seen before, and rows upon rows of tents. The entry in my dream diary is not at all descriptive apart from 'domes, beehive-shaped domes'. This is the search term to check. The results are back in seconds.

The second entry is 'History of Beehive-Shaped Homes'. My finger guides the cursor over the entry, hovering momentarily, before clicking. Uncertainty manifests itself in the form of a stomach roll. I'm not sure what I'm expecting to uncover and what it'll tell me, but I must see. 'Turkey, Syria, beehive constructions dating back thousands of years. Villages of beehive homes in Syria near Aleppo.'

Oh god, no. That's where I was on Monday, where Joel would appear to have been too. It makes sense. The tents, the refugee camp – but how? This is unreal, the meaning of it and the possibilities.

Standing up, I feel a sharp pain shooting through my right leg. Sitting awkwardly has left it momentarily dead. Limping through to the kitchen, I open the fridge door and grab a bottle of wine. One glass is poured and downed in seconds. Heady numbness is now spreading across my temple. A second glass, filled and downed, does nothing to stop the swirls and thuds mixing up my mind. Pouring a third and replacing the bottle in the fridge, taking a chocolate bar from the basket, I walk back through to the sitting room. My leg has now fully woken up, although both of them are now feeling rather wobbly.

Re-entering my password on my laptop once again I find, bang in front of me, the shocking search results. Nothing has changed, it's very clear. All the research I've done this week has been leading up to this. Souls and astral projection. This answers so many questions I've accumulated over the years and poses a million more. Taking a large swig of wine, I devour the chocolate bar in three mouthfuls, tremors reverberating through my body. The enormity of my discovery is sinking in. *What am I going to do? What can I do? What does this really mean? Are more aspects of my dreams real? The conflicts, the fights, and the biggest question of all, should I tell Joel that I've been stalking him?*

Chapter Twelve

Joel

After a long tiring drive back on Tuesday evening, Wednesday came and went with Emin working tirelessly transcribing the voice recordings made during our visit to the refugee encampments. The transcribing alone had taken him over eight hours. Come Wednesday evening, I hastily pulled together my article and several images, and sent them off to my editor for Thursday's print run.

On waking this morning, I called my editor, Ben, to discuss the refugee article and the potential religious phenomenon. Ben sounded dismissive and stated clearly that he was not prepared to run a story without further evidence or eyewitness testimony. None of which I have.

My day has been nothing but frustrating. With only quirky angelic sightings on the internet, I feel that maybe I've put too much time and emphasis on this unknown phenomenon. Ben is probably right, there isn't a story after all. It could just be a figment of everyone's imagination. I'm trying too hard to see something that isn't really there. I should be focused on the refugees and their misery and the most recent bombing in Aleppo just a mere two hours away.

In need of relaxation, I head to the hotel bar. The bar on the ground floor is stark, minimalistic and devoid of life – not at all inviting. It's barely after five and I place my first order.

'Beer, please,' I say, pointing to the local brew.

'Thank you, sir.' The bartender removes a tall slim glass from a top shelf, polishes it, and flicks the beer tap. A steady flow of clear golden-amber liquid pours into the glass leaving a shallow creamy foam head. I can taste it even before taking my first sip.

Drinking on my own isn't really my idea of fun. Being home with Elise is still some twenty-four hours away, but I need to relax. Having fulfilled my editor's wishes with the coverage of the refugee crisis, it's my own personal satisfaction that needs attention. I want more.

The refreshing beer works on easing my frustrations with my assignment, but does nothing to dispel the nagging thoughts that linger in my mind relating to the religious sighting. I rifle through a pile of Turkish newspapers in the vain hope of finding a distraction, realising that not one paper contains a word in English. Pushing them to the side, I resign myself to tolerating my own company, rather than looking foolish pretending to read.

Downing the last mouthful, I savour the sweet malty moreish flavour, and the bar beckons once more. A man dressed from head to toe in beige, wearing an action man multi pocket gilet, enters the foyer of the hotel and walks over in my direction taking up residence in the faux leather bucket chair opposite me. He looks like he has just been swept in from the desert, Lawrence of Arabia style.

'You don't mind if I join you?' he says in a distinctly southern American tone.

'Sure, have a seat. I recognise that accent. How far south do you call home?'

'Louisiana. You?' he asks.

'Florida,' I reply shuffling and repositioning in my seat, correcting my posture to make a good impression.

'Not much of an accent for a Floridian; where are you living now?' he asks.

'UK, for the past thirteen years. I'm Joel.' Lifting myself from my seat, stretching out my hand.

'Guy. Nice to meet you. What brings you to Turkey?'

'Work, I'm a journalist; and yourself?'

'Same; freelance at the moment, covering the conflict next door.' He gestures with an outstretched thumb as if Syria were only a couple of blocks away. 'I've been here for six months and am flying back tomorrow for a period of long overdue leave, first into Washington and then a few days later onto St Louis.'

'Wow, that's a considerable tour. Well, I'm in and out. I had a short gig – I made a couple of visits to refugee camps near the border but head back in the morning.'

'You don't fancy working the conflict itself?' says Guy.

'I do, that would be awesome, but as a freelancer, I've only been offered the emerging refugee crisis so far. What you're doing is where I've aspired to be since starting in foreign affairs a few years back.'

'It's not easy; it's fair to say that my home life is a little chaotic but the rewards for me make up for the sacrifice. Have you ever worked stateside?' asks Guy.

'In my junior days – nothing major, some local reporting. Since university though, which for me was in the UK, my base has been London covering Europe in the main,' I reply, settling back into my seat, the formality of our introduction now over.

'What made you stay in the UK?'

'Love,' I reply, picturing an image of Elise for a second.

'That will do it for sure. Well, I would say there are wider freelance opportunities if you were still in America. Syria for one, but also the military are still looking for embedded reporters to work in Afghanistan; that's far from over yet.'

'I monitor what's happening over there, but hey I'm out of the loop stateside. Without an introduction, those opportunities, especially the ones with the military, are unlikely to come my way. Drink? I'm going to get a refill,' I raise my glass suggestively and stand ready to head to the bar.

'Sure, beer, thanks,' replies Guy.

Armed with two beers, I return to my chair and the company of Guy.

'My dad used to be based at an airbase in Florida, MacDill; I grew up there. Do you know it?'

'Know it, yes, I've flown out of it. Cheers by the way.' Guy nods, raising his glass towards me. 'I did a tour in Afghanistan myself when it first kicked off, reporting for the Tribune. Back in 2001 I wasn't embedded, but got reasonable coverage. The military didn't want us tagging along with them back then, but that changed with the Iraq invasion in 2003. Many of my colleagues have had full access to the frontline, both in Afghanistan and Iraq.'

'There isn't so much a frontline in Afghanistan anymore,' I reply.

'You could say the war has evolved, but I hear occasionally that they're looking for journalists to cover stories from Bagram. Give me your details. If anything comes my way, I'll let you know.'

'Great, thanks. So what's next for you?' I ask, eager to hear what my new role model has planned.

Guy and I talk into the evening. Bidding Guy farewell and safe travels I ponder for a moment the idea of working in America, or in fact working for the Americans. If Guy is to be believed, there are untapped opportunities. He talked the talk so maybe, just maybe, an opportunity will present itself and finally my frustrations will ebb away. Right now, though, I focus on getting a good night's sleep before setting off on the arduous journey home.

*

Coming in to land, focuses my mind back on home; Elise and our weekend with friends. The weather descending is grey and overcast; another dull spring day in England. Accessing my weather APP I check out the current temperature and weather in Sanibel just wondering how Mom and Dad are doing. *Great it's ten in the morning in Sanibel and already 29 degrees. Blue skies and limited cloud with a 10% chance of precipitation. Shame I'm not heading to Fort Myers. I know Elise would be happier in the heat of Sanibel. She always glows when she's in the sun.*

With no luggage to collect I head for passport control hoping for a swift clearance. A quick check-in with Elise and detour via the supermarket and I'll be home and the weekend will truly begin.

Chapter Thirteen

Elise

Friday morning thankfully flew past without event. Philip was happy with the articles I had produced and I think he was a little too preoccupied to care. With my thudding headache, caused by last night's wine, still not having subsided, I pop another couple of paracetamol and try to erase the cause from the mind. My discovery. I need to forget it, for now anyway.

The familiar chugging noise of the black cab pulling up outside alerts me to Joel's arrival. A glimpse through the sheer voile in the bay at the front confirms it's my man. The sight of Joel getting out of the rear of the taxi causes a grin to grow across my face. Pausing, he pays the driver and grabs three carrier bags full of food from the back seat, and his barrel bag.

As the metal scrape signifies the turning of the Joel's key in the lock, I race towards the door. Stepping over the threshold I fling my arms around his shoulders, jumping my legs up and cinching his waist. Joel's strong athletic build clings onto mine, pulling me in close. Sliding back to the floor, my eyes remain locked on his face. Excited like a puppy meeting its new owner for the first time, I loiter whilst Joel secures the latch, having brought the bags in off the step. He removes his jacket and throws his keys on the hall table.

'Missed me then?' says Joel.

Flinging my arms around his torso once more he kisses my cheeks and moves onto my neck leaving my lips till last.

'What do you think?' I say, the warmth moving and sensitising my body. 'Um, now that is a lovely hello.'

'Well, I don't want to leave you, but I enjoy coming home,' says Joel.

Our lingering embrace is mobile as we shuffle in unison into the sitting room, and then, as if conjoined, fall onto the sofa with a thud. Like teenagers we're hurried in our touching and undressing as if making out for the first time. A dreamy few minutes pass, and I pull away.

'Why stop? Where are you going?' asks Joel.

'Henry and Amanda are due anytime, and as much as I love you and want you, you must shower and then start cooking. We'll have more time later.'

Joel looks at me, crestfallen. It's now he who has the sad, but oh-so-gorgeous, puppy dog eyes. I button up and straighten my skirt, still aroused and a little wired by all the hormones racing through my body. They so need to be unleashed but also need to be ignored and shelved, for now anyway. The reality is that if we continue, we would make love on the sofa again, which whilst lovely, is not ideal when friends are genuinely due any minute.

I leave Joel licking his wounds and walk through to the kitchen to pour him a glass of red wine.

'Do you want to take your wine upstairs?' I ask.

'No, won't be long,' Joel replies.

Whilst Joel is showering, I unpack the groceries and uncork a second bottle. Joel's swift return to the kitchen is announced by a subtle waft of musk from his cologne. We steal a gentler embrace, before he pulls away, having clocked the time. I leave him to it and watch the master at work from a distance. Pots and pans and chopping boards being used and filled, the food being transformed into dishes. Mushrooms, meatballs, sardines and chicken; it soon takes shape and smells delicious. *He's perfect, I have it all - when he's home.* I select a playlist, crank up the volume and draw in a deep breath, relaxing my shoulders and acknowledging that it's Friday; fantastic. The weekend begins.

One thing I learnt at university was the art of cocktail making. Back then we were less refined, and used cheap substitutes, but it's fair to say that the basics are the same. Armed with my expert mixer, I prep enough base to get the evening started. Gin, grapefruit and sugar are shaken and strained, which will be topped up with chilled champagne. We may have moved out of London, but when entertaining, and especially drinking, we know what we fancy on a Friday night. In particular we know what Amanda likes – the Champagne Queen herself.

Amanda met Henry through work. Whilst Amanda is a born and bred Londoner, Henry comes from a sleepier part of the world, Norfolk. I don't think Henry actually spent that much time in Norfolk growing up, what with going to boarding school and then university, but Amanda still considers him a 'bumpkin'. They chose careers with great earning potential and have secured themselves a luxurious lifestyle in central London. They own a modest two-bed apartment in a new development near Canary Wharf, which affords them easy access to the city and shopping districts. Amanda is not ready to give up her London living anytime soon.

I present Joel with a drink freshly made, with the champagne still effervescing in the glass.

'Mixing them, are we?' says Joel.

'Your red won't go cold, enjoy it.'

An abrupt *bzz* at the door signals our guests' arrival. *I swear Amanda can smell champagne a mile away.*

'Amanda, you look fab, come on in; Henry, great to see you, perfect timing. You could obviously smell the bubbles?'

'Oh, you know Amanda,' replies Henry, 'she's akin to a bloodhound when it comes to Moët or Mumm.'

Henry follows me into the kitchen whilst Amanda painstakingly removes her knee-high lace-up boots. Amanda is a sucker for the latest fashion, especially footwear, and tonight's are no exception – four-inch platform boots in black leather with laces up the back. Stylish but impractical, especially when not required indoors. Once removed, Amanda tiptoes into the kitchen wearing a cheeky smile as if she has been naughty. She pulls at her skirt and top and dances as if undressed without her foot attire, before finally taking a sip of my magic cocktail and relaxing.

Henry takes up sentry duty next to Joel, and soon the pair are deep in conversation about their respective working weeks. Amanda and I leave the boys to it and go into the sitting room where we slump in tandem on to the sofa. The sofa which, less than an hour earlier, was the scene of sexual arousal and heavy petting, but thankfully, under my stewardship, nothing else.

'So what's new in your world?' asks Amanda.

'Nothing much,' I reply. 'I've been researching dreams. It started off as research for an article, but I struggled to find an angle, so I've shelved that, although it occupied most of the week.'

'Well, I would've thought that particular topic was right up your street. All those fitful nights in university, when you'd wake believing you had gone ten rounds with Muhammad Ali. You're a legend for dreams.'

'Yes, it should have been, but it's more complicated, and I've concluded that it's not a story for the magazine. As my research developed, it felt as if I was psycho-analysing myself.'

'Ooh, that's deep, way too deep for a Friday night,' says Amanda, pausing and sipping her cocktail, wincing at the sharpness of the grapefruit.

'You're right, it's deep. The more research I did, the more I needed to walk away, so it's shelved for now as an article. I may look into them further in my free time, but sometimes the things I work on are too close to home. I ended up dragging out my diaries, the ones I started at university, and a few too many good and not so good memories came flooding back. Anyway, I pulled a few other articles out of the bag for Philip. He was content and has his own personal life to worry about: yet another first date tonight! Enough about me, what's happening with you? How's the money-making business?' I ask.

'Good, OK. Markets rise and fall, but I enjoy gambling, especially when it's not my money. The best thing is, I've not had any heavy losses for a while, so everyone's happy whilst their stocks are rising. The stock market is rather fickle like that,' replies Amanda.

'And Henry's work, how are things?'

'Great, as far as I know. We might both be in finance, but I don't understand half of what Henry does.'

'God, we are overdue a proper girly chat and catch up; we must have lunch or coffee in the next couple of weeks,' I say.

'It's a date, I'll pencil you in,' replies Amanda.

'Please do, it feels nice to be important enough to be pencilled into your diary.'

As we giggle together Amanda and I take synchronised sips of our drinks and sigh whilst trying to slump even further into the sofa. Our moment of calm relaxation is cut short by an exclamation coming from the kitchen, 'Girls, food is ready.'

That is our cue to join Joel and Henry and continue our evening next door.

*

'That was great, I'm stuffed,' I say, leaning back and rubbing my belly, gently caressing it as if I was proud and pregnant. 'I'm glad I put on a skirt tonight and not my super-skinny jeans – I would struggle to peel them off right now.'

Henry stretches his arms and long torso upwards and rubs his eyes. 'Yes, I have to agree,' he says. 'Not the bit about the skinny jeans or skirt, but I'm stuffed too. You really know how to put your guests to sleep, Hamilton.'

Joel looks at Henry with a slight frown and a wry smile and replies, 'Geez, thanks mate you can come again.'

As Amanda and Henry leave to go upstairs, Joel and I stack the dishwasher, and put the rest of the pans in to soak. We're not far behind them and, whilst having displayed plenty of passion for each other earlier, the excess food and wine has taken its toll. We both just strip and sink into bed under the duvet.

*

'Come on, sleepyhead,' says Joel. 'Our guests are up already so you need to stir too.'

'I can't,' I reply, 'I'm teaching my mum how to fly.' I bury myself deep under the duvet cover in response.

'Don't you think it would be better to teach her how to drive first?' replies Joel. 'Now fly up, fly out and fly down to see your friends. Pancakes will be on the table in ten minutes.'

Pancakes, yummy. Joel makes the most fantastic fluffy American pancakes, which, when topped with bananas and maple syrup, are truly divine. I never have understood the whole sweet and savoury combination, like bacon and syrup, but Joel enjoys it.

As I straighten and stretch under the covers, the distinctive smoky aroma permeates the house.

Walking downstairs and entering the kitchen, I'm greeted by 'Morning, Elise,' being cheerily voiced by Amanda and Henry. It's just remarkable how two people who consumed their bodyweight in food and alcohol last night can be so chirpy at nine in the morning.

'What is it, Elise, sore head?' asks Henry.

'No, not really,' I reply. 'I was midway through flying when Joel rudely interrupted me.'

'Oh, what was it this time?' says Amanda. 'A flying visit to the Eiffel Tower or a more salubrious part of Shanghai?'

'No, nothing exotic, just a flying lesson for my mum, but it wasn't working, and I resorted to putting a rocket backpack on her,' I reply.

Amanda and Henry both giggle and yes, I believe they are laughing at me, not with me.

'So what's on the agenda for you guys this weekend?' I ask as I flick the switch on the kettle, ready to brew myself a fresh tea.

'Nothing much. Henry has reports to finish. I think we'll be lazy. Catch a late lunch, early dinner in China

Town, maybe a show tomorrow, but not too much. What about you?' asks Amanda.

'Similar, but without the China Town and West End show. More like Bob's fish and chips and a trip to the art deco cinema. With Joel having been away we've some catching up to do, if you know what I mean,' I reply.

Amanda knows exactly what I mean. She knows I'm never keen on Joel being away and that I long for him, literally body and soul.

Once served, we devour Joel's scrumptious pancakes in seconds, the four of us imitating hyenas cleaning a carcass after a kill. Not a scrap of bacon, banana or syrup left. The feeling in my stomach is reminiscent of last night's indulgence. Looking across at Amanda whilst sipping my tea, I marvel at how well she looks. It's just after nine in the morning; we ate and drank the same last night and she's just packed away three loaded pancakes, yet she sits glowing and content. Her figure is slim and kept in check with personal training sessions and Pilates classes. On the rare occasion she enters her kitchen at home, it's only to prepare a new health-craze shake she's indulging in that week. Whatever her secret is, it works for Amanda, and she's the epitome of health and radiance.

It's a stark contrast to my pudgy over-indulged belly and body, which swells the instant I consume alcohol and more than a hundred calories. Joel and I will run later, once the pancakes have settled. That should at least blast away the cobwebs and get us some credit for fish and chips with a little less sprinkling of guilt.

Chapter Fourteen

Elise

As soon as Amanda and Henry leave, both Joel and I take to the sofa, Joel to study the broadsheet which has dropped through the letter box and me to read two recently purchased magazines. We've had little chance to chat since Joel's return, with Amanda and Henry staying over. The last sixteen hours have been a blur.

Sitting close together on the sofa, I can feel the warmth radiating from Joel's body. Joel is warm, whatever the weather. He rarely feels cold, and it's great for me in the winter months as he's a lovely addition to my thermal blanket.

The silence gives me time to reflect on last week's dream research – what questions it has answered, what questions remain, and what this means to me personally. For decades I have dreamt night after night, remembering fragments, sometimes complete dreams, but in effect never thinking they had any more relevance beyond subconscious mind games. It feels different now. I've a new understanding, which scares me. The more knowledgeable I become, the closer I am to my dreams. They're becoming my reality. But what does that really mean?

When I announced to Philip on Thursday that I couldn't write the dream article, I knew precisely what that meant. My time at *True Life* is coming to an end. A change is necessary. The dream research would never have made a feature; instead it has fuelled my weird and wonderful subconscious life. This dalliance I've been having with writing for the magazine needs to stop, and instead I need to pursue my genuine passion: books.

'I want to change jobs; I need a change,' I say.

Joel turns towards me, resting the paper on his lap. 'What's brought this on, what's happened?'

'Nothing has happened. I just desire a change. I've been giving the idea a lot of thought during the week whilst you were away and the time has come for me to fulfil my dreams, my aspirations. You know I love writing, but I can no longer write for the magazine. What interests me is publishing.'

'OK,' replies Joel. 'Slow down and take a breath. I know that's what you always said you wanted but your job with *True Life,* whilst not the best paid, is secure and works well for us now.'

'Yes, it does, but I'm not satisfied any more. Writing weird and wacky stories has been entertaining, but I need more. I've been working on an article regarding dreams, the meaning of which is too close to home for me. 'The Life of Elise Hamilton' will not be appearing on the front cover of the magazine anytime soon, so I've concluded I want a fresh challenge.'

'Good,' replies Joel.

'Good?'

'Yes. Look Elise, you must enjoy your job otherwise there's no point doing it. I get frustrated, but I have more freedom these days. Not being tied to one editor gives me scope to vary what I cover and keeps me at least content for now. If working in publishing will make you happy, then do it, leave *True Life*.'

'OK, so… If I start job hunting, it may take a while, and they might ask me to start at the bottom again, but you'll support me?' I ask, twisting to take in his response.

'Yes, I'll support you, of course I will. I love you and want you to be happy, so you must do what feels right. I'm hoping fresh opportunities will come my way too.'

‘Really. What opportunities?’ I ask, edging even closer, curious as to what he’s going to say next.

‘Well, nothing just yet. I made a contact, though, whilst in Turkey, who has worked with the military. He said that occasionally the military need embedded journalists. I want to return to the camps as refugees arrive daily. They’ll have more stories to tell, but I hope that maybe my contact might set me up with something else. Something different.’

‘The British military?’ I say.

‘No, the American. My contact is a fellow freelancer, an American staying at the same hotel as me. Guy had been covering aspects of the Syrian conflict for six months and was heading home for a break. We had a drink in the bar on Thursday evening, got chatting, and as it happened he knew MacDill Airforce Base too. You know, where my dad was based, where I grew up for a while. After a while Guy said he’d mention to a military contact he knew that I was interested in potentially reporting on the frontline and that I may get a call. That’s it, really, but it has potential, and if they asked me to go over to America to discuss it further, then I’d want you to support me. It’s what I’ve been waiting for.’

‘Yes. Great. All change then.’

Joel drops his eyes back to the newspaper and carries on reading. I shuffle back to my side of the sofa, a tiny distance suddenly created by this revelation.

I'm happy for him, really I am – I know he's longed for these opportunities, but a nagging pinch in the middle of my stomach simmers. Joel working abroad more, let alone with the military, sits uneasily.

'Talk to me about the refugee camps.'

'What do you want to know? I know you've read it, I've seen Thursday's edition of the *Standard* in the trash.'

'The article didn't seem complete somehow. Something was going unsaid. You were given plenty of access by the sound of it, but it wasn't your usual cut and dried exposé.' Joel pushes the newspaper to one side and eases himself off the sofa.

'I have a picture – let me get my phone.'

'A picture?'

'A bright light, probably nothing more, but rumours were circulating through the camps of it having religious significance. A few of the refugees described it as a bright white haze in the sky, not a star, more of a blur, with no sharp lines. They reported its movement as erratic, occasionally moving fast through the air, sometimes hovering. A few had convinced themselves it was an ancient religious sign. It sounds crazy, I know.'

'Did you see it?' I ask.

'No. But one man in Yayladagi snapped the picture on his phone. It's not great, a little grainy, especially as the only way I could get a copy was to photograph his phone. Look.' Joel hands me his device. Joel remains standing, looming above me waiting for my response.

I hold the phone, straining my eyes to make out the picture on the screen. A bright white light, a flash in the sky, but by expanding the image, the shape becomes clearer. A person; the figure of a human. No detail, just body shape, two arms, two legs and a head. The light dominates, though.

'What do you make of it?'

'The image? Well, I'm uncertain. Why's it considered a religious sign? It's a strong bright light, that's all,' I reply.

'Can't you make out the shape?' says Joel.

'No. What shape? If I stare long enough, I'm sure my mind will create an image for you.' I try to sound nonchalant without being too dismissive. My mind is unable to contain the possibilities. I'd done the research, I'd worked out that on Monday night I dreamt of villages and tents over Syria and Turkey. The dream research pointed to the soul flying to destinations. Astral projection and auras; but this image is too much, it cannot be.

'I can't understand how you of all people can't see it, the outline of a person. You have a more vivid imagination than anyone else I know.' Joel now pacing the room, frustration in his tone.

'Precisely, Joel, and I feel you can imagine it to be whatever you want it to be. The bright light is very clear though, just saying.' I place the phone on the sofa next to me and stare down at my magazines trying to not give myself away.

'Well, I need to delve further,' says Joel grabbing the phone, clearly wired by the image. 'The elders seemed convinced by what they'd seen. They referred to it as an angel from God. I'm sure there's more to it.'

'What does Ben, your editor, think?' I ask, looking back up at him.

'He's dismissive too, and doesn't want any more time or effort committed to researching a story which sounds fanciful.'

'So, what are you going to do?' I ask whilst patting the sofa, inviting him to sit back down.

‘I’ll go back. The Syrian conflict and emerging refugee crisis are far from over. I will resolve this potential phenomenon. Those men, women and children need hope and their faith believes this is a sign. If not for me, I need to find answers for them.’

Joel’s wired by this picture and struggling to comprehend it, looking to me for confirmation which I’m unable to give him, not because I can’t see the image – the image is clear – but because of what it means to me. My mind is awash with internet research, trying to piece together a logical answer. Right now I can feel Joel’s hurt, the pain caused by me not confirming what’s on the screen.

‘I agree you must go back, speak to more people, resolve it if you must. Let me take another look?’ Looking at the image once more, not needing confirmation, I struggle to find the words Joel needs to hear.

‘Maybe I was too quick to dismiss it, you could be right.’

‘Well, I need more than a copy. I require proof. I’ll speak with Ben tomorrow and see if he’ll support me going back as early as next week under the guise of another humanitarian visit.’

'OK, but totally changing the subject …' Without further words, I take the phone out of his hand and place it on the coffee table and then guide him towards the staircase. My body wants Joel in so many ways, but my mind is already focussing on its next adventure.

Chapter Fifteen

Joel

I wake early to a Monday morning filled with promise. My mind is racing with all the things I want to plan for the week ahead. Whilst the coffee is brewing I open up my tablet and arrange the kitchen table ready for a morning of calls. A call to my editor is first on the list.

'Morning Ben, it's Joel Hamilton, how are you?'

'Morning Joel, great thanks,' Ben replies.

'I wanted to arrange a time to come and discuss the refugee article with you, if that's OK?' I say.

'Sure, let me check my diary; great article by the way. Gave you a full page. The photos were impactive too. Right, eleven here at the office, is that OK? I can give you fifteen minutes,' replies Ben.

'Yes, great, thanks – see you then. Bye.'

'Sorted,' I say, once I've hung up. *One ticked off the list.*

'What's sorted?' asks Elise as she enters the kitchen and grabs a banana. 'You're doing business early this morning.'

'Just my meeting with Ben, the editor at the *Standard* about my article. He doesn't know it yet, but I want to discuss a return visit funded by the paper. He liked what I produced, so I have a chance.'

'Any other work this week?' asks Elise as she peels the banana teasingly.

'A few minor jobs. I haven't checked the agency drop box, but I've enough to keep me busy till Thursday. Some more articles relating to the refugees, the ones arriving in the UK, and two Crown court cases to cover. Nothing that should stop me heading back to Turkey if I can convince Ben.'

'Good luck with that. Are you coming with me to make the seven twenty-one?' asks Elise as she pulls on her coat.

'No, hun, I want to hang on and catch a later train if that's OK. I can get more work done here before my meeting at eleven. Are you going to tell Philip about your potential job move today?'

'No, not just yet. I must consider exactly what I want to do first and what's available. No hurry, although if I don't leave now I'll miss my train. Love you, good luck with Ben.'

'Love you too, hun.' Grabbing Elise by her arm, I pull her back close in to me. Softly, I kiss her porcelain face as if it were our last embrace. I never need an excuse. Neanderthal urges surge through me, even after a weekend spent mostly in bed.

'Now, be away with you woman, I have important work to do. I cannot spend all day smooching; well, I could, but go before I carry you back upstairs.'

'Don't tease me, Joel.'

'Look, have a good day and I'll cook Asian tonight, your favourite. I'll phone you when I'm on my way home.'

'Great, bye,' says Elise.

Once Elise has gone, I prep myself a shake and reawaken my tablet once more. I check all my email accounts and accept and decline several assignments. There's no news from Guy. Maybe I'm being too impatient; after all it's only been seventy-two hours since I met the man. He seemed genuine, though.

*

Riding in on a train after nine is luxury compared to the usual crush. The passengers are different too; wafts of lofty perfume fill the carriage and the chatter is not about the latest rise and fall of the markets but lunch dates and shopping trips to high-end boutiques. I defer opening my tablet for the quick hop; instead I savour the relative calm of the journey and for once look out the window to observe fleetingly the urban jungle passing by. Unlike last week when I flew home, descending beneath grey almost black clouds, this morning is brighter. The sun is peeking through a light cover of white cloud and its growing warmth magnifying on the glass. The reality is, though, that it's still cold. Our nearest star, whilst fiery and orange, is weak and far from ready to roast just yet, but today it matches my mood – optimistic and full of potential.

*

As I walk towards the offices of the *Standard* I consider for one moment what I'm there to achieve. I need to review my article; Ben was positive over the phone, that in itself is reassuring, and then I need to work on my persuasion tactics to convince Ben to fund a return visit. My angle is 'Religious phenomenon brings hope to refugees'. Selling it as a continuance of the humanitarian story might work. *My argument sounds weak though; who am I kidding?* Full of doubt, I've a meeting with an editor who I respect and only minutes to hone my spin. I trot across the road to avoid a cab, striding with purpose and pushing through the double glass doors as if I'm a force to be reckoned with. The heat, intense and dry, hits me instantly. Having dressed for the cool spring day outside, I'm not prepared for the apparent heatwave being experienced in the reception of the *Standard*.

'Morning, Geraldine. I'm here to see Ben Barker on the third floor. We've a meeting at eleven. What's with the heat?' I ask.

'The heat, Mr Hamilton, is us Brits not being able to work a thermostat. The maintenance team thinks it's a hoot. They run it like the military, radiators on full blast, September through May and then nothing. You can have freezing Junes sometimes, and today, well, I shouldn't go on; you're here to see Mr Barker not to hear me moan. I will call to say you're on your way. I liked your article, the one on the refugee crisis. Those poor children, they looked like they need a hot meal. Are you doing any more on that?' asks Geraldine, pausing at last to draw breath.

'Hope to go back again, only scratched the surface really,' I reply.

'You know where you're going, don't you,' says Geraldine, signalling towards the elevator.

'Sure do, thanks.'

As I enter the elevator I pull at my collar, loosening it without making it untidy, trying to vent heat which I've generated in reception. Ben is the editor for International Affairs, third floor. He's been with the paper as long as I've been typing up stories, which for me was eighth grade. He's a tough cookie with assignments. He knows the angles which work. If a hack doesn't fall in line quickly, they are toast in his eyes. I worked for the *Standard* before going freelance. Ben gives me at least half of my work, so is not a man to piss off.

'Morning, Ben,' I say as I walk into his open office which dominates a corner of the third floor. Light and airy with two floor-to-ceiling glass panes, it should be a modern minimalistic room, yet it is stacked high with books and papers randomly positioned in piles on the floor and an old fashioned leather inlaid desk at its centre. The walls are frittered with picture frames showcasing a who's who in the media world. Ben as always larger than life fully occupying the green leather executive swivel chair which he uses to travel around the room rather than walking.

'Morning, Joel, good to see you, take a seat. Excellent report last week, it paid off going to two camps, don't you agree?' says Ben.

'Yes, definitely, two separate set-ups and the refugees are at different stages of the transfer process with fresh ones arriving all the time,' I reply.

'Yes, there's no end in sight at the moment, so I want you to go back,' says Ben.

'Great; return, of course. Couldn't agree more.' I say, a buzz of excitement raising me in my seat.

'Well, I would like you to cross over the border just into Syria and try to follow the routes that the refugees are taking. You know, expand on their situation and see for yourself how they're coping before they get to the camps. Is it as challenging as they say?'

'Awesome. I also wanted to ask you about visiting the camps again, to follow up on that sighting, the phenomenon I told you about on the phone.' *Will he go for it or have I misjudged him?*

'Yes, the light. Um, not sure Joel, a god coming to save them?' Ben lifts his pint-sized coffee mug and gulps down half its contents all at once. 'I wouldn't print anything of that nature unless I had concrete evidence. We would be a laughing stock and we're not one of those wacky editorials which produce alien sightings every other week – you know the ones,' says Ben as he goes in for the kill, finishing off the remnants of his coffee.

'Yes, I know the ones.' Elise's magazine is a classic for that genre of story, and Elise herself has put together a fair few of those articles. 'I understand that it couldn't go to print without evidence, but I would at least like the opportunity to see if there's more to the story,' I say, hoping to sound convincing enough that I can find a credible angle.

'The priority is the refugees and the border crossings. If you get time, and it's your time, then I'll sign the papers for you to enter the camps, but don't get your hopes up, Joel. It sounds implausible to me and your career might come tumbling down on you if you write nonsense,' says Ben, his head now down, focussed on scribblings he is making on a blotting page.

'Sure. I promise to get you some exclusives on the crossings and routes. I'll make that my prime focus. How soon do you want me to go?' I ask.

'As soon as possible. If you've accepted work for this week, fine, but I would want you written off for me for fourteen days, possibly longer. You need time to make contacts. Are you up for it?' asks Ben.

'Yes, sure am. I can go this weekend. Friday works for me; I want the same interpreter though, but can the flights be more local? I wasted a lot of time driving to the camps on the border from Gaziantep. I suggest I head for Antakya this time and base myself in and around there.'

'You sort it and bill me. I want a roving report, several days' coverage. Images and video, if you can manage it, for the online readers. Use your interpreter for the video interviews too.'

'No problem, that all sounds doable, thanks,' I reply whilst standing ready to exit in a hurry, keen to start planning.

'It's important we get it right, Joel,' says Ben looking up from his scribbling. His tone earnest. 'The competition for this information is fierce. Don't get carried away with your god-like story. Stay focussed,' says Ben.

'I promise the coverage comes first. I'll sort the travel plans today and drop you a line when I've worked up an itinerary and accommodation options. I'll get started straight away. Cheers.'

I bounce out of Ben's office, and out of the overheated *Standard* building. The crisp air slaps my face instantly and the incessant noise of horns and engines batter my eardrums – the throng of central London. I need a coffee and access to the internet.

After two black coffees, I get myself back on track and head towards the South Kensington tube. A fifteen-minute hop from here puts me in Blackfriars, where I have a showdown with a judge and some drug dealers who are awaiting verdicts and sentencing. That should keep me busy for the rest of the day, but I can feel a long evening ahead planning for Turkey, especially if I'm leaving on Friday.

I've got my way, I'm going back. This time though I will get a little bit of what Guy has experienced across the border. Whilst I can't wait, I feel uneasy about what Elise will think. Her sudden decision to change job has come at the wrong time. *If I'm not careful, she'll think I'm putting myself ahead of us.*

Chapter Sixteen

Elise

'Morning, lovelies, how are we all today and how were your weekends?' I say on entering the office.

'Great, thanks,' pipes Jo.

'Good, darling,' says Philip.

'Good Philip? Not fabulous, not stupendous, just good? I want to hear how Friday went,' I say as I perch myself on the corner of his desk.

'Well … not being one to kiss and tell,' replies Philip.

'Jo, are you listening too?'

'I wouldn't miss it for the world,' says Jo as she rises from her desk and quickly advances towards Philip's station.

'Well … Friday night was fab. Drinks only, I'll have you know. I took your advice for once but, well, what can I tell you. His name is Mark, he's younger than me but into similar things. This salad bar job is temporary. He's a photographer and has work exhibited but the money is irregular, hence the lettuce leaves,' says Philip.

'OK, all on track so far. So, are you seeing him again?' I ask.

'Yes. I am, we have. We met up again Saturday afternoon, and he took me to a gallery where a sample of his work is on show. We had dinner out and, well, I said goodbye to him at breakfast this morning.'

'Philip. You may well look coy and embarrassed hiding your face. You are a tart,' I say.

'Go there, lover boy,' says Jo.

'It's all marvellous, girls. It was breakfast at his and we're catching up tonight. He's just so lovely and so into me,' says Philip.

'I'm pleased, really I am. Look after yourself. We care you know,' I say as I head for my desk and settle, having hung my coat.

'Thank you, darling, I know you do. I appreciate it. Anyway, how was your weekend with your lover boy?' asks Philip.

'Great, so nice to have him back, very relaxing, but he's likely to be off again soon and …'

'And?' says Philip who has now taken up residence on the corner of my desk.

'Well, he's looking at reporting further afield and so may be away for longer periods,' I reply.

'How do you feel about that?' asks Jo.

'OK, I suppose – it's what makes him happy. He's been chasing the dream of working in a war zone all his life. Maybe once he's finally got up front and personal in a conflict situation, it'll be out of his system. No, it's all good, really. I support him, I do.'

Smiling and sounding confident is something that I need to get used to doing. I need to convince everyone that I'm happy for Joel, including Joel, although deep down in the pit of my stomach I ache a worrying ache – worried what could happen to him whilst he's away, worried about me and whether I'm going mad. *Could my dream really have taken me to Syria the other night, what does it mean?* I'm worried about all my dreams and occasional recurring nightmares and worried about change, the change of job and leaving Philip and Jo and the safe world of *True Life* behind.

'Your face betrays you Elise; he'll be fine though, I can feel it in my water,' says Philip.

*

With the mailbag done and my emails up to date, I collect together ten leads for stories in a folder.

Grabbing my tube and Greater London map, I set off in search of truth.

Once away from the office I plot my route around London and the surrounding area and prioritise the stories to be investigated according to success value. Whilst still cool for a spring day, it's not bitter and makes a pleasant change from being tied to a desk. By late afternoon I've secured two possible runners, which, with some tweaking, will make worthy articles for one of the autumn editions. I take respite for a while in a tube station café and utilise the free Wi-Fi to research jobs in publishing. I need to work out what I am capable of and more importantly, what I really want to do.

*

As I approach our front door a little after six I'm surprised to see the inside of the house fully illuminated. I wasn't expecting Joel to get home before me, but it makes a pleasant change from the previous week when I entered a dark and uninviting home each night. As I turn the key in the lock and step in, the lovely aroma of Asian cuisine fills the air, exotic smells – five-spice, soy sauce, limes and ginger – all permeating through the hallway.

'Hi hun, I'm home,' I shout as I drop my coat and bags on the bench. Entering the kitchen at the back of the house, I can hear the gentle hum of the extractor fan drawing up the steam billowing from the wok below.

Wandering through to the front room, I find that the door is ajar. As I enter, Joel, who is standing by the window with his ear pressed to his phone, turns towards me. He's engrossed. From his expression, the call is still ongoing. He throws me a glance and a half smile and turns back towards the window. Not wishing to disturb him further, I leave, pulling the door behind me and pop upstairs to get changed.

By the time I reappear in the kitchen, Joel is back at the helm, shaking the wok with such ferocity you would think it has done something wrong.

'It's caught a bit, sorry. I think it should still taste nice though: grab two plates, would you,' says Joel.

'Sure.'

Joel serves up straight away. He thinks eating off cold plates is a cardinal sin, so encourages me to sit and tuck in immediately. Three or four mouthfuls in,

I reluctantly slow, finishing my mouthful, and ask after his day.

'Great, thanks; actually, to be honest it couldn't have gone better,' says Joel.

'This is lovely, by the way,' I say interjecting. 'That's good; so was Ben on board for you to return to Turkey?'

'He sure was, and I didn't even have to ask. He wants me to go over the border this time, into Syria, and report in more depth on the routes that the refugees are taking,' replies Joel.

'Really, Syria. OK, and what about the image you captured, what did Ben say about that?' *Hopefully nothing, please say he was dismissive, please say he doesn't want it pursued.*

'Not a lot. He's not keen on me pursuing it and thought it was a story better suited to your magazine than his paper. I felt a little embarrassed if truth be told. Apparently, though, if I use my own time and not his then I can revisit the camps. He's sorting the paperwork,' says Joel.

'How soon?' I ask, although not entirely sure I am ready for the answer.

'As early as Friday if I can arrange the travel plans for Ben to sign off. This time for at least two weeks, as it'll take me a while to negotiate for me and my interpreter to have access to the Syrian side,' says Joel.

'A couple of weeks, OK.' I try to sound pleased, but inside I'm in turmoil, the trotting escalates. I know he wants to go back, but not this soon, and for so long.

'You'll never guess what though – this put the icing on the cake to make it a truly awesome day,' says Joel, beaming and placing his fork on the side of his plate.

'No, what?' I daren't ask, I don't want to hear. I've an idea what he's going to say before he even opens his mouth.

'America has come calling. Guy came through. That was him on the phone earlier. He knows a man who knows a man, you know how it works – well they're looking for an embed,' replies Joel.

'A what?' I ask.

'An embedded journalist to work with the military,' says Joel.

'What, for the Americans in Europe?' I ask.

'Well for the Americans, but in Afghanistan,' replies Joel.

The nausea rises, the turmoil now chewing my insides. My head tries to fathom what Joel is saying and my heart wants to leap from my chest. First Syria, a potential conflict zone, and secondly Afghanistan, a full-on war-torn country where Americans are equal to Hades, the slayer of the underworld. It's fair to say he won't be safe in either country, and for that matter nor will I.

'Elise, are you OK? You disappeared for a moment there,' says Joel.

'No, I'm fine, just trying to comprehend what you're saying. First Syria, then Afghanistan. It's a lot to take in, Joel. Excellent news for you, maybe, but you know how much I worry,' I reply whilst stirring the contents of my plate, no longer interested in eating. Joel might be the MasterChef in our house, but he's just served up a dish which makes me feel sick.

'It's going to be OK, don't worry. Firstly, I'll just be over the border in Syria and secondly, the Afghanistan thing, well, it's potentially exciting, but a long way off becoming reality. Guy says I need to go over to America and meet with the military advisor. Then there would be an interview and if all goes well, then maybe by June I could be off on that jolly.'

Jolly is not a word I would use to describe entering conflict zones, with or without military protection. Joel buzzes around all evening, researching and booking flights for Turkey and sending off emails regarding Afghanistan. There was always a possibility that his dual nationality would be of benefit, but tonight for me it's the thing taking him away, further away than I've ever felt. Even lying in bed next to him I sense a growing distance. His dream is potentially his new reality, whereas my dreams, my subconscious ones, are potential future nightmares.

*

As the week progresses and Friday draws closer, my anxiety grows more intense. I spend most of the week out of the office occupying my time with article research and writing. Some stories seem a million miles away from the dream research I had started less than two weeks ago. I haven't totally shelved that, though, and with Joel planning more trips overseas I feel drawn towards it again, needing to pick up where I left off. Knowledge is power. The military has strategists; I have Google.

On Friday morning Joel and I stand at the station waiting for our respective trains to take us off in different directions. I hold Joel tight, tighter than I have before. I can't stop my eyes from smarting as I absorb his bodily warmth, feeling his touch on my lips for that last time in what will be a long two-and-a-half weeks.

Reassuringly Joel holds my face in his hands, breathing warmth over my skin. This will be longest absence we've experienced since he stayed back in America after our gap-year travels, the spring and early summer before he secured his first UK job. All those years ago that absence seemed like an age. After he moved to the UK and we lived apart for months, that distance between us never felt like this. Joel might not see it, but to me this is different. We have grown together over the years and I fear that Joel's work now, for the first time, has the potential to pull us apart.

Goodbyes done, it's time to go. Letting him go, I head for the platform. Another day, another dollar, Joel would sometimes say; today is another day, another dimension for me.

Chapter Seventeen

Elise

The two-and-a-half weeks whilst Joel is away flies by. The speed at which time evaporates surprises me no end, but so does the manner in which I can control my dreams. My dreams seemingly propel me into the desert almost every night. I believe knowing where Joel is, actually helps. Joel said that he was not going too far over the border of Turkey into Syria and somehow neither do I. It's as if the dreams recur; night after night, familiar desert plains, landmarks, and landscapes. The sky is clear with little to observe. If I cannot see anyone, maybe they can't see me. Maybe I'm not really there after all, and it's all mind games, with me making convenient and maybe even coincidental connections which don't really exist.

Nevertheless, I channel my time and energy in to finishing the dream research. At home, just like before when Joel was in Turkey, I spend the evenings on my laptop. My TV dinner is perched on the sofa and a faithful glass of Sauvignon Blanc keeps me hydrated. The revelation that my soul potentially transcends to real locations around the world is a lot to comprehend – it's scary whilst at the same time exciting. The evidence, though, is growing. My nightly excursions into Syria and Turkey, countries I've not consciously visited before, afford me insights not routinely remarked on in tourist guides. My recordings in my dream diary resemble those of an explorer, highlighting unseen and untouched territories. This fractured part of the Middle East is now ingrained in my subconscious.

I focus on astral projection and auras. What surprises me is how much information is available on a topic dismissed in scientific terms and only supported by pseudo-science. There's no mention, though, that anyone has made a connection between their conscious and subconscious worlds in the way that I have. Auras are interesting. Joel captured a bright white image. If that was an aura, my aura, then a white or silvery aura is thought to be possessed by someone who is sensitive, spiritual, intuitive, possessing psychic abilities and of a practical nature. I prefer that description to that of a black aura, which just spells death and destruction. Auras, reportedly, are created by the vibration of our very atoms and a combination of electromagnetic, microwave, infrared and UV radiation. Science at last.

On Joel's return, he does not mention once a sighting of a deity, god or hovering bright light. Whilst he's seemingly put the religious phenomenon to bed, I still need clarity.

Joel's downtime in Syria allowed him to make applications to various bodies, including the Afghanistan International Security Assistance Force for a 'media visit'. He also floated to Ben the idea of the *Standard* being his sponsors. The *Standard* has a sister paper in America called the *Globe*, and Joel sold it to Ben as a win on both sides of the Atlantic.

In the days following Joel's return, our relationship warms up again. Joel's on a high gearing up for his visit to America to complete his application. I feel relatively calm too. With Joel lying beside me each night, I experience little or no dreaming at all. I still have my doubts about Afghanistan and how my subconscious will cope with another absence, but that is hopefully some way off for now.

Joel's plans for America include hops to New York, Washington, and Sanibel Island, Florida. I can't help but be a little envious. We were saving hard for a visit to see his parents on Sanibel. I would want for very little on an island that provides such warmth and so many shells. The thought of Joel visiting without me leaves me feeling a little empty. Whilst the *Standard* and *Globe* have agreed to sponsor him, we still need to fund his initial application and flights ourselves. If he gets the attachment, then the military will jointly fund the project as they want Joel to work for them, not just with them. They will also control what Joel reports on and how and when it's published.

The waiting game begins.

*

Amanda and I have a date to meet in one of Amanda's favourite places, her very own coffee house. It isn't quite Amanda's but the amount of money she's spent there over the years, she should own shares or they should name a coffee after her. As a regular she only has to step over the threshold to hear the holler from a barista shouting 'tall Americano with room'. Amanda need not reply, but just smile in the barista's direction and virtually by the time she reaches the counter it's ready. Service with a smile. Coffee, on the other hand, is not my drink of choice. It used to be, a long time ago, but I'm now free of stimulants – barring the obvious wine, champagne and cocktails of course.

Several years ago I associated late-night coffee drinking with my overactive dream cycles, so rather than wait for the men in white coats to take me away, I quit – quit the habit, the obsession, and the social scene that accompanied it. I handed in my membership card for the coffeehouse and went into hiding. To start with, I literally just drank hot water, going cold turkey. Once 'clean' I re-joined the 'club', but my poison of choice became green and herbal and now minty. Little did I realise at the time that caffeine had absolutely nothing to do with my dreams. I, however, feel healthier and am not spending as much time or money in the den of iniquity. As the tea drinker amongst a group of hard-nosed coffee quaffers, I always seem like the driver, the safe one with no additives. I feel no residual buzz or shake associated with a hard double shot.

As I enter the coffee house, I spy Amanda seated in her favourite spot near the window. She occupies an oversized camel tone leather chair that looks as if it has comforted far too many customers. With her coffee positioned front and centre on the table and her mobile phone in hand, she is head down, texting. I stride over to her and as she looks up to acknowledge my presence she simultaneously points to the barista and says, 'There's one in the pot for you.'

'Great,' I reply.

The handsome and somewhat short barista, probably all of nineteen years old, smiles and hands me a short mug with a mint blend tea. *Perfect.*

I return to Amanda and sit down on a worn, fraying bucket chair opposite. The original jacquard print is faded and reminiscent of my mum's old hall carpet. Stretching out my whole torso, I kick off my shoes, freeing my toes from the shackles that restrained them all day.

'Pink, ooh summer's arrived,' says Amanda.

'Yes, darling,' I reply. 'Pink seemed the way to go. It definitely makes them look better and gives my feet the illusion of being tanned.'

'You know my motto,' says Amanda, 'no rain, no roof.'

'Yes,' I say. 'But that normally applies to sports cars, not shoes versus sandals.' Amanda rarely wears closed-toe shoes or boots after April and reluctantly puts on trainers only because the gym insists on it.

'Anyway, how are things?' she asks. 'Last time we caught up you were working on dream world aka *The Life of Elise*. I recall it wasn't going so well.'

'No, it wasn't. My research, what I discovered about dreams, resonated maybe a little too close to home. My fear was it would be more of an autobiographical account of me than an article.'

'What's wrong with that? After all, you probably qualify as an expert. What you've experienced in dreams can't be rivalled.'

'If only you knew.'

Amanda smiles and takes a long, slow sip of her coffee, ingesting the aroma and savouring the kick, her eyes broadening momentarily.

'You're obviously itching to do more on it, but you fear something,' says Amanda.

'Yes, I'm scared. I fear being judged and ridiculed. When you and Henry were last over at ours you were both laughing at me when I recounted my dream. The one about me trying to teach my mother to fly,' I reply, cupping my mug with both hands and sipping carefully at my tea, trying to avoid the floating bag which still remains.

'Yes, but we know you, and you do make us laugh, you're so sincere about your dreams. I can barely remember what I had for breakfast, let alone what I was doing overnight. Whereas you, well, you're more connected in that way.'

'I'm not sure if you truly mean connected or you're trying to be polite. It's hard for you to understand. There's far more to it than you realise. *There's far more to it than I realised.* Anyway, anyway, I'm going to change my job. I decided several weeks ago that I need to move away from the weird and wacky. I posted my CV off to a few publishers just to test the water and am waiting for responses.'

'You've got a book in you; I've always said you could write a book, you've read so many, so why not write one?'

'Well, one step at a time. I need to find a job first and I may have to start at the bottom of the pile again, making tea. I told Philip and Jo only last week so I'm under no pressure there, although I would like to secure something sooner rather than later.'

'You shouldn't dismiss writing a book. I can see the cover now: 'Best Seller by Elise Hamilton'. It has a certain ring to it.' Amanda strikes a Hollywood pose for my benefit.

'I'm not sure I like the idea of having my name up there in neon lights.'

'Well, use a pseudonym then. How about Henrietta Taylor or Juliette Bardot – both very sophisticated. No one would ever guess it was you.'

'Thanks a lot, my best friend, and number one fan. Anyway, do I really look like a Henrietta? My mum and dad have a wooden carved hippo they affectionately call Henrietta. My backside can be broad on occasions, but I'm not a hippo.'

'No one's saying you're a hippo, but you get my drift; a false name, a little intrigue, and after all you can choose any name because the whole point is, it's not you.'

'Another?' I say to Amanda as I stand up and point to her coffee mug.

Surprisingly, she replies, 'No,' followed by, 'make mine a peppermint tea too, please.'

'Ooh,' I say, 'is this a conversion in progress?'

'No,' she replies. 'I just need to cut back.'

Having secured our two herbal infusions, I walk back over to Amanda and once again slump into the worn but comfortable chair. The conversation has been one sided, all about me. It's time to move on.

'Anyway, I've been meaning to ask what your secret is, your health secret. You looked positively radiant the other week and even the following morning after all that alcohol we consumed. Are you on a new eating regime?'

Amanda does not reply. Her head tilts forward towards her drink, and then she rummages in her oversized bag. She looks up and simultaneously pulls out a small piece of paper which measures only about four inches square and hands it to me. There, in black and white, blurred and grainy, is the image of a baby. A tiny baby.

Instinctively, I let out a shriek of delight and lunge forward, embracing Amanda. 'OMG you're pregnant, that's fantastic, it is fantastic isn't it? Please say it is.' I seat myself on the edge of my chair, waiting for the reply.

'Yes, it's fantastic, I'm pleased; we're pleased.' Amanda puts her hand to her mouth and laughs nervously, tears well in her eyes.

'Oh no,' I say, standing and throwing myself at her once more. 'That's brilliant, I'm so pleased.'

'You are?' says Amanda.

'Yes, of course, why would you think I wouldn't be?'

'Well, it worried me to think things would change with a baby on the scene.'

'No, don't be silly. They do a brilliant line in cocktail dresses for babies these days; have baby, will travel – that's my motto.'

'That makes me thrilled, thank you Elise.' Amanda's toothy smile is reignited on her face once more.

'But hang on, this image would suggest you're... I don't know, a couple of months?'

'Thirteen weeks give or take,' replies Amanda somewhat sheepishly.

'But you were drinking cocktails and wine at ours like they were going out of fashion.'

'I know I was and I feel so bad. It wasn't planned; don't get me wrong, Henry and I are over the moon. We always thought one day we'd have kids but never set a time on when. I was drinking because I didn't know then, but the doctors and midwife have assured me that I won't have pickled the baby. The crucial thing is that I stopped as soon as I knew. I've reduced my coffee intake and actually entered my kitchen and cooked several healthy meals. See, you should be proud of me.'

'Well, you look great so it obviously suits you; and Henry, he's coping?'

'Yes, he's over the moon. I think his family thought with us living in London it would never happen. Now it has they are cock-a-hoop.'

'That's such brilliant news; I can't wait to tell Joel. We must get together, all of us, soon, before you balloon and no longer want to be seen in public. What am I saying – as if that will ever happen.' My voice trails off at the mere suggestion that Amanda would ever balloon.

'You're right, it won't happen, I can't wait to buy trendy maternity wear and party frocks with elasticated waists. You'll see, I'll party to the end.'

'Ooh, how exciting. I get to be cool Aunty Elise. I like the sound of that, and of course there will be awesome Uncle Joel. Now aren't we grown up.'

'So, let's have a toast.' With that Amanda and I raise our cups. 'To new beginnings, a baby, and a new career – cheers.'

When I leave Amanda an hour later and walk towards the tube, there's a spring in my step. I can barely conceal the excitement. My beaming expression is drawing attention, but I don't care. I've been worrying and fussing over my dreams, my subconscious life. Yet in the real world, right in front of me, this new life has been created and is growing. I want to be part of that world. I need to let my dream obsession go and focus on the here and now.

Chapter Eighteen

Joel

Seeing Mom and Dad again for the first time in ages is a genuine treat. They always carry a golden wheat glow regardless of the season, one of the many benefits of living in a year-round warm and sunny climate. Stepping into the kitchen of their cosy diner makes me feel at home, like the old days. Prepping dishes alongside the resident chef is an education, I'm careful to memorise the dishes so that I can treat Elise on my return. The potential anxieties and complexities of working in Afghanistan melt away for a short snapshot of time. Growing up on Sanibel, with nature on the doorstep, limited distractions and the safety net of the sea around the island has done little to prepare me for what I will probably witness and experience in Afghanistan. Challenges with the environment, the people and the threats are all bound to change my life forever. It's what I've always wanted though. *That's what I Keep telling myself.* I never wanted to be a soldier growing up, but I want to experience the adrenalin rush that deployment into a conflict zone gives so many.

Forty-eight hours is not enough time on the island to do it justice. When not helping at the diner I take several long strolls along the sandy shell-encrusted beaches, consuming the air in large cavernous breaths, capitalising on the purity. The warmth and strength of the sun is intense and my skin prickles as it adjusts to the freedom that living in shorts on an island brings.

With several wildlife sighting reports completed, I pin them to the diner notice board. Ospreys nesting and dolphins playing. Island life is simple, we are the guests, and the wildlife are our hosts.

Adopting the 'Sanibel stoop', I collect shells, varying sizes and colours, some faded and aged by the sun and some fresh and vibrant as if just plucked from the sea; one shell for each day that I'll be away. All for Elise. The shells are Elise's favourite aspect of the island, coupled with the warmth. Over the years, Elise has spent hours walking, stooping and shovelling for shells. Repeatedly she would comment how no two are the same, wonders of nature which retain so much beauty long after life has left them. I feel bad that she's not with me, and the news that I'm taking home is not going to be met with joy either.

Dad's tense when he drops me off at the airport in Fort Myers. His time served in the air force taught him many things about combat zones. Whilst he wouldn't show it in front of Mom, there's an edge to him as he hugs me and shakes my hand to say goodbye. His eyes betray him. He fears what he imagines I might encounter, scared for his son who, regardless of age, is still his boy. So, the hug and the look which says it all is what sends me off on my journey home via Miami and then overnight to London. With any luck, I'll be home before Elise and can prepare my mom's new signature dish.

*

Hearing the keys turn in the lock, I reduce the heat on the grill and hob and pour two glasses of a tasty New Zealand Sauvignon Blanc. Wiping my hands, I head to greet Elise.

Once she is free of her jacket, I capture her in my arms and pull her in tight, afraid to let go.

'I've missed you so much, it's great to be home,' I say.

'Me too. You look so well – just look at your sun-kissed skin. It's so unfair. I resemble a vampire compared to you,' says Elise.

'Well, people say they have muscle memory, with me its pigment memory,' I reply.

'You even smell of the sun, the beach and the sand. It's as if you bathed in it,' says Elise, and she inhales and absorbs me.

Elise's touch arouses my senses. Her perfume, subtle and sweet as candy, is just vaguely detectable on her soft neckline. I feel edgy, a pressure forms on the notch in my throat. Elise is not going to like what I have to tell her, I can sense her reaction before I even start the conversation. It's the intense look in her eyes, her longing which gives her away.

'I've cooked something special tonight – my mom's new signature dish, minus the grouper but the principle and 90 per cent of the ingredients are the same. Come through, the wine is already open and poured.'

Walking back into the kitchen, I check on the grill and stir the sauce, then pass Elise a glass. 'Cheers.'

'Successful trip, then? You sounded pleased when you left Washington.'

'It did go well; let me serve up and tell you what's going to happen.'

Explaining to Elise how the interview and form filling went is the easy bit. My sponsors, the *Standard* and the *Globe*, came through. I satisfy the powers that be with my credentials, and living in the UK presented no issues as both of my passports are up to date.

Explaining how quickly they offered the position and how soon they want me to work out in Afghanistan is a little trickier; not as tricky as trying to reassure Elise that I'll be OK, when I know very little regarding the assignment.

'It's great that you've got it. I cannot believe you're going in June, but why can't they tell you more? It's no secret where the military is based, and why; it's the war, the conflict, isn't it?' says Elise, clearly tense from my news.

'I don't know exactly. I had to sign lots of confidentiality agreements and standard operating procedures. The *Standard* and *Globe* also had to sign contracts. I will work for the military and the papers.

The military, though, will maintain control in the main over any reporting,' I reply.

'So, you won't be free to report on what you see?' says Elise.

'No. That's one of the fundamental conditions of the attachment.' I pause a moment to finish my wine and top up both of our glasses. 'I'll get briefed when I arrive on the ground in Bagram. Apparently I'll then have some familiarisation training, whatever that is, and everything I write they vet before being released. They control my reporting. Everything, even phone calls, are recorded, encrypted and routed via Langley. There'll be no sex talk or, come to think about it, no talk of any sort. I won't be able to discuss my role or tasks, and if I do I'm out.'

'And you still want to go? You've always fought against suppressing the truth. Why agree to such terms?'

'I want to go, Elise. This is the only way I could ever afford to get this kind of opportunity. The military is covering half the costs, without which the papers would never support me. There'll be plenty of opportunities post-attachment for independent reporting, but as yet I've no idea what operation I'll be covering.'

'I still cannot believe it. June – that's in no time, and the one thing you haven't told me is how long. How long will you be gone?' Elise's face is now flushed, her concern evident from her questions and those eyes betraying her internal emotions.

'Three months, maybe more. They gave me a rough end-date of mid-October.' Elise's face drops in an instant. I know I've pushed my agenda recently and been away far too much.

'It's three months,' I say. Elise is still seated at the dining table, her face pale and eyes empty. I push the table to one side and pull my chair in close; our legs entangle. Holding her face, my favourite part of her body, I search deep into those eyes, trying to draw her back out. 'Three months, fourteen weeks, no more than a hundred days. Treat them as sleeps to D-Day, a countdown to my return. I promise I'll be OK.'

Elise tilts her head in towards my shoulder. She's trying hard to mask her tears, but as my shirt grows damper, I know she's crying. Lifting her face towards mine, I slowly kiss each tear away, tasting the salty droplets. Each one I capture and savour.

'I love you, Elise; I'll be safe and come back, I promise.'

'I love you too, Joel, I'll just miss you for a hundred sleeps; that's lots of dreaming.'

'Make them nice dreams, dreams of me, of us, of wonderful times and places.'

Elise is quiet. She buries her head once again in my shoulder and sobs quietly whilst I hold her until I walk her upstairs to bed.

*

'You're up early,' I say, savouring every minute I can under the duvet.

'Well, work beckons, here and now,' replies Elise.

'You never said how the job hunting was going,' I say.

'Well, with your bombshell last night there wasn't time. To be honest, I didn't feel like making the effort,' replies Elise.

'Elise, you knew it was a possibility when I flew out for the interview.'

'Yes, a possibility, but June, and three months, Joel. You barely returned from Turkey before going to Syria, then America, and now Afghanistan. We've hardly seen each other these past few months. I feel as if I'm living here alone most of the time.' Elise flushes from the chest upwards as if a pot is simmering and ready to boil. 'I'm sorry. I just need to absorb what's happening here. I need to go,' says Elise.

Elise doesn't give me her usual lingering parting kiss. She turns and leaves the bedroom and heads down the stairs. Feeling an utter idiot, jumping out of bed grabbing shorts and flip-flops, I race behind her to the door.

'Wait Elise, wait up.'

As I reach the bottom of the staircase, the front door slams shut. I grab my keys from the hall table and step out into the morning light. Elise is only twenty metres along the road when I catch her.

'I'm the one that should say sorry. Sorry for leaving you so many times and sorry for not realising what it's doing to you. You've nothing to apologise for. I'm the one being an ass, I promise I'll make it up to you. I love you so much and once this assignment is complete, I'll be home, I promise. This is just a blip with my career, not with us,' I say.

Elise stands listening to me but not wanting to look at me. Her neckline is still flushed. When she lifts her head, I can see her glazed eyes. Elise grabs me tight and places one peck on my cheek and says, 'We'll talk tonight; by the way, call Henry.'

It's favourable that she kissed me, but I'm far from off the hook.

Chapter Nineteen

Elise

April evaporates, and May and June merge with hot and cold days both inside and outside our home. Amanda and Henry's baby news helps, breathing fresh life into our extended family socials. Baby-centric conversations draw the attention away from Joel's impending departure.

Joel keeps himself busy focussing on local news stories, biding time, keeping Ben happy at the *Standard* and our bank balance even happier. To be honest, my head stays buried in the sand. Whilst Joel is home my sleeping and dreaming are under control and carefree, but I know that will change the minute he leaves.

The CVs that I sent out in April reap rewards with one publishing house, Jones Butler, offering me a job to start straight away as their new editorial assistant.

The night before Joel's flight, we stay in and Joel cooks. Dinner feels like the last supper and in my mind it probably will be the last balanced meal I get for a while, cooked in our kitchen anyway.

'Are you OK, Elise?' Joel asks.

'If I say "no", would it make a difference, would you cancel your plans and stay?'

'If you felt so strongly about the Afghanistan assignment, I would've listened.'

'Yes, you would have listened and we would have talked it through, followed by you reassuring me that everything would be OK, no different to now. Saying no was never an option.'

'I don't want to leave you like this,' says Joel.

'But you will. There's nothing that you can say which will convince me it will be OK, you know I'm worried. Afghanistan is a war zone, a place which has been at war for decades, just different parties in the mix; and they definitely do not want the Americans there.'

'The war is technically over, they're winding things up slowly,' says Joel.

'If that's the case then what are you going to do? What is your assignment really about?'

'I'm not sure, Elise, but I'm excited to get involved in some minor way. Growing up in a services environment, seeing families separated, and some torn apart by war was shocking, but my family emerged on the other side and so will ours.'

'Our family; you're not getting broody, are you? All that baby talk with Henry.'

'No, I'm not, but their baby is another exciting thing happening in our lives that we can truly get involved in, and then there's your job. I wish I was going to be around more to support you.'

'Joel Hamilton, you may be right in what you say, but I'm not letting you get off lightly. Three months away means you owe me big time and you can start by coming back in one piece so I can put you to task.'

'Well, I promise you I'll return and count sleeps as you count those shells. As I need to get in some credit, I've a surprise for you. This was to be my parting gift tomorrow at the airport, but now seems the right time.'

Joel hands me an A4 white envelope, unaddressed.

'Ooh, this is more like it.' Unpeeling the envelope I rummage around inside, pulling out a folded piece of paper.

'Careful,' says Joel.

On instruction, I carefully remove the paper and unfold it. A plane ticket falls into my lap. Leaving the note for a moment, I focus on the ticket. *London Gatwick to Tampa Florida 15th October.*

'Joel, this is wonderful, thank you.' I leap towards him to plant a hug, pausing for a moment. 'You will be there too?'

'Yes. Look, I said mid-October; my flight back into America arrives two or three days before yours, so I'll be at Tampa to collect you, I promise. We'll then have two weeks together for me to devour you in every way possible on Sanibel.'

'God, I love you, Mr Hamilton,' I say, smothering Joel in kisses and a tight embrace. 'This has bought you some credit; and your parents, they're OK with us descending on them?'

'My parents are well on board. I made the plans a few weeks back. They're eager to see us both. Remember, their home is your home too.'

Once my excitement from the surprise calms I read the information, carefully absorbing the idea of our stateside reunion. Whilst blissful, part of my consciousness has already set to work fathoming the one hundred sleeps, trying to determine if they will be nice dreams or scary nightmares I have to contend with.

*

Leaving Joel with a memory of my smiling face is crucial. Watching him walk through the security gate to the departure lounge causes a nerve behind my eyes to pinch. The smile, though, remains fixed, accompanied by a wave until he's no longer in view. Turning back towards the exit, I release the dam and allow the pressure to ebb away down my face. Last night I was nothing but a mood Hoover and had focussed on my selfish feelings without considering what Joel might feel too. This is his opportunity to fulfil a dream and my sulky, childlike behaviour dulled the moment. Joel's parting words were nothing but positive, promising regular calls and that he'll be safe and count the days to meeting me in Florida, which will be great. I know he did that for my benefit, which at the time I appreciated.

During my waking daytime hours, I throw myself into my new role at Jones Butler. Dozens of manuscripts in varying shapes and forms accumulate on my desk within the first few days. With deadlines set for reviews and assessments, I quickly become accustomed to speed reading. The change of task makes a pleasant change, especially with the genres varying daily. Whilst I miss Philip and Jo, it's nevertheless refreshing to start a week by reading a love story or a thriller, rather than trudging through the mailbags looking for the next best alien abduction story. The change in my working life is positive. Since Joel's departure though, I haven't formed a plan to cope with the sleeps which lie ahead.

Although I've learnt a lot these past few months about dreams, and my dreams in particular, I'm still not a hundred per cent sure if I've proved my theories sufficiently. What I know is that Joel being in Afghanistan will be very different. This time he's literally in a war zone and has the potential to be at the front and centre of the action, my worst fears, or should I say nightmares, being realised. There are two options. Option A – allow my dreams to run wild, to take me wherever, maybe Afghanistan each night, and fly, float, run or walk, all uncontrolled. No planning. Gift myself the luxury of falling asleep and letting my subconscious take over. Or, option B – I can take control. In taking control, though, I have to ask myself what that really means. Taking control even in some small way makes more sense, but potentially carries more risks. Having discovered after all these years that my soul actually goes, physically and tangibly, to places, do I want now to place myself in Afghanistan?

Joel, at least, has the military there to protect him. What or who will I have, and do I need protection? In the past I've experienced dreams where I've punched, kicked and fought my way to escape, and ran and flown. All amazing things, but my psyche is still trying to fathom all the links. If my soul physically transcends to a place, a country, as with Syria and Turkey, that would suggest that when I've previously had fights with people and escaped, my actions and interactions with people were real too. They've always felt real. Some are exhilarating and I want to relive them. Others are exhausting, scary and I need to end them, wake and forget.

Not wanting to jump to too many conclusions, I need to finish the research and see if a plan presents itself. Cranking up the laptop at home with the TV on in the background is becoming an all-too-familiar routine. If anyone ever views my search history, it will make interesting reading.

The aura research talked of the vibration of atoms being responsible for the aura itself. My little knowledge of physics will not win me any prizes, but I can vaguely remember covering something in school regarding humans comprising atoms. Seven billion billion billion atoms, to be precise, which are a lot of moving molecules. Comprehending that our rigid bones, skin and blood could actually all be moving is difficult.

Searching through the many pages on the internet, scanning for answers, one snippet catches my eye: 'electromagnetic repulsion'. The premise is that atoms never physically touch each other – the closer they get, the more they repel. The research suggests that we, humans, animals and plants never touch anything, not even each other. Instead, we float a tiny indistinguishable distance above or away, suspended by the repulsion between the very fabric of our being. The grey cells within our brains interpret the physical world for us, which allows us to believe we're touching and feeling when in the physical world we're not.

This quantum physical explanation regarding our atoms goes some way to confirming my flying and soul theories, insofar as, if we never really touch our beds and our atoms are literally floating, we could be flying. *Could that really be what's happening to me, I so want and need to believe it to be true.*

Overlapping my research with lucid dreams and whilst not wishing to pick out the definitions which suit my rationalisation, I find one of interest. There's one explanation that talks of the individual's capacity whilst lucid dreaming to control themselves, their environment and the meaning of a dream as long as the dreamer remains focussed. Whilst lucid dreaming, physical laws need not apply. *Physical laws need not apply.*

I finish a tiring night of research by looking into the energy produced by the human body. How could a camera capture an image of a person in the night sky? Would a glow, an aura, truly be visible if the origin was a soul, a dreamer?

Humans produce an average of a hundred watts of energy at rest and need about 2,000 calories to do so. I scan the sitting room, looking for appliances that give off a hundred watts of energy. The glow from the forty-watt bulb in the table lamp is soft and subtle, but a one hundred-watt bulb would be bright, unbearably bright. That's my glow. There's some logic to it, and some science. But, if I had offered Joel this explanation to his religious phenomena sighting, in Turkey three months ago, he would have thought I was mad. I know he felt embarrassed pursuing it, he said he had been uncomfortable talking to Ben about it, and after his Syria trip was quick to dismiss it further. Am I trying to make connections to fit a scenario which suits my own agenda of rationalising my dreams? Is this my desperate attempt at clinging onto the idea that I'm important to Joel's life, knowing full well that he is pursuing his dream which does not include me?

As I switch off the laptop and ready myself for bed, I feel the first twinge of nerves climbing the stairs. What am I really going to do, and have I the control that all the research has lead me to believe? Will I just observe, or if my soul really wants me to watch over Joel, as that seems the only rational explanation, then will it also want me to protect him physically if required? Could I end up facing a combatant hell-bent on killing, one who will not discriminate between man and woman?

Man or woman? Another question crosses my mind as I reach the bedroom door. *What am I?* I know what I am, obviously I'm a woman, but from memory and notes in my diary I occasionally experience a dream as a man. The character and action has been one of a man in a man's body, so it begs the question, what do I look like in my dreams? This is a question that I have until now never asked myself. There are no mirrors, either, in my dreams, as I far as I can recollect. The entire dream unfolds through my eyes.

Switching off the light and pulling a loose sheet over me, I lie still, wondering and staring at the ceiling. My mind is racing with the endless possibilities, too wired to rest and sleep, and maybe just a little scared of what will happen when I close my eyes.

Chapter Twenty

Joel

On arrival at Bagram in Afghanistan, I'm shown my sleeping quarters, which comprise a small bunk bed housed in a plywood unit within a larger prefabricated chipboard hut. The hut contains twelve internally secure units each with a set of bunk beds. The decoration is limited to graffiti on the ply wood. Scribblings made by the endless number of soldiers who have taken up residence over the years. I take up the lower bunk and unpack my toiletries and clothes using the upper bunk for storage. There's a tiny plywood desk and shelf, but little else in the way of furniture and comfort. Having been instructed to unpack, and report to the sand coloured poly tunnel briefing tent opposite, I waste no time.

On entering the briefing tent, I'm greeted by a man who introduces himself as Lieutenant Rogers. Lieutenant Rogers is dressed head to toe in military fatigues, and sports a regulation buzz cut which sets off his strong jawline and large frame.

'Hamilton, now that you have your bunk, we need to get you briefed and give you familiarisation training before deployment,' says Lieutenant Rogers.

'Ok,' I reply. 'What training do you have in mind?' I ask. Having not been told what aspect of the military operation I'm reporting on, I wonder what training a journalist needs in order to take photos and write reports.

'Well, if you want to be part of this operation, all of it. Rollover, fire dampening, first aid. I don't know what you think you're here to do, but we can't carry passengers, not on this operation'.

'Lieutenant Rogers, that's just it, I haven't been told what I'm covering.'

'You will. I have an operational briefing pack for you to digest and return. Once you have familiarised yourself and met the boys over the next couple of days, we will add seasoning to what's in the pack. Understood?' says Lieutenant Rogers.

'Yes, understood.'

Lieutenant Rogers thrusts a brown envelope towards me, together with a small A5 ring binder. The binder contains maps and a layout of Bagram Airbase and an itinerary of training for the next three days.

'Hamilton, you will be privy to very sensitive intelligence on this operation, your life and the lives of the men you will work with, depend on operational security remaining tight. You are a guest here, do not abuse the privilege we have given you. Now, the boys should be back so go over and introduce yourself. Be warned, they have a tendency to give civilians grief when they first join the platoon so don't expect them to give you a warm welcome. Welcome to Operation Rattle.'

As I leave the temporary briefing tent and walk back to my accommodation hut, just for a second I pause. I knew it would not be easy, but a pressure pushes down on my shoulders, my spirit feels flat. Echoing in my ears, Elise's words of encouragement. *I've left her behind, I need to make her proud.*

On entering the accommodation hut the banter being exchanged between the soldiers ceases and the room falls silent. I'm not sure if I should speak first.

'Dude, you must be Hamilton, the Emby.' A young Latino looking soldier announces.

'Yes, Joel, that's me.' I feel like the new kid at an old school.

'Well, we don't stand on ceremony round here, not unless you've got red, gold or silver bands, eagles or stars all over you, and then only because of the formality. We get three square meals a day, but if you're not liking the chow, there's always fried chicken available on Main Street. I think you've got rollover training with us tomorrow, so I recommend you don't eat lunch, not unless you have a strong stomach.' With that the Latino soldier puts his left hand on my shoulder and offers me a handshake with his right followed by, 'Welcome to Bagram and welcome to Operation Rattle. I'm Arturo, Corporal Lopez officially, but just Lopez amongst the boys. Be prepared to be called a host of names over the next few days. Once they get to know you, it will settle down. They're a good bunch, really.'

'Thanks Arturo, I wasn't sure what to expect.'

'Expect the worst,' replies Arturo, immediately followed by 'Listen up boys, this is Joel Hamilton our new Emby. I've explained the rules of engagement to him, now it's up to you to break him in. Outside in five, it's time to see if Emby can throw a ball.' Arturo then turns back to me and says, 'Sorry mate, if you're going to ride with us, then you have to do everything with us, rule number one.'

'Great.' *Fuck.*

*

The afternoon unfolded without event. They put my skills with a basketball to the test, but being tall, American, and an ex-high school hoop captain, reduced the pain. My names to date; Emby, Embed, Bed, Hammo, and Hamilton are all far from original and not at all offensive. I think what Lieutenant Rogers and Arturo said to me, was part of the banter, they were on the wind, maybe?

Taking to my bunk for some light reading and an early night seems surreal. I dreamt of getting this opportunity, and here I am living the first night of my dream. My briefing pack details the platoon structure with Lieutenant Rogers who I've already met overseeing the marines, field operations are to be lead by Captain Duncan Wilson with Major Simon Dunedin having full oversight and control. Operation Rattle is clandestine in nature with US Marines working alongside local Afghan Intelligence Police.

Hoping for more, but with my reading complete, I loosely pull over a sheet, close my eyes and wish to fall asleep quickly. The overhead strip light remains illuminated and some of the men are still milling around between bunks. Slightly reminiscent of my university days, I try to shut out the peripheral conversations and focus on Elise, her skin, her smell, her body. God, I miss her. Visualising her form is what will keep me sane for the next three months.

*

I'm woken abruptly to the sound of cans being rattled and a cold wet sensation on my feet.

'Come on Emby, if you're late, we're all late. Get a move on,' says Corporal Short – Shorty to his mates.

I snatch my feet inwards towards my chest to prevent a further soaking and launch myself off my bunk in response to my orders. Feeling dazed and disorientated I pause momentarily to absorb my surroundings, pinching myself mentally, reminding myself where I am. Thirty minutes later, I'm sat with thirty marines wolfing down ham, eggs and tepid tea.

By nine a.m. I'm pulling on fire-resistant overalls, and being shown how to manhandle a fire-extinguisher, and the most effective way to dampen flames. Remembering what Arturo had said to me yesterday, I opt to miss lunch and instead mentally prepare my stomach for the rollover training, not that I have a clue what that is.

As a platoon, we snake on foot around Bagram Airbase, reporting for Mine Resistant Ambush Protected Vehicle (MRAP) Egress Simulator Training, which is taking place in one of the many hangars. This affords me an impromptu tour of the base. Bagram is huge, it's a city, swollen with military personnel and civilians. Numerous hangars, control towers and prefabricated structures dominate the landscape. There's even Main Street with shops, takeaways and a barber.

The MRAPs will be the platoon's transport of choice, and therefore, everyone who rides in one has to go through the rollover simulator. The MRAP is a solid looking modern day tank which comes in various sizes, shapes, and which has various attachments, including armoury.

On arrival at the training hangar, I'm given a helmet, body armour and safety goggles. Being a Floridian, I'm used to safety briefings before going on rides, but this is very different. The stark warning given by the trainer is that this training "could" save our lives, not "will" save our lives, but "could". To quote, "This will increase your chances of survival in the event of an actual rollover". *Fuck.* For the first time in 36 hours, my stomach twitches. I'm not sure if it's nerves because of the training, or nerves because of the reality which lies ahead. A reality, which is yet to unfold.

With six of us being put through the simulator at any one time, I have to wait my turn. When my name is sung out with Lopez, Shorty, Fox, Jones and Pearson, I follow their lead and climb into the back of the sand coloured metal tin attached to a rotating frame. With my seatbelt fastened and my arms crossed I listen for the holler 'Rollover, rollover, rollover,' and then follow the lead of whoever makes the first move. We don't just do this once, but several times, each time being held at a different angle presenting a different exit route. As I exit for the last time, I feel my legs wobble slightly and I stumble forward onto my knees. I hold in my stomach, draw breath and stand to see Arturo smiling.

'Well done Emby, not bad for a virgin, most throw up the first time.' Little did he know how much I was straining to avoid being sick. Two hours later, having missed lunch, I tuck into dinner.

Chapter Twenty-one

Joel

By day six, I've completed all my training and received two briefings which explain Operation Rattle in more detail. The platoon of marines I'm accompanying for the next three months, is to be deployed to counter the growing number of smuggling cartels trading in weapons, drugs and people. I'll be reporting directly on the impact Operation Rattle has on disrupting supply chains between Afghanistan and Pakistan, across their immense 1500 mile border.

It's Nineteen hundred hours' local time. The residual warmth from the long hot sunny day lingers in the air as the sun sets. The sky is clear and partially illuminated with swathes of pinprick-sized diamonds and a crescent moon. As we walk from our sleeping barracks across the open compound to the briefing tent, I'm more than acutely aware of my environment. The city is enclosed by razor-wire fencing, high walls and watch towers ready to take out an insurgent attack. Occasionally a brave lone wolf will launch a night-time assault, which is usually silenced within moments of the first cracks being heard. Soldiers have been injured, though, just walking around, which makes me feel quite vulnerable regardless of the number of weapons possessed by the platoon.

On entering the briefing tent, I seat myself on a chair to the side of where the platoon has all taken up residence. Twenty of the thirty-strong team are present. Just enough chairs are laid out in rows in the centre of the tent. At the front, is a small square wooden table. Sitting on top is a laptop computer and projector. Behind the table is a large portable screen. Lieutenant Rogers stands next to the table, adjusting the screen image. The black-and-white, slightly shaky image is an aerial photograph of tracks through the Hindu Kush Valley leading to a remote village called Prakh.

During an earlier briefing, I'd learnt that the smugglers and insurgents – the Taliban – favour the inhospitable territory of the Hindu Kush mountain range and use off-road routes, predominantly at night. Drone and satellite imagery has identified, via laser marking, several valuable targets, and provides the marines with their own off-road map.

Bagram Air Base is ideally located for access to the Hindu Kush range. Access for the marines is via roads through the main Salang and Tang-e Gharu Passes. The soldiers can then deviate and follow their own private road map, leading them onto the smugglers' routes. Being summer, all the passes are open, but the military has a small window of four months before snow falls again.

As Captain Wilson enters the tent all the soldiers rise to attention. I do this instinctively. Whilst I'm not a military man, I feel compelled to follow their lead. Captain Wilson waves his hand towards us and says, 'As you were.' Captain Wilson is a man in his forties with over twenty years' military experience. He's seen action in Helmand Province and has lost honourable men and women because of roadside bombs and insurgent attacks. He volunteered to take on a third tour specifically for this operation.

Once seated, the room falls quiet and the overhead lighting dims. The only noise is that of the power generator outside the tent humming away. Lieutenant Rogers takes a quick roll call of those present. Captain Wilson opens the briefing detailing the objectives and then Lieutenant Rogers takes over allocating tasks. I'm assigned to Squad B, riding along with five men and a sergeant in one of the MRAP vehicles. Squad A comprises six men and a sergeant, and Squad C carry the remaining seven men. The soldiers are a mixture of ranks and expertise. Corporals and specialists with weapons-handling and explosives experience.

'Here are the specifics,' says Lieutenant Rogers. 'Intelligence indicates that two vehicles will be transporting munitions destined for Prakh. They will be using this minor track detailed as Route A99 on your maps'. Lieutenant Rogers using a long cane points to a barely identifiable wavy line on the projected image. 'If the information is correct, there will be six men, all heavily armed, riding in the vehicles. The aim is to intersect the vehicles before they reach Prakh. We do not want these weapons getting into the hands of the Taliban, understood?'

'Sir, yes, Sir.' The marines respond in unison.

'The men are to be detained,' says Lieutenant Rogers.

'Sir, yes, Sir.'

Lieutenant Rogers covers my role last saying 'Hamilton, you will shadow Corporal Lopez, he's our best linguist so get used to buddying up with him, because he'll be your translator. He's not a bad shot either.'

‘He’s not a great one though,’ says Shorty. That comment being followed by jeers from the men and “You make a lovely couple,” followed by a humming of “Here comes the bride.” I look across at Arturo, who quite obviously has heard and seen it all before as he shrugs his shoulders and says ‘at least I can string a sentence together boys.’

‘That’s enough men, quieten down,’ says Lieutenant Rogers taking back control of the room.

The briefing over, we’re told to “grub up” and be ready to head out at twenty hundred hours.

Chapter Twenty-Two

Elise

The underground is packed as usual. Thursday signals the start of a long weekend for some commuters. Having finished early in the office, I now wish I hadn't. Being crammed into a sardine tin full of damp bodies, all of whom seek solace from the onslaught of rain, is no fun. With bodies warm, steam rising, odour strengthens. Relief comes as the doors spring open at Paddington, allowing the tin's occupants to spill out, including me.

Not being in a hurry, I choose deliberately to miss the first Reading train. The slow, round-the-houses train suits me better tonight. This also increases the likelihood of me getting a seat.

Once aboard I settle myself on a pair of seats, stretching my legs at an angle and slumping down in an effort to relax. Plugging in my earphones, I select a serene playlist for the journey home and then place my oversized bag on my lap. Wrapping my arms around the soft leather like claws, I hug it gently for comfort and security.

The train itself is relatively quiet, with only a faint hum from the engine. The commuters are a little noisier, but this subsides as they settle into their seats. Conversation starts between a group of girls behind me and two men. Nothing to disturb my moment of solace. As I close my eyes, the seat to my left is still free. The train, as expected, is not full to bursting point, no one needs to stand as we depart the station. On pulling away, the hum of the engine grows into a drone, rhythmically pulsating faintly in the background, interspersed with muted conversations and the relaxing tone of my music.

Joel and what he's doing centre in my thoughts. He's now been away for ten days. Whilst I know where he is, he's unable to furnish me with any more detail on the assignment. During our brief conversation Saturday, he in his inimitable fashion reassured me all was well, but I still have my own nagging doubts. The last phone call we had was rather stilted, both of us more than acutely aware that the call was being monitored. Hearing his voice and detecting, through the frustration, his excitement at this opportunity made me feel warm and comforted to a point. He's living his dream, and for the past few nights so have I.

Option A – relax, do nothing – was never going to work. I realised that virtually as soon as I fell asleep that first night. Option B – take control – made me finally understand the meaning of the word control. Control is not as simple as using restraint or knowing one's direction. No, control means influence, check, and dominate. My soul dominates my dreams, and it controls the direction they go in, which, since Joel's departure and arrival at Bagram Air Base, has been Afghanistan.

I haven't consciously chosen to go there, but that's exactly where I end up each night. Sometimes I'm high above Bagram, sometimes on the ground. I walk around unchallenged, maybe on the pretence of being a soldier, or at least viewing the surrounding scene through the eyes of a soldier. Military personnel busy themselves, with a constant flow of vehicles in and out. Bagram is, as I have seen from the air, a compact city, a conurbation, active twenty-four seven.

Whilst fleeting, my observations allow me to become more and more familiar with the terrain. On waking each morning I record as much detail as I can in my diary to remind myself or, in effect, brief myself, for the following night's sleep. It might be just my dream, but I'm creating a mental picture of what I believe to be Afghanistan and this is the closest form of reconnaissance I can do.

With Afghanistan being three and a half hours ahead of British Summer Time, just for a moment, I wonder what Joel will be doing right now. Truth be told, I think of him all the time, but being tired from my night-time excursions, I close my eyes, relax my shoulders, slow my breathing and free-fall.

*

The more I thrust upwards, higher and higher, the darker it becomes. The night sky is abundantly full of intensely bright stars with barely a patch of cloud; instead the sky resembles a blanket of glitter.

Instantly recognising the mountain range, I fly fast and low, searching for landmarks which might help build my virtual map of the area. Tracing the dirt tracks below, I traverse the landscape. Vast open stretches of barren land are surrounded by jagged, intimidating mountains.

Ahead, way off in the distance, the glow of artificial lights barely impacts on the night sky. Communication towers on hillsides are lit modestly.

A fog of dust rises in the air, dispersing in every direction. There is movement on the road, the track below.

Approaching quickly, I focus on two vehicles racing. Their tyres rumble as they spin in the dirt – the origin of the fog is identified. A trail lingers behind them.

Two vehicles, utility type, are in convoy with little or no distance between them. The lead one clearly has a mounted weapon in the rear, and the second vehicle carries an unknown cargo. Both career along without headlights.

A person sits in the open cargo area of the first vehicle, the one with the mounted weapon. A male. He too holds something, but I'm too far away to make it out.

I match their pace; the view becomes clearer. The first vehicle bounces as it races; the mounted machine gun is now clear, the chain of ammunition present in the chamber.

Unseen, swooping towards the rear of the second vehicle, I grab the tailgate, pulling myself on board as it speeds up, keeping close to its partner in crime. The vehicle veers left and right, swerves and bobs furiously along the track; the dust cloud forming behind obliterates and obscures the landscape, and wafts into the night sky. The road is riddled with potholes, my favourite things in the world.

Steadying myself, one hand on the side of the open-back truck, I grab at the tarpaulin covering the cargo. Moving the heavy, damp diesel-tainted sheet to the side reveals one enormous stack of rifles, handguns and ammunition in open wooden boxes. Cartridges and magazines all piled indiscriminately on top of each other. The rear truck is packed several weapons deep, forming a mound.

Feeling vulnerable with my feet down, I need to gain height. Propelling and forcing myself upwards, I move swiftly away from the truck as it speeds from under me. There is nothing to halt its journey or divert its path.

Faintly in the distance a glow emanates and softly illuminates a village, or maybe a town.

I track the vehicles as they bend and flex with the terrain. Surprise is my weapon.

Raging like a bull, motoring forward, I pass vehicle two, then one. Swooping, I land steadfastly on the unmade road in front of the oncoming trucks. Fifty metres and closing, I stand boldly upright, front and centre. The hot tyres give a muffled screech, the sand storm erupts, with the grit, stone and rubble flying sideways as they stop – dead.

The passenger, a man shouting, jumps down from the rear of the first truck, now just inches from me. Both front doors fling open and out step two more men, armed, all shouting and approaching fast.

First the driver; I give a swift right hook planted squarely across his jaw. My ears ring with the shouting, but they look confused. I'm distracted momentarily by the warmth of the radiator; the front passenger from the lead vehicle is upon me. Lunging forward I kick out at the centre of the target, forcing him back into the bonnet. The man from the back of the truck raises his weapon, a rifle, and then shots ring out around my head. I go in for the tackle, taking him down off his feet, his head slamming into the bumper as he falls. Three down, two more to go. Two men emerge from the second vehicle. Standing side by side, they look perplexed, waving their arms and their weapons. Grabbing the fallen man's rifle by the muzzle, I swing wildly towards the pair, connecting with their ears, their necks and their shoulders, until they buckle forward.

The men now unconscious, I discard my weapon.

Climbing into the rear of the lead truck, I search frantically for anything which can be used to restrain them. I pull a length of flex and a second length of frayed rope from near the base of the machine gun and jump down onto the dusty ground. Dragging at their shirts, I pull the men across the dirt, lining them up just off the road as if dominoes. Weaving the flex and rope into knots and forming a chain, I make sure the men have nowhere to go anytime soon.

The odour of diesel is strong and hangs in the air. Carefully removing the headscarf from one man, I jump up into the cab of the lead vehicle looking for matches or a lighter.

There's rumbling on the road, rubber turning and getting louder. Something is approaching in the distance.

With matches to hand, I rip and tear the scarf in two and stuff one piece into the petrol tank and then move swiftly to the second. Striking two matches at once, I hold them under the rag until it catches. Sprinting back to the first vehicle I repeat the process, looking back tentatively to see that the rear one has taken well enough.

Thrusting upwards, I climb fast, putting distance between myself and the ground. With both rags alight, I climb into the night sky. Flames from both petrol tanks fade and dim. Holding my position, I wait. The power of vapour takes over, and there is a whoosh as they ignite and explode, propelling me further away into the air, into the night sky with a jolt as if I'm being resuscitated.

Falling back under, I'm gone.

Chapter Twenty-Three

Joel

Having left the base at twenty hundred hours, the two hours spent cocooned in the MRAP seems more like ten. They designed the MRAP to carry up to ten soldiers, but that figure never took into account equipment. The sergeant sits upfront with the driver which leaves five of us in the back. The soldiers all equipped with Berettas, carbine rifles and automatic weapons. They also possess ammunition, grenades, night-vision gear including helmet mounted sights, radios and individual first aid kits. Each MRAP has a machine gun locked and loaded and carries essential fire extinguishers.

I limit my equipment to my notepad, camera, video and voice recorder, not forgetting my flashlight. I've been provided with fatigues, a helmet and body armour with the word "Press" velcroed on the back. I look like one of them, but am clearly not.

Lieutenant Rogers said that the intelligence was being sourced from the Central Intelligence Agency (CIA), and that whilst on live operations, we would receive accurate location data every fifteen minutes. A drone flying high in the sky is shadowing the targets, and is providing our American-based intelligence colleagues with the best visual picture possible, which they relay to our vehicles. The drone has identified two large heat signatures for the smugglers' vehicles and five smaller ones for the smugglers themselves.

With Prakh now behind us, having taken a circuitous route to avoid detection, we're now back on course head-first towards the target vehicles. My view is limited apart from a slim channel through the front windshield. I'm in effect imprisoned in the belly of a metal beast.

It's been less than ten minutes since the last update and the chatter on the radio suddenly escalates. Our driver slows behind Squad A, and we wait. Not having been able to make out the full radio report, I can see from the expressions on the men that something is wrong. My eyes catch a glimpse through the windshield of a bright orange glow on the road ahead.

Pausing briefly, we ease forward again, our vehicle accelerating to stay close with Squad A's. I can make out flames up ahead. Enormous balls of fire are burning intensely in the night sky.

The sergeant bellows, 'Listen up people, listen up, the targets have been immobilised. They're on fire. The eye in the sky reports an explosion in the last couple of minutes. We have a change of task, we now need to secure the scene and assist in recovery if possible. Eyes front people, keep alert.'

A nervous spasm turns in my stomach and a fresh rush of adrenaline brews inside me. Subconsciously I fiddle with my camera and I can hear myself mutter, 'Geez, what's happening.' Arturo leans across and places a hand on my helmet, pushing down gently as if to hold me in my seat.

With a smile he then says, 'Don't worry, it's plan B. It looks like our targets have been blown up or something. Keep your head low, wait till I give you the nod, then come and join me.'

'What the hell is plan B?' I ask.

'Never you mind, just follow my lead,' says Arturo. Nausea engulfs my throat and unanswered questions confuse my mind. Why the change and what should I be doing? The soldiers seamlessly adjust to the deviation as if they know that in their world nothing is fixed in stone. They're flexible and versatile and stay pumped and ready to go.

Within seconds of processing this change in tactics we're there upon the fire, with the intensity of its glow. As the vehicles won't be moving anywhere, no one will escape tonight. The ring of steel that we would have created around them is no longer necessary. Instead, Squad A's vehicle manoeuvres cautiously off-road around to the left of the burning mass. Its new position is now in effect behind the vehicles back on the main track.

The sergeant shouts, 'Deploy left and right, go.' Simultaneously, the rear doors fly open. Four men who have been keeping me company jump down out of the vehicle, swiftly moving forward towards the inferno. The sergeant, turning to me as he exits, shouts 'stay,' as if I'm a dog. Whilst feeling fractionally scolded for my mere presence, I know that until they declare the scene safe, I'll be a burden and an added vulnerability to them. The driver joins me in the vehicle's rear and takes up point manning the machine gun from the top turret of the MRAP. The tactics having changed do not lessen the risk but heighten them. Whatever or whoever has caused the explosion could still be in the area and unless it can be determined quickly that they self-combusted we're on attack alert.

For me, time stands still: I can do nothing but wait. Outside, hurried voices and crackles of snatched radio transmissions dominate. The soldiers from all three MRAPs are now deployed front and rear. Shorty, a corporal from Squad B rushes to the rear of my vehicle and snatches out two fire extinguishers. I slide towards the front of the vehicle to get a better view of the scene. Soldiers are attempting to dampen the flames with little success.

Through the smoke and glare of the flames, Arturo runs alongside the vehicles in my direction.

'Right, sergeant wants you out and at the front with me, it's time to go to work,' says Arturo.

'Sure,' I reply. I stand, albeit hunched over, and shuffle to the rear of the MRAP. Approaching the front vehicle, a burning mass, I feel the radiating heat scorching my skin. I peer through the smoke into the cab to see if there are any bodies, the smugglers caught up in this inferno, but it's empty.

The roadside grabs my attention. On the dusty dirt, five men lay roped together. Arturo gesticulates towards the men on the ground.

'We need photos in situ as they are now, individually and collectively, then we will sit them up, got that?' says Arturo.

Nodding and without hesitation, I take the lens cover off my camera and start snapping away. Mentally, I record the scene in front of me for my own records and my military report.

The men lay alongside each other, their wrists bound to the front. The rope is long and continuous, having been woven between and around them, and the knots are neat and regimented. Square and slip knots, the same as ones shown me many years ago in Scouts. Whoever tied them must've been in a rush, and yet everything is so calculated. Each man's hands are bound exactly the same way and the same length of rope left loose between them. The men don't appear to have attempted to get themselves free; they're dazed as if drugged or drunk.

Once finished I turn to the vehicles. Both having been fully engulfed, fierce orange flames having eaten the metal, glass, rubber and plastic, the flames are now struggling to find anything left worthy of digesting. The powder residue from the fire extinguishers coats everything.

In the back of the tail vehicle is a molten heap of metal, twisted and glued together, barely identifiable as weapons. The smouldering heat gives off a foul choking stench. A faint glow emanates from the back of the pile, not wanting to die down like the rest. The glow is not diminishing but brightening and intensifying. Recalling the briefing, the cargo was weapons and *ammunition,* and that glowing intensifying mass has yet to have its day.

I yell, 'Ammunition,' without thinking.

Shorty turns to me, his eyes wide, and his grip still tight on one extinguisher. He knows instantly what I'm saying. He bellows, 'One in the hole, hit the decks.'

The wrench to my arm comes simultaneously with the blast, dragging and throwing me to the ground. Arturo hollers in my ear, 'Brace.' Clasping my head, I throw myself crunching into the foetal position as the deafening noise rockets through the air. The ground vibrates beneath me as if there's been an earthquake. My breath is stunted, my eyes welded shut, the air cracking and popping. The heat is intensifying and the sky raining sparks and shards, burning hot, singeing my hands; my camera is still strung around my neck, pressing into my throat.

Rolling onto my stomach, I low crawl, blinded, away from the vehicles, the burning inferno. There I remain with nothing but the whoosh and roar of the flames, cracks and muffled dust-choked voices symphonically lingering.

I wait. Seconds, moments pass, my hands clasped tight on my helmet and ears. Dirt and dust now tickle my nostrils and grind in my teeth. Daring to open my eyes, unhinge my shutters, I squint and take in my surroundings, focussing on movement around me.

A slap on the back alerts me to Arturo shouting, 'All clear.'

There's another muffled voice calling out, 'Head count, eyes up.'

Twisting up, I glance around as one by one the soldiers emerge holding their helmets, checking they're still intact, their register being taken. Pulling myself up and shaking myself down, feeling dazed, I feel a wave of nausea pass over me. My ears ring incessantly, my face is sore and my bare hands stinging. *I should have kept my gloves on; hindsight is great, but frankly fucking useless in reality.*

The vehicles are now being devoured before my eyes, the fire having been given a newfound momentum. Crackles and smoke billow into the atmosphere and an increasingly putrid and toxic smell sucks the life out of the air. The metal and rubber melt, eaten away by the all-consuming flames.

'Are you good?' says Arturo, with another slap on the back.

'Yes, sure, all good,' I respond. I'm lying but I'm not really going to say, 'Fuck no, I nearly had my head blown off. My hands are a little sore, can I go home?' No, 'All good,' is the way to go.

'Great,' says Arturo, giving me the thumbs up. 'Back to work. The sooner we sort through this mess, the better.'

'Will do,' I reply. My mind is now processing the range of possibilities of what just happened. *I mean, we're off plan, spontaneously working the problem. We cannot seize the vehicles – no problem, the men being detained – no problem, the weapons being vapourised – not great but no problem. No, the actual problem, Joel is how, why and who?*

Checking my camera, blowing dust from the lens and squinting to check the last image I captured, I'm relieved to find it still intact. If I pick up from where I left off, the images will tell the story – the change in intensity of the fire, the spread and what remains. My role is more of a crime scene investigator than a journalist. Whilst my pictures will speak volumes, it's Arturo who is getting to do the questioning, and he'll be the one writing the report.

As the dust settles and the air clears sufficiently to see beyond the end of my reach, I observe the soldiers operating as a well-oiled machine, chugging away, hard at work. They show no signs of strain or deviation from orders.

'Are you done?' shouts Arturo, bringing my mind into focus.

'I think so, there's not much left to photograph here,' I reply.

'Right, I need you at the front with me now.'

There's an urgency in Arturo's voice as he beckons me over. His eyes stay fixed on me as I cautiously manoeuvre back around the vehicles to the front where the detained men still lay tied on the ground. All the men are now conscious.

'Your recorder, Joel. I need your recorder. I don't have time for notes and I want to get basic details from them before we ship out. We don't have much time,' says Arturo.

'Sure, what's the rush?'

'The sergeant says we are taking these guys with us now. There's significant movement ahead in Prakh and we need to get off these roads and out of here before we are engaged, understood?' replies Arturo.

'Yes.'

They pull the men up into a seated position, still bound, bloodstains on their upper clothing and their head coverings. One male, absent of a turban, has a trickle of blood running down his temple. The detainees try to speak all at once, motioning with their bound wrists towards their heads. One man pulls one way, jerking the hands of another.

Above the sound of garbled Pashtun, the radios spring to life. Flurries of exchanges which mark a change in the behaviour of the soldiers. Men deploy front and rear, extending their cover range. The tension within these fifty square metres of Afghanistan is rising.

'Time's up men,' shouts the sergeant from Squad A. 'Eye in the sky says we have three minutes to exit. If not, they'll intercept us in approximately eight minutes. Split three and two and load now.'

'You're done,' shouts Arturo. 'Back to the MRAP now.'

Without hesitation, I scurry away from the detained men, not looking back, and climb quickly into the stationary tank. The driver joins me seconds later and then the roll of flex which had been used to bind the men is thrown inside, landing at my feet.

Arturo peers in and says, 'Scoot down, you have company.'

Gingerly, two of the five detainees climb up into the MRAP, aided by Arturo and another corporal. Their hands are still bound, but by plastic cuffs. Their faces speak the universal language of fear; their eyes are piercing and mouths clasped tight. The eagerness displayed moments earlier to talk and tell their story is gone, replaced by the realisation of the situation – their situation. Their liberty is now lost in the short term to the military but potentially in the long term to their leaders, the cartels, or even insurgents – whoever wants them silenced.

Seconds later the metal beast roars into action, the throatiness of the engine a welcome sound. Slowly and cautiously our driver manoeuvres around the smouldering, barely recognisable utility vehicles, placing us back on track, now heading towards Bagram.

The radio transmissions stay constant. The eye in the sky, being our guardian angel, observes from up high. Whilst heading in the right direction, our progress is slow. We're driving blind, our lights off and our path lit only by the moon and the stars. The brightness of the moon that illuminated the carnage earlier is now gone, replaced by a moon less vibrant, more obscured.

The only sound inside the MRAP is that of the radio chatter. Everyone else remains silent. The detainee next to me shakes his head, which is resting in his hands, his mind possibly pondering his circumstance.

The radios crackle upfront, sporadic words identifiable. Feeling not only blind but deaf, my own internal anxieties play out in the form of backflips in my stomach.

Arturo, seated opposite, listens intently to the chatter, his ear pressed to his shoulder, his thumb and forefinger adjusting and fine-tuning the dial of his personal radio.

'Contact made, movement at the scene, several vehicles, lots of bodies and they appear to be searching the area, but have not started off in our direction yet,' says Arturo.

I don't respond, just listen. Arturo's report is punctuated; a piecemeal attempt at joining the radio traffic together. Nervously we sit in silence, relieved that the distance between us and the scene is expanding. Timing is everything. Only three minutes have passed; the scene of carnage, now swarming with unknowns and smouldering glowing vehicles, is a distant vision. The acceleration of our MRAP comes at the exact point that Arturo gives his next update.

'Movement, towards Prakh, two are now heading in our direction, closing,' says Arturo.

As the MRAP accelerates, the road up ahead illuminates, our driver having decided that lights are necessary if top speed is to be achieved. The little exposure I've had to the MRAP has taught me one thing – top speed is a mere sixty-five miles per hour and that, tonight, is just not going to happen. We're, after all, an enormous lump of metal, not a rally car.

Instantly the gunner takes up position on the machine gun and the soldiers ready themselves for contact. The engine noise intensifies as our speed increases, amplified through the centrally located open turret.

Selfishly, I consider the reality of my situation. *I don't even have a weapon to my name; we're fucked.*

Whilst they fit the MRAP with restraints, they're not routinely used by the soldiers. You're hardly weapons-ready weapons-hot if you have to undo your seatbelt first. As a consequence, those that are not restrained bump and jolt in their seats and grab fixtures and people to steady themselves. I sit welded to my seat as do the two detainees. The journey becomes more and more unsafe as we plough along the unforgiving terrain, hoping to put enough distance between us and the unknowns.

Not just a couple of minutes, but tens of minutes pass. The jerking and swaying are relentless. With more crackles and splintered dialogue comes the news, via Arturo, that I want to hear. 'They've stopped, desisted, and are turning around.'

Not one word, not a sound or a whoop, but some gasps of breath, the patting of helmets and the wiping of brows speak volumes.

There's no deviation from path or reduction in speed, our course plotted in front of us; our goal of Bagram lies ahead.

Chapter Twenty-Four

Elise

My music is still faint but rhythmic. Conversations low and private apart from one.

'Stop staring William, it's rude to stare. William.'

Who's William, and what's he doing? Who is he staring at, that causes someone so much concern?

'William, will you turn around and face forward, I won't tell you again.'

An intriguing one-way conversation. What have I missed? Peeling open my eyes and stretching out, releasing my grip on my bag, I subtly turn and scan the carriage. There, next to me, is a small boy. The seat is oversized compared to the proportions of its occupant. *Is this William?*

I remove my earphones and pack them away, placing my bag on the floor between my feet. Plucking my phone from my inside jacket pocket, I check it for emails and messages which I might have missed.

Distracted by a noise – munch, munch, I drop my eyes towards its origin. I glimpse the boy, eyes wide, staring blankly at me whilst stuffing fistfuls of crisps into his tiny mouth. As our eyes meet he sharply turns away.

The train slows and draws to a halt. Looking up momentarily, I clock the station name and then reconnect with my phone, although more than acutely aware that I'm being watched again.

Twisting this time with a broad smile on my face, I say, 'Is it William? Hi, I'm Elise.' The little boy jerks his head away. His eyes drop as he turns to his left towards a smartly dressed young woman.

'I'm sorry,' she proffers, 'You fascinated William.'

'Really, why?' I ask.

'You were mumbling and shuffling in your sleep, and then suddenly jerked awake, that was all. He was just hooked,' she replies.

'Oh. Oh, I'm sorry. God, I hope I said nothing inappropriate or swore, did I?'

'No, nothing really – nothing audible, anyway. I think he found you interesting, that's all. His dad snores and he's used to that, but you were definitely mumbling,' she replies.

'Oh god, how embarrassing.'

The warmth rises in my cheeks, the confinement of the carriage overwhelming. William turns back towards me and our eyes meet.

‘Well, William, I’m Elise and you caught me talking in my sleep, nice to meet you,’ I say.

William doesn’t respond. I smile broadly and detect a slight raising of his cheeks as if he’s smiling, although it’s not clear. Crisps are still being forcibly piled into what must be a cavernous mouth for a child no older than four. Trying to make light of it I turn to his mother one last time and say, ‘OK, well I’m glad I kept him entertained.’

Forward facing, focussing on the rear of the seat in front of me, I feel my embarrassment at the hands of a four-year-old is apparent. The back of the seat, whilst uninteresting, provides me a blank canvas on which to paint my dream, my meanderings that William observed. The trucks, the men, the fireball and the explosion. A dream yet again of Afghanistan, but this time some sort of conflict and action. The idea, though, that I’ve been there now, not at bedtime, not whilst in bed in my home, is shocking.

I continue to focus, eyes forward, ticking off the stops until I reach home. My embarrassment is obvious to all. Once at Reading I briskly walk along the platform, through the barriers and exit out into the fresh evening air. I resist looking back to see if I’m being followed, a slight paranoia setting in.

Home is unwelcoming when I step through the door. No warmth, not even the glow of a timer light. My mind has still not cleared from the events on the train and my acute embarrassment at the hands of a small boy. An adult would at least have had the decency not to stare, thus not alerting me to my mishap.

While the memories are fresh and vivid, I grab my diary and start recording images and actions and people. They are random at first and then a picture, a story, unfolds of what I've been party to. Ten days in and the action has begun. My reconnaissance is over.

Chapter Twenty-Five

Joel

Just after one a.m. we drive through the guarded gate at Bagram. My first experience outside the wire has been awesome, whilst also being scary and well and truly fucked up. God even the journey home was tense and exciting.

Safe behind the concrete walls and razor wire for the first time since we left base five hours earlier, my stomach settles, the twitching subsiding. Feeling physically and mentally drained, I jump down out of the vehicle, my knees buckling slightly, unbalancing me. Arturo, my trusty aide, grabs my jacket and steadies me.

There to greet us is Lieutenant Rogers, and he requests an immediate debrief with the three sergeants. He orders the rest of the men to transfer and process the prisoners, moving them to the on-site detention centre. As Lieutenant Rogers walks away, he pauses and turns back towards Arturo and me.

'Hamilton and Lopez, I would appreciate your input too on this debrief, as the interpreter and the independent on this operation,' says Lieutenant Rogers.

Arturo swiftly responds with a sharp, 'Sir.' We follow on behind the lieutenant, leaving the rest of the men to process the prisoners. The base still buzzes even in the early hours of the morning. Our return has not gone unnoticed. It's unusual for platoons to return in the middle of the night, especially with prisoners. More so when they're not attached to the regular fighting arm of the 101st Airborne Division.

The hot debrief comprises a verbal report primarily from Sergeant Cox, Squad A. The summary describes the scene as we found it, followed by the explosion and our exit. Arturo summarises the first statements made by the men.

'Sir. My assessment of what happened is sketchy. I need to transcribe the recordings for detail. The men were all willing, eager even to talk, and complained of injuries caused by assaults to their heads. Hamilton has images of their injuries, nothing severe, small minor head and face wounds. Difficult in the light to confirm cause,' says Arturo.

'How did it happen, what did they say?' asks Lieutenant Rogers.

'Well sir, this is the sketchy bit. Two of the men from the front vehicle claim a blinding light appeared on the road in front of them, forcing them to stop. When they got out to see what it was, someone or something knocked them unconscious and they've no more recollection,' replies Arturo.

'The others?' asks Lieutenant Rogers.

'Similar story. The men from the second vehicle say something metal hit them. A butt of a gun, maybe. They saw the others drop but do not know what attacked them,' replies Arturo.

'Did they see the vehicles ignite?' asks Lieutenant Rogers.

'No. They were dazed when we arrived and scared, that's for sure. I'm not sure if scared by what happened or the consequences of what has happened,' replies Arturo.

'Do you believe them?' asks Lieutenant Rogers, who considering it's one a.m. is firing questions back and forth as if he's on a game show.

'It's hard not to. It's easy for them to deny seeing the assailant and failing to describe who attacked them. But we cannot dismiss the injuries and the fact that they were all bound and their cargo destroyed. As they're so scared, it could well have been rival smugglers or rebels in the area that seized an opportunity,' says Arturo.

'Yes, but why not steal the guns, why incinerate them?' says Lieutenant Rogers.

'Fair point, but I don't think the men can add anything further,' says Arturo.

'OK. Hamilton, would you like to comment as an observer?' asks Lieutenant Rogers.

'Sir. Well, their wrists were bound with a combination of rope and flex, which suggests to me it was a spontaneous decision to secure them. Also, to be brutally honest, why not kill them? The smugglers don't value life, so why were these men left relatively unharmed? That's not usual for these cartels,' I reply. It feels good to be asked for my opinion, something six days ago I couldn't have imagined happening.

'Anything else?' says Lieutenant Rogers.

'Just the rope and the flex. Someone knew what they were doing – knots I mean. I've seen those knots before when sailing with my wife and in the scouts. They were neat and strong and even if tied in haste, someone gave thought to the style of knot used. The men, whilst bound securely, were all left with sufficient rope between them to move if they needed. The rope caused little or no marks on their wrists either; not the thoughts and actions of smugglers and killers. Whilst spontaneous, it was clever really,' I reply.

'We're not here to admire these people, Hamilton,' says Lieutenant Rogers. *And in that instant, I'm put back in my box.*

'No. I didn't mean that, sir, but think about it. They're alive, all with minor injuries, and were moved a safe distance away from the vehicles. Also, all bar one man had a turban, which is odd, don't you think? Look,' I say. I hastily grab my camera and scroll through the digital images until I arrive at an image of the five men bound together. Four are clearly sporting turbans and one, well, clearly not. I offer my camera to the Lieutenant for him to inspect for himself.

'Yes, Hamilton, your point being?' says Lieutenant Rogers.

'Well, I bet you'll find he had a turban if you ask him. If so, where is it? Why take a turban?' I reply.

'OK, thank you Hamilton. And the fire? Sergeant Cox, anything obvious that caused it?' asks Lieutenant Rogers.

'No, sir. Heavy smell of diesel in the air, but after the explosion there was barely anything left. What hadn't been previously burnt was destroyed as soon as the ammunition exploded,' replies Sergeant Cox.

'OK. Is there anything identifiable at all?' asks Lieutenant Rogers.

'My images, sir, were taken before and after the ammunition exploded. I have quite a few of the vehicles,' I say.

'OK, well we should have the download from the drone first thing. I would like another briefing at oh-eight-hundred-hours to review the footage before we do a full debrief with the platoon, understood?' says Lieutenant Rogers.

'Sir, yes, sir.'

'Hamilton, I need not remind you that this does not go any further. There's no story, no article coming out of this debacle. You may get to print some misinformation on the fire, but not a word is typed until we've done a full review. The detainee interviews need to be conducted first, understood?' says Lieutenant Rogers.

'Yes, Lieutenant Rogers, understood.' Whilst it's frustrating to be gagged in this way, this operation has placed me closer than ever before to a combat zone. The adrenaline buzz alone is reward enough for now.

As we all stand and walk towards the exit, my mind churns over the possibilities of what has happened. My expression gives me away as Arturo slaps me on the back once more and says, 'Time to rest that brain of yours; plenty of time to think tomorrow.'

Arturo is right, I am knackered and hungry, but food must wait till the morning.

*

The night is brief. Seven a.m. arrives all too quickly. A quick shower followed by a visit to the canteen, and I'm ready for the eight a.m. briefing.

Exactly as it was a few hours earlier, the three sergeants, Arturo and I wait in the briefing room for Lieutenant Rogers. As he enters we stand quickly to acknowledge his presence and he waves us back down.

'Right, first things first, health and wellbeing update please. How are the platoon, Sergeant Cox?' asks Lieutenant Rogers.

'Sir. All present and correct. No injuries, just Hamilton, who has minor burns to his hands,' replies Sergeant Cox.

'Hamilton, have you seen a medic?' asks Lieutenant Rogers.

'No need, sir, just spark burns. They stung last night but are better now, sir, thank you,' I reply. *Nothing is getting in the way of my reporting, not even burnt hands.*

'OK, let's move on to the detainees; Lopez, what's the update there?' asks Lieutenant Rogers.

'Sir. All seen by medics, minor contusions to the head and in one case neck, no breaks and no stitches required,' replies Arturo.

'And have they said anything else since they arrived?' asks Lieutenant Rogers.

'Sir, I followed up on Hamilton's comment about the turban and can confirm that the man had been wearing one, and we cannot account for it,' replies Arturo.

'OK. Let's see if this helps then, although what you're about to watch makes for uncomfortable viewing,' says Lieutenant Rogers.

Four minutes and thirty-eight seconds later Lieutenant Rogers pauses the video stream. Nobody says a word; the confused faces of all present stare at the bright image on the screen. Who'll dare speak first and offer their assessment? I sit frozen, my sore hands restrained under me, awaiting a response.

Arturo bravely clears his throat and raises his hand as if to request permission. 'The men said a bright blinding light had stopped them in their tracks, so this concurs with their account.'

'Yes, Private Lopez, that much is obvious, but can anyone offer a less obvious explanation?' says Lieutenant Rogers sounding frustrated.

Sergeant Cox proffers his explanation. 'Well, it looks like Iron Man is now doing our bidding; who's next, Captain America?'

'Very amusing, Sergeant, but not what I would expect to come from the officer in charge on the ground last night,' replies Lieutenant Rogers.

'No sir. Sorry sir,' says Sergeant Cox shrinking inches down into his seat, trying to be invisible and hiding from the Lieutenant's glare.

'Hamilton, you're quiet,' says Lieutenant Rogers.

'Well, sir, it explains the turban,' I reply.

'How so?' asks Lieutenant Rogers.

'Well, the white thermal image moves back and forth between the vehicles and where the men are lying,' I grab the remote and reverse the frames. 'See,' pointing to the screen as the flickering bright light shifts around. 'It makes one visit back to the men before returning to the vehicles and— boom. The turban was used to ignite the vehicles; not quite Iron Man's style,' I say casting a sideways glance to Sergeant Cox who is smiling albeit through gritted teeth.

'OK, right, point taken regarding the turban, thank you Hamilton, but I'm not sure you all quite see the serious nature and implications of these images. The vehicles were tracked and monitored the entire time by the drone. The men were all accounted for and then this additional unexplained thermal image. Whilst weaker than the rest, there's no mistaking its presence. It appears and miraculously disappears,' says Lieutenant Rogers.

'What does Langley say, sir?' I ask.

'Langley, excuse the pun, are spookily reticent to comment and want the equipment checked for interference and hacking. Whatever Langley says, we still need to account for who disarmed these men and destroyed their vehicles, and how. Operation Rattle's risk assessment will be right off the charts if we don't, and we'll have to ground the team,' replies Lieutenant Rogers. 'Let's move on.'

The visual feed re-starts but the vehicle inferno distorts the surrounding images, its thermal signature wiping out the smaller ones. The recording shows our presence and the second larger explosion, but nothing can explain where the unknown thermal image came from or disappeared to.

'That's it,' says Lieutenant Rogers. 'Considering the lack of intelligence available on this one, I see no point in sharing this visual recording with the wider platoon. I want you to think on this, please, and we'll carry out a further closed briefing at eighteen-hundred hours. Maybe after interrogation the detainees might provide some answers. Let's get the boys in and run through an operational debrief, and leave it at that for now.'

Arturo turns to me and without saying a word; his expression says it all: 'what the fuck?' I know my expression concurs.

The room quickly fills as the full complement of men enter and take seats. The debrief starts with a high-level overview of intelligence to date and then deals directly with operational aspects, efficiency, equipment and procedures. My eyes wilt and glaze over as the soldiers report on their actions and status, and the sergeants make notes.

My mind is plagued by the image on the screen – the bright light. Whilst a thermal image, it reminds me of one I've seen before, not in Afghanistan but in Turkey. That image was captured on a phone and believed by religious elders to be a god, a saviour – a belief which I'd dismissed, but now I'm not so sure. They are similar and dissimilar in their nature, both unexplained. This time, though, I want answers.

Chapter Twenty-Six

Joel

Over the following days I'm privy to several briefings, all discussing the events leading up to and after the explosion of the vehicles. No further operations are sanctioned, and the platoon is getting restless knowing that they do not have the full story.

Additional satellite imagery drew a blank. They identified no mysterious planes or vehicles within a five-mile radius of the scene. The rogue thermal image was too small and faint to be anything other than a human or animal.

The flex and rope were examined, along with my photographs of the knots, and how the men were restrained. All that was concluded was that a proficient knowledge of knots had been used, and the materials were indicative of local farmers.

Intelligence assets, though, report tensions between two prominent smuggling gangs, one blaming the other for losing the weapons, and accusations made that the men were kidnapped and killed.

The military embargo all reports, records and intelligence. I'm not allowed to produce any article for circulation. I'm envious somewhat of Arturo, who is called in to support the interrogation, whilst the remainder of the platoon and I wait for orders. One positive, is that I'm now "Hamilton" amongst the platoon, and no longer Emby and Hammo. I think when I sounded the alarm, immediately before the ammunition ignited, I earnt myself some credit. Since then, I have definitely felt more part of the team.

*

Light relief comes in the form of my sanctioned Saturday telephone call to Elise, my one weekly pleasure. It's as private as anything can be on base. Whilst I have a personal phone, I'm not allowed to use it, and Wi-Fi is really expensive, which means most of Saturday evening if we are not deployed is spent queuing for access to the secure satellite phone.

'God it's wonderful to hear your voice, Joel. I can call you Joel, can't I?' says Elise.

'Yes, you can. They encrypt the line. It's great to hear you too,' I reply.

'You sound weary; how are things?' asks Elise.

'OK.'

'Just OK?'

'Yes, actually just OK and frustrating, but I can't say a word, Elise, apart from it's been a terrible week at Red Rock,' I reply.

'OK, that's not code is it, you know, Red Rock as in Ayers Rock or Mars?' says Elise.

'No, Elise, don't read anything into it. I'm not in Australia or on Mars, you know where I am.'

'Sure, yes I know where you are, but – oh, never mind. I'm sorry things have been, well … frustrating. Things will improve, I'm sure,' says Elise.

'It makes a change to hear your optimism for once, rather than…'

'Don't say it, I'm not a pessimist. Wanting things to go well for you and being an optimist doesn't mean I won't worry or don't care. Nothing has changed on that front. I worry about you and I know things are challenging where you are: believe me, I understand,' says Elise.

'That's good to hear. How's work, what's new?' I ask.

'Not a lot really. A bit tiring and I've started bringing work home. Only manuscript reading, but it gives me some focus on a quiet evening rather than nodding off early, which I can well do without,' replies Elise.

'Why?' I ask, wondering just for a moment why Elise needs to avoid nodding off before getting into bed.

'Nothing, really, I'm just pleased I have work to keep me occupied,' says Elise.

'Anyway, I hope you're still counting the shells,' I say.

'Of course. I can't wait, but according to my ready reckoner there are still eighty-six sleeps to go until I fly,' says Elise.

'And fly you will. It'll be great. Look, I'm sorry, Elise, time's up. This is a hotline tonight. Love you lots, stay safe and I'll try to call same time next week.'

'You too, stay safe, love you loads and watch those roads at night. One bounce in the wrong direction and anything can happen,' says Elise.

'Thanks for the advice, love you too, big hugs.'

*

Sunday comes and goes, and another working week starts. And yet, that isn't really what it's like. All days seem to merge into one long week, that merge into one long month and the time keeps ticking on by.

Since Operation Bizarro, as it has affectionately been named, we've seen little time outside the wire. The men keep themselves occupied cleaning and checking equipment, and training, both physical and technical, ever ready for the next deployment. I've even joined their weight training session, and when the sun is at its peak, and I have nowhere else to be, a few rays might have come my way. Going from full on tactical operation, to gym work and sunbathing doesn't seem right though and for different reasons, we are all itching to be the other side of the wire.

Rather than leave anything to chance, all platoon vehicles and MRAPs are speedily fitted with common data links. These provide a direct feed from the drone, thus cutting out the middleman and the delay. Langley has concluded that the rogue thermal image was a member of a mountain-based group. Because of their superior knowledge of the terrain, they moved around unseen to the naked eye. This technology will give us on the ground everything that the eye-in-the-sky sees. Less room for error next time, is the accompanying warning.

Somehow all the analytical and intelligence bods at Langley squarely place the blame at our door. We missed the lone wolf attack and allowed them to slip through our fingers. Langley's assessment sits uncomfortably with the team and with me too. Having been there that night and seen those images, I'm less convinced.

*

The briefing is called late at twenty-one hundred hours. Five MRAPs this time will head out south, driving for just over an hour to a reportedly abandoned farm compound, a prior stronghold for the Taliban. Intelligence coupled with drone satellite imagery has identified significant movement of trucks in and around the compound only days earlier. Three small thermal images remain – close-up satellite pictures captured three men identified as armed Taliban fighters patrolling the perimeter of the farm.

Intelligence suggests that munitions have been transferred to the compound to be used for a future planned assault in the area. Rather than get the 101st Airborne to go in, our platoon is tasked with neutralising the fighters and, once located, disposing of the munitions.

Typically, the access roads are mainly single track, one route in, one route out, so there's every possibility the Taliban soldiers will call for backup as we approach. A quite sensible question had been asked as to why we don't use a Hellfire missile and take the target out from a safe distance. The reason given for not deploying this tactic was collateral damage. Those in charge insist we get confirmation of the existence of the munitions before taking action. So, instead, we're to neutralise the obvious Taliban threat, clear the building for hidden persons or unidentifiable thermal images, confirm the munitions and then manually blow it up. They don't even want a shallow crater left which could show a military strike. Operation Rattle commanders want total deniability.

Just after midnight Squad A, upfront, slows their MRAP causing a concertina on the road behind. The radio chatter is light, short and concise. All eyes inside our MRAP are focussed on the video images being fed directly from the drone high above. As long as the drone keeps on target, so will the military. Three thermal images are clear – one outside patrolling the perimeter, and two inside stationary, possibly asleep.

Our approach will not go unnoticed for long. The spray of gunfire upward into the night sky sounds the alarm. Our cover blown, we speed up towards a shabbily-fitted iron gate. Squad A barge through sending the gate flying and leaving a trail of dust in its wake, clouding our view as we motor on in. Swiftly we're followed by Squad C. Squads D and E stay outside to protect the rear and our exit route. Whilst the men are primed for deployment, I feel definitely like a passenger on this mission. I will only be allowed out of the MRAP once the compound is secure. With that in mind, I focus intently on the screen, memorising the images and internally recording every second of action as it unfolds.

The thermal images inside the compound building are now mobile and making their way towards the rooftop; the watchman, having retreated inside, moves swiftly to take high ground in an upstairs room.

Deploying left and right, the soldiers from all three squads engage forming a pincer movement towards the primary structure, ready to enter, search and eliminate.

I remain seated in the MRAP with Arturo monitoring the feed from the drone. At 20,000 feet not only has it got our immediate location tagged, but has a broad eye on the approach in case Taliban reinforcements move our way.

Whilst there are only three insurgents, they're tenacious, unwilling to give ground, their firepower equal to ours. They are holding back the advancing troops, the shots cracking and ricocheting around the compound. The soldiers' night-vision capability gives them the edge. Four marines make it to the entrance and inside. As they enter, there is a slight loss of vision and I can feel myself holding my breath waiting for them to reappear.

From the relative safety of the MRAP, the scene, the operation, is in full execution under our watchful eye. For a fraction of a second it feels like I'm watching an action movie, the security provided by the MRAP distorts my perspective and the reality of my situation. In the blink of an eye, I'm back in reality, with a fixed stare on the monitor as one gunner lights up the sky and the roof of the structure, firing off a rocket-propelled grenade, or RPG, aimed accurately at two of the Taliban insurgents. This silences a significant proportion of the shots which have been ping-ponging around the compound and in the general direction of our vehicle. Holding my breath, I detect a slight pause in the platoon's advancement.

Confirmation is being sought via the radio that the four soldiers who have entered the building have not been caught up in the resulting collapse of the structure. Arturo gives visual confirmation that all is well as we observe their thermal images weave through the maze of rooms.

Images advance in formation towards the third remaining Taliban fighter who is cornered in an upstairs room. The Taliban fighter is wildly firing through a hole in the concrete where a window may once have been. Silence follows a flurry of cracks. The third man is down and dead; there will be no prisoners tonight. The soldiers now need to confirm the existence of the munitions and do a last sweep of the structure.

With the thermal images on the screen all accounted for, we're ready to go to work.

'You're up, follow me,' shouts Arturo.

Holding my helmet firm, I jump from the MRAP and scuttle behind Arturo as he zigzags across the open compound. I activate my helmet camera and record the activity in front of me. The spotlights on the MRAPs are illuminated now the scene is under our control, thus providing necessary light. A fog caused by disintegrating rubble obscures my view ahead and dances in the light beam. Inside I keep close to Arturo, only inches behind, treating him as cover; my handheld camera is now out and primed. With limited artificial light inside, it's hard to make out a clear path to the soldiers. As I follow in Arturo's footsteps, it's the voices of the men that draw us towards the bounty.

'Over there, Lopez,' shouts one marine.

'Bingo,' replies Arturo.

The mound of boxes is crammed full of bullets, magazines and rifles piled high to the ceiling. This is a significant haul, one that needs destroying and rendering unidentifiable in the next few minutes.

A clean sweep of the compound and outbuildings confirms no further occupants. Collateral damage is negligible. The building itself has history written on its walls. Not in ink, or carved out of the stone, but the scars of fighting, of the previous battles between troops and enemy fighters. The stone is riddled with bullet holes, internal and external walls demolished by the constant bombardment of lead. This compound was once a home, a thriving farm, more than likely filled with warmth, but somehow over the passages of time it has been turned into this outpost for combat.

With dozens of photographs taken of the munitions, I shout, 'Done,' towards Arturo.

'Time to exit then,' replies Arturo.

I scoot behind Arturo as he navigates back towards the exit and across the compound towards our MRAP.

Behind, three soldiers strategically place plastic explosive in the room with the munitions. They've also left a cookie trail of dynamite throughout the building. The soldiers unravel an extended detonation cord out across the open compound and out through what used to be the iron 'keep 'em out barrier'.

The MRAP containing Squad A manoeuvres, heading out and motoring away from the compound followed by ours and the other three.

Crackling on our radio signifies the count down. 'In two, one detonate.' Simultaneously, the screen on the video feed goes black and then bright white as the blast rockets behind us. Plumes of cement and dust billow into the night sky leaving a low-level orange glow lighting up the barren land.

Whilst there's no sign that Taliban reinforcements had been alerted to our presence, that has all just changed. The noise from the initial explosion is followed by a symphony of cracks and whooshes as rockets and magazines burst into life. Debris and fireballs rain down an umbrella of fire on the desolate landscape.

Confident in their work, a confirmation code is broadcast across the radio to all MRAPs and the order is given to return to base.

The return journey promises to be potentially as treacherous as our advance. The route, whilst a well-trodden path, is fraught with dangers, and the fire in the night sky is a signal beckoning all-comers.

The feed from the drone steadies as the air clears. The fire is powerful and will burn for hours to come. I find the distance growing between us and the fire comforting, although it feels oddly strange to still view the aftermath in real time. The drone will observe and record long after we have left and will capture any activity and reaction to the explosion covertly, photographing and tracking all interested parties.

As the distinctive runway lights of Bagram Air Base come into view, I sit back and relax my shoulders, breathing deeply, readying myself as if to enjoy a fleeting nap. My temporary home is in touching distance, my safety net soon to be wrapped around me once more.

The steady but throaty engine of the MRAP keeps a respectful pace, tucked neatly in behind Squad A. The silence and my rest are suddenly broken by a burst of life over the radio. My eyes flick straight to the drone feed, which is still high above our target, not over us. Braking harshly, we stop and our sergeant barks orders into the rear.

'C's down, gunner turret now, two back, two recovery, A's got point, D and E are holding position behind,' he says.

Another language: another lesson in ignorance. There are no orders for me as the men deploy from the rear, exposing the MRAP rolled on its side behind, now off-road.

'What the fuck?'

'IED possibly. Stay here,' says Arturo.

'You bet,' I reply. Whilst confined to the back of the beast I switch my helmet camera on and grab my handheld camera, capturing the scene now presenting itself to the rear. The MRAP was chosen specifically because of its ability to withstand a blast from an improvised explosive device, but echoing in my ears and my memory, is the stark warning given on our rollover training.

The MRAP looks solid; there hadn't been a loud bang to accompany an explosion. One by one the men cocooned in the rear climb out, all apparently unscathed. The driver and sergeant climb out, also looking unhurt. Their rollover training was put into action.

The vehicle is beached on its side, seemingly intact but down.

'Potholes. Can you fucking believe it?' says Arturo.

'Potholes, seriously?' I reply.

'Fucking potholes, Hamilton, these metal beasts have a high centre of gravity and just fall for them time and time again. They withstand an IED but a pothole is its real nemesis, hence the rollover,' says Arturo.

'A pothole?' I say again.

'Unbelievably yes, you know,' says Arturo.

'No. I know what a pothole is, but you're having a laugh,' I reply.

'Do I look like I'm laughing? You can stop recording. The last thing we want published is a headline "Military flounders at the sight of a wrinkle in the road". We'll be a laughing stock,' says Arturo.

I switch my helmet camera off straight away. Arturo is not amused, and this seemingly untimely incident leaves us vulnerable only metres from safety, and will require a recovery vehicle being called out to get the MRAP back.

Whilst a success until now, the longer we sit here, especially as daylight dawns, makes us sitting ducks. Not the end any of us wanted to our evening.

Chapter Twenty-Seven

Elise

Surprisingly, the weeks since Joel's departure pass at a pace. July was a non-event weather-wise, with as many showery days as warm ones. Early August showed some promise, but there's talk of an Indian summer this year as we skip into September.

Work wise, I'm having a ball. I'm writing, or at least editing, fine-tuning stories, checking the chronology. It's refreshing and rewarding.

Catching up with Philip and Jo over lunch a couple of times has been illuminating. Philip's love life is developing into a steady relationship, with Philip being a permanent fixture in Mark's apartment. Jo is single again and looking for Mr Right but is all too eager to snog Mr Wrong, and a new member of staff has joined their weird and wacky team.

Since Amanda's baby news she and I meet regularly, and slowly she is developing a neat, all up-front bump. A blossoming mum-to-be who, by the sounds of it, is spending a fortune on baby clothes and accessories, although she is adamant she doesn't know the sex.

Joel and I speak weekly. It's short and sweet and rather veiled. Joel has instructed me not to give him any more advice but refuses to elaborate on why. He sounds more content though.

For the past few weeks, since my train embarrassment, I've strictly controlled my sleep routines. Confining myself to my bed at home at an appropriate time, usually after ten. That way I avoid any unsolicited gawping, and by rights on Afghan time it'll always be after 1.00 am when I visit, if I visit. Therefore it should be quieter and thus I'm less likely to get into trouble.

Night after night, though, without fail I return to those skies, mountains and villages. Soaring high and low, I traverse the terrain unseen, unhindered, unchallenged, and not once seeing Joel. I start to wonder whether I'm really there. Doubts are creeping in, pulling my theories apart. After all, what am I doing? What actual evidence is there that they're anything more than dreams?

Missing Joel dearly, the loneliness playing on my mind, I finish my hot tea and down the paracetamol and the antihistamine once again, hoping that the pill combo will dull my senses and knock me out for a while. Antihistamine always seems to make me drowsy during hay fever season, so why not now? I've nothing to lose and everything to gain – that being a good night's sleep.

*

The higher I fly, the colder the air feels. The air is thinning out and the sky becoming one with space beyond. The mountain tops below me are permanently snow covered, rarely touched by man, too high and treacherous for the unskilled.

Free-falling fast towards the sharp rugged peaks and into the deep cavernous valleys, I slow and stall to take in the sight below. Camouflaged and barely visible at night is a remote military base. Wafts of smoke creep out into the chilly air from a chimney laden with camouflaged netting. Below, large imposing guns blend into the scenery. My eyes strain to make out the lines and structure of the camp. Quiet and still their work continues; eyes peeled forward facing.

Unseen and unheard, I swoop below and past, flowing with the tracks, descending towards more occupied territories.

An enclave in the trees is a diversion for me. It's invisible from the ground but on show from high above, with three vehicles stationary. Six men are walking around.

Dropping to the ground, I seek cover behind a cluster of tall conifer trees. The vehicles are clearly visible, having a distinctive utility shape and size that create shadows on the barren dirt ground. It's a circle of emptiness surrounded by forest and shrubs, as if manually cleared of all vegetation, hidden from the outside world. Access is limited to narrow tree-lined tracks, one in, one out. No signs, no distance markers; it's a place with no name.

The men are now huddled on the ground, resting on their heels. Puffs of smoke rise from the group. The glow of their cigarettes is evident in the night's blackness.

Slowly and cautiously leaving my cover, I tiptoe towards the cluster of vehicles, parked facing inwards in the shape of a cloverleaf. Ducking down in the centre of all three, I absorb the warmth emanating from their engines.

Carefully depressing the handle on the first door, gingerly pulling it open, I will it not to creak. Scanning quickly, I see a bounty of weapons, knives, handguns and a rifle abandoned in the passenger footwell. I grab a knife, retreating and keeping low and close, moving to the rear to check the contents. Clear plastic bags, filled with a brown-blackish resin, line the back, all loosely covered by hessian sacking. There are upwards of twenty, maybe more, the size of large ripe pumpkins.

I move swiftly to the next vehicle; a quick look confirms it to be empty, both front and rear, then the third. No chances to be taken with this one. A peer into the cab will suffice. More weapons are strewn across the seats, the confirmation that I didn't need that these are bad men. To the rear, a cargo is hidden once again under layers of sacking and woven matting.

There's a sound so alien to the environment it's almost unreal – a whimpering, a faint sob emanating from beneath the coverings, then movement, albeit slight, only distinguishable in the star-studded light.

Lowering the tailgate slowly and quietly, I slide aside the top matting, causing whatever or whoever concealed thereunder to wriggle and then freeze. Peeling back the sacking, there's a small pair of feet in open-toed sandals attached to what appears to be a young child, lying on their back. Their hands are bound to the front, and a scarf is tied across their mouth.

I should not be here, and neither should the child. Swivelling sharply, I check where the men are, counting five still seated, huddled, but one missing.

I beckon the child forward, their eyes meeting mine, the fear and sadness pouring out of their deep brown windows onto the world. There's no reaction, no movement, just a hard stare right through me.

Beckoning once more and stretching forward to grab the child's wrists, I feel goose bumps travelling down my spine; the child's stare is so intense and unnerving. They raise their bound hands slowly towards me, but not at me – through me, with outstretched fingers pointing. Realisation dawns – something or someone is behind me. I sharply turn 180-degrees, and an arm swings furiously with a clenched fist. A burly, angry looking man is intent on striking me down. Jolting back, averting the first blow, does nothing to stem the onslaught.

My heart is racing faster, pounding in my chest. In that instant, drawing breath, I resist the urge to fly, to rise and escape.

The blows rain down, hitting my head and shoulders. Cowering, I raise my forearms, protecting me from the deluge; the thuds, whilst contacting, are not forceful. Regaining focus as a wide arching blow is approaching, I move to block it, realising in that instant that I'm still holding the knife from the cab. I thrust it forwards; the male arches back, sucking his oversized belly inwards, narrowly missing the blade.

He lunges forwards, his face boiled red with anger, both arms now outstretched and rotating. He's swinging wild punches, causing me to stumble back, hitting the tailgate; our commotion is sure to alert the other men.

Steadying myself, I unconsciously drop the knife and seize the moment to attack. Leaping forward, I grab at his throat with both hands; his blows continue to land on my head and back. I squeeze. His arms are still flailing, his round face looming large. Slowly his arms drop, his resistance weakening but his weight increasing as he slumps. As he loses consciousness, his eyes close and saliva bubbles from his lips. He falls forward, his knees buckling; my grip is maintained around his throat. Once on his knees I release him, allowing gravity to take over. The man's body is now slumped forward, face down in the dirt.

Turning towards the child, I hear a noise. My senses are heightened by the engagement. A low hum is a little way off but definitely there, and steadily increasing in volume as it approaches; not on the ground, but in the air.

Beckoning, my arms outstretched once more, I grab the child's wrists and pull them towards the lip of the truck, seeing for the first time a young girl. She's pretty with black olive hair and a tanned but dirty complexion, wet with tears. Gently untying the scarf covering her mouth, I raise my finger to my lips, 'quiet.' As I lift her down from the truck, it's evident that she should not be here. They have taken her as part of the deal. Her clothes, whilst soiled, are tidy and the lace embroidery on her kaftan is intricate.

I cannot take her with me. My only option is to hide her from the men and hope that the humming, which I suspect is a helicopter, is the military who will find her.

I turn to exit back to the woodland; an almighty blow to my right knee stops me dead. My head jerks towards the ground. There on his knees, holding the knife which I had discarded moments earlier, the man who I thought I had taken care of. His arm is pulled back towards his ear, ready to launch a further attack.

Moving the girl behind me for cover, I raise my arms forward instantly to block the oncoming blow and seize the opportunity to snatch the knife, before throwing it to the ground once more. My rage wells up, my heart is pumping; I grab his throat, squeezing like I have never squeezed before, powering my grip with my anger, my mind. The man is losing consciousness. I continue to squeeze, the colour draining from his face until I hear it again; not it – them. The humming is now much louder, more rhythmic, pulsating; the men, no longer huddled, hear it too, and have risen to their feet.

Dropping the man down like a dead weight, I grab the girl's bound hands and step forward to run to the trees.

'Shit.' My leg, my right leg, heavy and lame, is not budging. Blood oozes – my shin and calf are covered. Instantly I feel the pain, the tingling, burning sensation piercing my senses, and the nausea sweeping across me. Willing it to move, raising it off the ground and forward, I make for the trees, pulling the girl in my wake. I seek cover behind the conifers and pines and the wood beyond the enclave. Pulling the girl in behind me, I crouch down, the ground now vibrating as overhead the sky lights up, the pulsating hum now a booming thrum.

Dust and dirt are being blown outwards. The men, her captors, are barely visible through the storm created by the downdraught and there are men, more men, military men, boots now on the ground encircling the glade.

They were always coming; I'm here by chance.

It's time for me to go. They'll find the girl. Her small face is still wet from tears, her nose running and her eyes dark and hollow. I run my hand through her hair gently and reassuringly. Taking her hands in mine, I say, 'It will be OK, you are safe now, and these men will help you, I promise.'

There's no response, no reaction, just blank, empty tear-filled eyes stunned by fear and shock.

The urge to rise, to thrust and fly is overwhelming. The pressure, the rush and intensity increase and I'm no longer there, gone into the night sky, higher and higher; no looking back and no hesitation, just gone.

Chapter Twenty-Eight

Joel

'Alpha Sierra One to base – we have control, six detained and no resistance, two outstanding. AS2 and AS3 also deployed.'

'Control received, AS1. Are Ground Sierra One and Two on scene?'

'AS1 to Control, GS1 and GS2 on site and deployed.'

'Sir, it's time for you to get out now, sir. Corporal Lopez requests your presence by the vehicles.'

'Thank you, Corporal,' I reply. Holding my helmet before jumping down and exiting the bird, my feet are finally on solid ground. The experience of riding in the Chinook is by far the best so far and the noisiest. The constant piercing whine is still ringing in my ears. It's impressive, though, the aerial assault, as the troops dropped and deployed, dispersing and seizing their targets who barely had time to realise what – or who – was upon them. Two are still outstanding, but the all-clear has been given for me to join Arturo and capture my story.

The intelligence from the briefing is so far correct and supported by the live drone surveillance feed, providing up-to-the-second images and thermal scans.

As I walk towards the vehicles, several troops are shadowing the detained men, all kneeling, their hands behind their heads. I spot Arturo over by a lone detainee who is kneeling but flopped forward.

'This one's not with it at all, he's dazed or drugged; he's out of it, anyway. Go to work, fill your boots, contents the lot and make sure your head cam is on at all times,' says Arturo.

'Will do.'

Methodically, I snap and capture the scene. My flash is working intermittently, confused by the artificial lighting being beamed in by the Chinook. The three target vehicles, all utility type, are parked facing inwards. They're unlocked and their engines, whilst not running, give off a little residual warmth. With every angle captured, inside, outside and underside, a three-dimensional picture is being formed which will later bring my story to life. I photograph the contents front and rear. Knives and guns are in the cabs, hessian sacking is strewn on the ground and there are large plastic bags containing a brown substance, ball-shaped, crudely tied, bunched up together filling the rear of one truck. A knife lies discarded on the ground nearby where the dazed detainee was kneeling.

The rotor blades on the Chinook finally slow and draw to a halt; the silence and the stillness of the glade is apparent. Faint muffled crackles over the squad radios and Arturo's familiar Hispanic accent even when speaking Pashtun tickle the air. The detainees are silent and unresponsive, their faces wizened, yet their bodies strong.

The chemist amongst the platoon, Private George Jones, is tasked with seizing and testing the contents of the plastic bags. If the intelligence is to be believed, it's raw opium, not yet processed, gathered up from a number of farms in the area. It's the last of the harvest destined for a refinery and onward sale to the west.

'Hamilton, here please; can you record the test and seizure of a sample for me?' says George.

'Sure.' My head cam captures the full procedure from start to finish, but I snap an additional book's worth of shots to corroborate the process and for my portfolio. The plan, according to the briefing, is to burn the haul in situ, including the vehicles and weapons, and to seize only portable evidence, papers, identification and money if found.

'Pure, unrefined, not worth much now but if processed worth a mint,' says George.

'How much do you reckon?' I ask.

'Hard to say; let's weigh one. That should give us an idea of the total haul,' says George.

George produces a small set of luggage scales. The method is crude but effective at determining the size of the haul. They record the drugs seizure in pounds, so there's no need to be accurate to the last ounce.

'Thirty-three just shy of thirty-four pounds, give or take. Video the count of the bags and I'll dip sample a few to be 100 per cent sure it's all opium. If we weigh the odd one or two we can then work it out,' says George.

'Twenty-seven, got them all. Now, Genius George, you can do the math.'

'That's 918 pounds, knuckle brain; or maybe you prefer we call you Emby, smartass,' says George.

'No, Hamilton or Joel are OK; so what's that going to be worth, then?'

'Well, not as much in its current state. How ripe it really is we'll never know; it's late in the harvest, bordering on over-cooked, especially with how dry it's been. For seizure purposes, though, we work on its potential having been processed and marketed in the west as heroin. I would estimate $4,000,000 give or take; not bad eh?' replies George.

'Not bad at all, so what's next?' I ask.

'Well, we light the touch paper and, boom, that's what, but before we have a party, we have to off-load it all and make a funeral pyre. I'll get us some willing helpers,' says George.

George paces off in search of willing bodies to help with the unloading and returns, what seems like moments later, with two men. Forming a mini chain gang, the bags are unloaded and re-stacked away from the vehicles. The pyre won't be lit until we're ready to leave. The fumes and smoke are likely to create a toxic haze which, if inhaled, might render the team incapacitated and vulnerable. Instead, it'll be the team's last hurrah as we wave it goodbye.

Leaving George and the others to prepare the pyre, I walk out from the centre of the glade and embrace my surroundings. Radio traffic is light, the men all deployed in search of the outstanding targets or thermal images.

Exploring the glade beyond the immediate vicinity of the now militarised zone, the light dims naturally and the woodland beyond casts shadows all around. Walking the perimeter, I skirt the clean lines where the open glade meets the dense woodland beyond. I strain my eyes to see through the trunks of the trees and over the fallen branches, forming a wooden leafy cobweb of camouflage at various levels. Pitch black and eerily quiet, the never-ending woodland has the potential to swallow you up.

Faint rustles in the undergrowth stop me in my tracks. My heart is reigniting, a gentle but steadily increasing drum in my ears as my anxiety levels rise. Dismissing the rustles as only a rodent or snake, yet with the unknown and unseen ahead of me, I step back to return to the comfort blanket of the armed soldiers. My 180-degree step is met by Arturo, who is closely followed by several of the platoon.

'The thermals show over here for the outstanding target; fall back, Hammo,' says Arturo.

'I just heard something in the trees, I had assumed rodent or snake, not target,' I reply.

'Put it this way, Hammo, it would have to be a fucking enormous rat to show up on the scan,' says Arturo.

'Got you, falling back.'

As I retreat behind, the men all fall silent. A number of hand signals and gestures are exchanged between them as they advance and spread out towards the darkness of the woodland.

A rare breeze sweeps through the glade, causing the tallest of the trees to wave and sway in unison. As the trees steady, the rustling can be heard once more emanating from behind the base of a tree and under cover of densely matted undergrowth.

As the troops advance towards the spot, the rustling stops dead, accompanied by a sharp intake of breath.

Arturo stands firm, several metres back, and his voice booms loud and large issuing orders in Pashtun to the shrubs and the woodland beyond. Seconds pass and the undergrowth rustles more vigorously. As if born within, a small figure unfurls from the ground, arms limply raised and wrists clearly bound, shielding their face and wiping tears from their eyes.

Not a man, but a child.

As the child advances, the soldiers fall back oh so slightly, keeping a safe distance. Arturo's dulcet tones albeit softer engage the child, encouraging them further away from the woodland and into the openness of the glade.

Rifles and side arms train on the child's body. The rustling is now replaced by wet whimpering; the child, as if overcome, is no longer able to contain their emotions and shuffles closer and closer towards the soldiers and the safety of the military.

Arturo gestures towards the child to lower their arms and do a 360-degree turn. Wearing a loose kaftan, sandals and scarf, the child complies, unwittingly demonstrating no hidden weapon or explosives. This child poses no risk and the soldiers' weapons are lowered simultaneously, sparking an intake of breath.

Arturo slowly approaches the child, now recognisable as a girl, and continues to speak softly in Pashtun; his hands, free of his sidearm, are now lower and more welcoming, offering comfort. The child's face is now clear, fear etched across it. Her hands are still bound as she falls to the ground on her knees, exhausted and terrified.

'Here, give us a hand – get us the medic,' says Arturo.

Running forward to help, I grab her ankles, Arturo lifting her under her arms, and we carry her weightless body over to one of the MRAPs for attention.

'One down, one to go, then?' I say.

'No, we've lost the eighth signature, it disappeared more than ten minutes ago, vanished,' replies Arturo.

'So they're all accounted for?' I say.

'For now, yes. We need to wrap this up and get out of here,' says Arturo.

'What about her?' I ask.

'I suspect she's been stolen or was a prize to sweeten the deal. If she talks, we may identify her, but she's in shock and unlikely to say anything for a while,' replies Arturo.

'The men?' I ask.

'They might talk and say where they got her from, but we don't do bargains with them so they've nothing to gain by talking; we'll see,' he replies.

A flurry of activity ensues. The detained men are separated and loaded on to the MRAPs. The girl is secured in a medic-harness and loaded on to the Chinook. All but three of the soldiers clamber aboard as the twin rotors start up in unison.

'Hamilton, do you want to capture this for posterity?' says George.

'Where do you want me?' I ask.

'Well, we've rigged the vehicles to blow, but the opium is trickier. Call me old-fashioned, but that needs to burn in situ, not be blasted to kingdom come. Snap away and as soon as it takes hold we'll board the bird and then, kaboom, the trucks go up too,' says George.

'Awesome,' I reply. Like a kid at a fireworks display, I find bonfire is always the most mesmerising part. I capture a timeline to incineration.

'Move, Joel, she's going nicely and we cannot hang here too long before we feel the effects of more than just the smoke,' says George.

'Sure.'

I scramble up on to the cargo hold of the Chinook and strap on a safety line and then wait for the explosion.

The opium burns bright, its natural oils fuelling the fire, the smoke rising into the air below us as we gain height and distance. My eyes and head cam are still trained on the scene below as the countdown begins, then, in George's words, 'kaboom'.

Once clear, the cargo doors are sealed and the journey back to Bagram begins. Tonight we're taking a circuitous route back. We'll shadow the MRAPs below, monitoring their progress as they first negotiate the narrow tracks of the Hindu Kush and then steadily weave their way along the roads home.

They, after all, have the prisoners, valuable in their own right, as potential intelligence sources. All security measures need to be taken to get them and the soldiers back in one piece.

We have our own valuable cargo, a girl stolen and traumatised; but somehow she escaped, survived and is safe. She, too, will have her own story to tell in the morning.

Chapter Twenty-Nine

Elise

Waking with pins and needles is not unusual. Often I sleep on an arm or hand and wake to find half my body numb. A combination of shaking and flopping my dead limbs ensues, slowing reawakening my extremities, thus allowing me to continue my slumber.

That familiar numbness is upon me, but unusually this time it's my leg playing dead with a subtle soreness and extra weight, those familiar prickles accompanying the insensitivity. Wriggling my upper torso, trying to flip the switch to my nerves and grabbing at my pyjama bottoms, does nothing. Lifting the leg and dropping it repeatedly, hoping to jump-start the system, has no effect.

A few thumps to my upper thigh does the trick. A warmth starts to simmer in my toes, spreading slowly through my ankle and up my calf. Temporary paralysis is scary as hell, but thanks to my crude DIY physio, disaster has been averted once again. The warmth is now rising through my upper thigh, my skin sensitised to my touch once more. Stretching out I lengthen my torso to reaffirm my new-found mobility, only to pull both knees back into my body, tight to my chest, cradling them. A residual ache is lingering but not painful enough to prevent me from drifting back into the abyss.

*

Sitting up sharply, my ears are pierced by a high-pitched sound. Confused, I turn to check the time and swipe to switch off the offending alarm. With no alarm set the night before, it's evident that the rude, unabating punctuated *bzz* is coming from the front door; on a Saturday morning, of all things.

Ignorance is bliss as I flop back down, burying my face in my pillow, hoping that the next time I wake I'll feel like I've slept. A second later, the loud *bzz* pricks my ears once more. The noise is vibrating through the house.

Feeling like a zombie and unable to put it off any longer, I know that whoever is there will not go away until I rise and attend to their needs. Stretching, awakening my limbs, pulling myself up, I grab my robe from Joel's side of the bed and swing my legs around in readiness to decamp and descend. My soles brush the carpet and as soon as I have placed my feet and stand up another alarm bell goes off, this time in my body. A most intense pain is piercing my right leg. My previously dead right leg is now alive and hollering at me with a sharp throbbing sensation above the knee.

As if sensing my discomfort and determined to ruin my morning, the short sharp *bzz* resonates through the house once more. 'I'm coming.'

Lunging forward, I make for the bedroom door, leaning with my arm outstretched to grab the handle. The throbbing in my knee turns to a stabbing, sharp, piercing hot pain. My knee buckles and my grip on the handle is the only thing keeping me off my knees.

'Bugger, shit, I'm coming.'

Using the handle and the door frame for support, I drag my leg upright and shake it in the vain hope that the pain subsides as quickly as it arrived. Stepping forward gingerly, cursing under my breath with each planting, I shuffle across the landing towards the stairs. Gravity takes hold, my descent quickening and propelling me to the front door. 'I'm coming, I'm here.'

Unlatching, I pull the door open in haste. 'Yes?'

'Delivery for you, madam. The sender insisted we delivered today,' says the man.

'Who's it from?' I ask.

'Doesn't say; sign here, please.'

Loosening my grip on the door frame, I grab the plastic wand, scribbling my signature on the gadget imitating a Magna Doodle.

'Here, this is for you,' says the man, handing me a medium-sized cardboard box.

'Thanks. It's light, are you sure it's not empty?'

'We just get paid to deliver, madam, sorry,' he replies as he turns and walks back to his waiting van.

Once the door is closed and secured, I pick up the feather-light box and hobble into the kitchen. My knee is still sore and very present in my mind, but curiosity is now getting the better of me and the desire to open the box is growing.

With the kettle on and the biscuit tin open, I sit down and study the box, just pondering for a moment its contents and fathoming its sender. It can't be Joel – he's unlikely to send me anything from Afghanistan. Joel's communications have been so limited, and that includes the internet. I like surprises, but this one has me guessing.

As the kettle switches off, I stand up and am reminded once more that my knee is in pain. Hobbling across the kitchen, I make a brew and then return to the table and my parcel.

Carefully unpicking the tape around the edge of the box, keeping the label intact, I lift the cardboard flaps as if handling a bomb. Mounds of oversized bubble wrap burst out as if finally unchained. Removing it layer by layer reveals nothing, until two-thirds down a white envelope is addressed to Elise Hamilton, me.

Somewhat perplexed by what seems like unnecessary levels of packaging, I cautiously lift the envelope from inside the box. The envelope is of fine quality heavy-weight ridged paper and has my name lovingly inscribed in black ink on the front and is sealed with wax.

My caution is now replaced by excitement at the idea of this potential gift. Pulling at the wax seal, I split it open; the contents are revealed. Several pages of heavily scented paper are typed and folded and a plastic card is attached with a large pink paperclip.

As I unfold the papers, the contents are clear – a membership card and vouchers for the luxury spa De Vere's. Gym membership, beauty therapies, tanning salon all included. The paperwork, being official in tone, explains the membership and entitlements, but the vouchers are all handwritten.

One handwritten, separately folded note falls out of the 'terms and conditions' page, with 'Elise' inscribed in Joel's unmistakable cursive scrawl. Warm yet shivering, I carefully unfold the note. It reads:

Elise,

I have now been away over half of the time. Those shells are no doubt collecting dust on the windowsill, and this morning you will have awoken one day closer to meeting me in Florida.

I can't imagine how hard this has been on you; I love you with all my heart. I'm nothing without you and having your support these past weeks has enabled me to cope, knowing that you're always there for me. You have helped turn my dream into a reality.

I miss you now as intensely as when we parted after our first kiss, the longing I felt then I feel now. I miss the way you breathe when you're sleeping, fitful but content, peaceful but chaotic. I miss being your comfort blanket, your protector.

With only six weeks to go (if they have delivered this on time), I want you to have some fun and relaxation at De Vere's. Spoil yourself and rejuvenate, ready for our reunion. I love my English rose but thought you would enjoy a little sun boost before hitting the beach!

I can't wait to reacquaint myself with you in every manner possible. With all my love,

Joel

x

Reading the note a second and a third time, wiping away the tears, my mind fills with images of Joel and my heart aches. 'God I love you, Mr Hamilton.'

Six weeks – no, forty-six days sounds better. *Forty-six days and I'm a wreck. Just look at you, Elise, all pink-eyed and snotty. Baggy pyjamas, your robe, a mug of tea, and a tin full of biscuits. Maybe this is not so loving of Joel, but a gentle reminder not to let yourself go. No, he wouldn't think like that. But I'm pale, a bit wobbly in places and sleep, or lack of it, has replaced any beauty regime I might once have had.*

Flicking through the paperwork once more, checking the details of the membership, the start date looms big and bold. Today. Standing from the table, intending to refill my mug, I'm reminded why today might not be the day to start at the gym – my leg.

'Shit.'

Hobbling across to the kettle, I get the urge to take a peek at what is causing me so much pain. Pins and needles never normally cause this amount of residual discomfort.

With my tea bag and water replaced, hobbling back once more to the table, I slump down. Once seated, I roll up the leg of my pyjamas and there it is. Four inches above my right knee, a large red throbbing welt. Swollen and sore to the touch, heat radiating from its core, this welt won't calm soon. Instead, it'll develop into a deep purple bruise swiftly followed by a sickly brown-yellow one and finally a shadow under my skin as a gentle reminder for weeks to come.

A reminder of what, though? Just like the hundreds of unexplained bruises I've had over the years, so many unaccounted for, no obvious cause. Why and how – who knows? What have I done? What has caused this, and so deep? The pain is still unnervingly sharp.

Sipping at my tea, staring down at my leg, flashes of recognition flow through my mind – flashes of a dream, a vivid, very real dream.

Trucks, men, a girl, a fight, a knife, a stab – no it can't be; now a bruise. No, no, no, it's not real, Elise.

The pain, though, the throbbing, the dead leg from earlier – that's all real, all here and now. I'm not asleep, and yet I've got an injury that aligns itself with my dream.

Shooting from my seat, willing my leg to move normally, the pain real but ignored, I race to the front room to get my dream diary. It's still on the coffee table; I grab it and walk back into the kitchen.

I start to write, to remember, and to record details – jottings and then more vivid recollections.

> *Afghanistan, mountains, glade and 3 vehicles.*
> *Brown resin in bags (possibly drugs).*
> *A girl, young, olive-skinned. Scared and crying.*

What happened to the girl?

> *A girl on the back of a truck, tied, hands bound. Men, 6 men, guns and knives in the truck. A man punching and swinging.*

Placing my pen down slowly, I raise my hand to my head and gently caress it through my hair. There are tender spots down towards my nape and my neck; it feels stiff.

No, it cannot be. Shaking my head in disbelief, I tremble, shudder, and rock, staring at the words written on the page in front of me.

A man punching and swinging.

I remember now. Vivid powerful images are before my eyes. My pen poised, I write.

> *Swinging punches, I block to defend and grab his throat, squeezing and overpowering him, and then there's the knife, my leg.*

Where did the knife come from Elise? Come on, think.

> *The knife. I took it from the cab of a vehicle. I had the knife; I lunged at the man but dropped the knife. OK, think.*
> *The girl. I hid the girl in the trees and bushes. The military, a helicopter arrived and then nothing.*

OK, focus on your leg.

Closing my eyes, clearing my mind, I focus on my leg, the pain, the intense stabbing, piercing feeling. Taking a breath and opening my eyes, I write.

> *The man stabs my leg and is still holding the knife, prepped to lunge again when I grab him and throttle him until he loses consciousness. Blood oozing down my shin and calf, I make it to the trees with the girl, and then nothing.*

Cold and trembling, I place the pen down on the completed page in my diary and stare down at the words on the paper. My head is numb and hot and my nose blocked, yet wet. As I stare at, and through, the paper, the words are no longer relevant, it's all about the meaning.

I've just made and rationalised a connection between my dream world and my reality, and my leg, this welt – soon-to-be bruise – is it. It's the evidence that I've sought all my life to make that connection, the one which spells out clearly to me that my dreams are real and that somehow my conscious and subconscious are intertwining on more than a cerebral level.

This is the stuff of gods and Mesopotamians, of Greeks and the ancient Chinese, of prophets and the Bible. This is real, and yet somehow I still feel a small nagging doubt. My rational and irrational brains are at odds. A war has begun where 95 per cent of my fibre and being believe it to be true and 5 per cent thinks me mad. A nutter. The next *bzz* at the door will be the men in white coats.

I need help. I need reassurance, and I need Amanda, my oldest friend. She will believe me.

Chapter Thirty

Elise

An hour elapses before I pluck up the courage to call the one person I hope will help me.

'Amanda, I need you, can you come over, now?'

'Elise, what's the matter? Are you OK?'

'No, I'm not. I need you, now. I'm not feeling great. I'll explain more when you get here.'

'Right now? I'm in central London shopping for baby bits.'

'Yes. I need you, Amanda, I wouldn't ask if it wasn't urgent.'

'Elise, you're scaring me, are you at home?'

'Yes.'

'Sit tight, I'll catch a train and be there as soon as possible. Elise, you are OK? You're not going to do anything silly or dangerous, are you?'

'No, I just need you. I'm going mad and I need to talk, please.'

'Of course, I'm on my way.'

Phoning Amanda is one of the hardest decisions I've ever made. There's no turning back. Amanda will want answers now, and when she sees me, will have lots of questions.

Slumping to the floor in the kitchen-diner once more, laying my mobile on the ground next to me, I know I look a wreck. I don't need a mirror to tell me that. My eyes are sticky where yesterday's mascara has run and my chin is wet from the mucus pouring out of my nose, a continual stream. I cried for an hour before phoning Amanda, and the realisation that maybe I'm mad is killing me.

My mind whirring, I calculate the possibilities of what I now know – well, what at least 95 per cent of my mind knows. The other 5 per cent has already granted me access to a secure facility, no questions asked, and it's that 5 per cent which I fear. The 95 per cent to me is becoming my new reality. What will Amanda think, though? Will she agree with the 95 per cent segment or join the 5 per cent and make a swift phone call to a psychiatric unit? Doctors and social workers and maybe even police could descend any time. I've no idea how this might end.

The floor is cold and uninviting, and yet I feel no drive or energy to lift myself to a more comfortable place. The longer I sit shivering, the more the floor feels like home. It gives comfort in its simplicity, allowing me to hug myself, sway and wail, and not once passing judgement. My mind is strangely absent when the now familiar *bzz* sounds. Pausing a moment in my zone, I then stand and wipe, yet again, the underside of my nose to remove the endless gloop. At this rate, I'll probably dehydrate, my brain actually melting away; that might solve the whole 95 per cent versus 5 per cent thing.

As I shuffle through the hall, I hope it's Amanda. I'm not expecting anyone else and if by chance it's a stranger, then they'll get a shock. Unlatching the door, I open it just far enough to see Amanda on the doorstep trying to get as close as possible into the door but hindered by her bulging bump.

'God, let me in, you look awful,' says Amanda.

With the door secured and Amanda safely over the threshold, without saying a word, she throws her arms around me, pulling me in as close as she can. Her hug is tight and reassuring.

'I'm sorry,' I say, wiping my face, 'I've left a snail's trail on your jacket.'

'Never mind about that; look at you. What's happened, Elise? I hate to say it, but you look dreadful.'

'Come through to the kitchen. It's where I've been resident for the past couple of hours.'

Unable to ask Amanda to sit on the floor, I offer her a chair at the table and then walk back to my wall, and patch of kitchen floor, which I've grown fond of. Slumping down to the floor and hugging my knees in tight, I let go; an outpouring of tears cascades endlessly down my face. Amanda stands quickly and rushes over, bending down towards me.

'Come here, what on earth's wrong? You need to tell me.'

'You'll think ... I'm mad.'

'We're all a little crazy, you no more so than I, so you need to tell me.'

'God, it even sounds crazy to me; I'm not sure where to start.' I struggle to find the words, my mouth salty, my head throbbing and my face hot.

'If I tell you, please don't judge me too quickly. I need you to listen and, well, be open-minded.'

'OK, what's this about? Are you and Joel OK?' asks Amanda.

'Yes, well apart from him being away. He's done nothing wrong and technically there's nothing wrong with our relationship, but it relates to Joel.'

'He's still in Afghanistan, isn't he?'

'Yes, that's part of the problem. Look, I'm going to say it quickly to start with and we can go from there.'

Grabbing the roll of kitchen paper which has formed part of my armoury on the floor, I wipe my face as dry as possible. Just deciding to tell calms me somewhat. Amanda sits herself back at the table, unable to stay squatting any longer.

'I dream, you know I do. Well, of late, I believe – and this is the hard part – that I can fly.'

'You've always flown in your dreams,' says Amanda.

'Yes, I know, but to all intents and purposes I went nowhere. But here's the thing – I believe my soul leaves my body and I arrive in Afghanistan; although it doesn't have to be Afghanistan, it has been lots of places, but at the moment it's Afghanistan, and, well, I've been watching over Joel and may have got involved in the odd one or two military operations.'

'In your dreams?' says Amanda.

'Well, yes, whilst I'm asleep dreaming, but actually there. It's real, it's not a dream.'

'Elise, you sound a little crazy; help me out here?'

Feeling slightly offended, I stand up from my zone abruptly and walk over to the chocolate basket. I've been putting off attacking a four-pack since my discovery, but if there ever is a need and justification for chocolate it's now. I rip open the packet and undo the first bar, biting it into half at once. As I munch through the chocolate, I pace the floor waiting for my mouth to clear enough to continue. Amanda patiently sits poised at the table.

'Amanda, it makes sense to me,' I say.

'Well, it doesn't to me,' replies Amanda.

'Look. The first time I knew this was happening was when Joel went to Turkey and Syria, when he did the refugee reports.'

'Yes,' says Amanda.

'Well, I'd been there too. Nothing happened, but I recorded in my dream diary a dream where I flew over dome-shaped buildings. There was a desert and a larger conurbation and then a tented area. Immediately after the dream, it meant nothing, but when I read Joel's article, well, it made sense. That was the same time I was doing the dream research and had just looked into astral projection. Before he came home, before he could tell me about his trip, I researched areas in the world where there were dome-shaped homes. I found beehive houses in Syria near Aleppo. Aleppo is a city near the Turkish-Syrian border, and the tents, the rows of white tents – that was one of the refugee camps.'

'And you think that means you were physically there?'

'Yes – well, my soul, and that's not all. Joel, as you know, was keen to go back to Turkey to do more research. Well, that was because he had been told on his first visit of a deity or god flying over the camps near the border. A bright white light. To top it off, an image, a photo exists, and whilst grainy, it shows a human form. That was me. The image confirmed it for me then, and it scared me shitless; but now, well, put it this way, 95 per cent of my brain believes my soul is truly travelling the globe.'

Amanda's smile is no longer present, her usually healthy glow fading and her eyes intense.

'I know it's a lot to comprehend, but it's true. Look, let me tell you more. Since Joel's been away in Afghanistan, I've visited there night after night. I feel somehow connected to what he's doing. Sometimes in my dreams I'm on the ground in Bagram but there have been a few occasions when I've run or, should I say, flown into trouble. Maybe I've done things I shouldn't have, but at the time it was all part of the dream, I was none the wiser.'

'What are you talking about Elise? I'm struggling here.'

The more I speak the more confident I feel; sharing what I've learnt is empowering my 95 per cent. The madness, the fear, the 5 per cent, is fading fast.

Grabbing my diary, I open it to show recent entries. 'Look, I record everything in my dream diary. When Joel returned to Syria, I attempted to avoid him so he wouldn't make me into the story. With Joel being away in Afghanistan, I fear for him daily and this has been my way of watching and helping him. These entries are accurate accounts of what I've seen and done. Whilst you might see them as the ramblings of a madwoman, I now know they are evidence of my new reality.' Opening up my diary, I place it in front of Amanda.

'Are you sure, Elise? As imaginations go, you've a very active one. I'm trying to work with you here and if I wasn't pregnant would definitely want alcohol to continue, but look at you. You look like you haven't slept for days. The bruises – where did they come from? What has happened, what are you not telling me?'

The bruises. Now it's time to explain the bruises. Those black and purple swellings which have confirmed my 95 per cent. Grabbing at another chocolate bar and taking an almighty bite, I begin, but as I speak chocolate flies out like spittle all over my chin. Once wiped, I continue.

'I've always bruised easily, you know that, and sometimes I'm clumsy, but – and wait for it – last night during my dream I intercepted a group of smugglers. I got there before the military. I found a girl in the back of one of the smugglers' trucks, scared, petrified and alone. As I was trying to help her, one of the male smugglers saw me and we ended up fighting.'

'Elise, my god,' says Amanda.

'Well, to cut a long story short I made him unconscious, which is another matter altogether, but only after he stabbed me in the leg. I've suffered injuries in dreams before but have never really equated injuries to bruises until now. Anyway, I got the girl to safety, but I remember the look on her face – she was really looking at me. Me, dressed in pyjamas. I must sound crazy, but it's true. When I awoke this morning, my leg felt dead. Only when I got out of bed did I see this humongous welt on my leg in the exact position he had stabbed me, here.' I point to the large reddish-purple swelling on my leg, touching it gently to demonstrate its tenderness to Amanda.

'It's this which has now confirmed for me, well for 95 per cent of my brain, what my soul is doing at night.' With my second bar of chocolate gone, I head for the third.

'Stop,' says Amanda. 'Enough with the chocolate; what does a girl have to do to get a tea around here?'

'Oh god, I'm sorry, so sorry.'

There's a pause in my storytelling whilst the kettle boils and I make myself and Amanda tea. As I pass her a mug, I take a seat at the table next to her. I sit reading the lines on her forehead. I reach out, clasping her hands around her mug, holding them tight.

'Amanda, I need you to tell me what to do. I'm not mad and yet I have this niggling 5 per cent of grey matter that's telling me to pursue the logical explanations rather than what I truly believe. I'm more scared of that than anything else.'

Amanda says nothing. Instead, she stares into her mug and stirs the herbal tea bag around in the water.

'Elise, the 95 per cent part of your brain that you've been listening to and that you believe is your reality – are you comfortable with what it represents?'

'Yes, I am, I don't want to stop. Obviously, I don't want to keep getting hurt either, but it feels more real to me, my dreams excite me, I believe there meant to be.'

'Then that's it. Listen to your instincts and ignore the 5 per cent. You're not mad, Elise, a little cuckoo, but I love you to bits and I do not believe you're mad.'

Jumping from my seat, I throw myself at Amanda. 'Oh my god, you do not know how much I needed to hear you say that. I needed someone to tell me I was not mad.'

'No, I don't think you're mad, you're crushing me a little though.'

'Sorry.' I take a step back towards my seat.

'Elise, you look awful though, and cannot continue like this. What will you tell Joel?'

'Well, Joel and I still won't see one another for a few weeks. This morning I received the most wonderful and thoughtful surprise from him. A membership for De Vere's and vouchers for the spa. I would start today, but with the bruise and, well, you're the one looking at me. You're right, I'm a mess, but I'll be better by the time we meet up.'

'But will you tell him, Elise? Will you share your secret with him, the man who you believe you're stalking?'

'I'm not sure. I need to get it under control first, and that's difficult. I need proper sleep, not the kind of sleep I've been experiencing. I know it's my fault. I've made it worse by trying to get to sleep early so I can link in with the Afghanistan time zone. In doing so, I've placed myself in danger and probably been a hindrance on more than one occasion. I'm so drawn to being there, being with him and near him, I can't help it. And yet telling you was hard enough. In all our years together, whilst he's known I'm a dreamer, it's something that we haven't shared, haven't talked about. I wouldn't know where to start with Joel.'

'Right, well you need to work on minimising the effect it's having on you; fewer battles, and your diet. You need to kick the chocolate and get some meat and vegetables into you so you can heal quicker.'

'Look who's talking now; you've been pregnant, what, six months? and already turned into Martha Stewart.'

'Yes, without the prison term!' replies Amanda.

Chapter Thirty-One

Joel

Forty-eight hours have passed since we rescued the girl, detained six smugglers and torched over $4,000,000 worth of drugs high up in the Hindu Kush mountain range.

Arturo has been pivotal to all the interviews, including the girl's, and whilst they're all talking, what's being said is of limited value. None of the men speak about their roles in the smuggling cartel or who's in charge. They fear their bosses more than the military. One man persists with a story of fighting a woman who was trying to help the girl, and of being strangled. He also claims to have stabbed this woman before passing out. His story makes little sense, and it's being explained away as the ramblings of a man who has smoked too much of his own product. That's until the girl finally talks. The girl's story is far more enlightening and worth listening to.

Painstakingly Arturo works with a female soldier to elicit her story, background, where she has come from, and who her family are. The circumstances of her kidnapping are horrendous. The girl's father is believed to have been killed at the hands of the smugglers for failing to harvest a sufficient crop in payment of debts. The mother was beaten, and the child taken to prevent further loss of life to the family.

Traumatised, the girl continues explaining that a person, believed female, helped her from the truck into the woodland to hide from the men. Whilst vague, she describes a top worn by her rescuer – a top with long sleeves and the number '99' on. The girl when given some paper and a pencil, draws the shape of the top, the number '99' and the outline of an emblem. She describes a fight between the woman and one man, and seeing blood. After two days of interviews, Captain Wilson instructs soldiers to take her home. I feel slightly envious of Arturo who has been present during all the interviews. Normally, as the journalist, it would be me getting the first-hand accounts.

The information gleaned from the detainees and the girl never form part of a larger debrief, but Arturo feeds me snippets, including providing me with a photograph of the images drawn by the girl. I've so many questions and only half a story. What Arturo says, though, just begs more questions.

During one of the wider briefings, a summary of the operation covers its success and deals with the outstanding thermal image by proposing two theories. Theory one: that it was a large wild animal, not a rodent or snake as I had imagined. Theory two: that someone is possibly living feral in the mountains and maybe, just maybe, is acting as a vigilante. To be honest, neither theory sound convincing.

The other issue for the military is that whilst they've not lost ground and the intelligence was correct, they do not enjoy being the ones not holding all the cards. The overall mood of Operation Rattle personnel has changed. Captain Wilson takes over the daily briefings and Lieutenant Rogers is seemingly demoted to carrying out the roll call and nothing else. Whenever the men lose focus, and the chatter escalates, Lieutenant Rogers severely reprimands them with a growl.

The men walk around as if they've lost a competition. They're sulking in effect. When playing ball, they play for themselves, selfishly hogging the ball as their testosterone overflows. The tight team is fractious and in need of a task to focus their minds.

Little is being said, but we're told to be ready to ship out to new coordinates, the details of which will be shared only when we leave Bagram.

I can do nothing but sit tight and write. Whilst embargoed, I'm still able to catalogue the photographs I've obtained, write up my notes and interview the soldiers to gain their perspective. The digital images provided to me by Arturo sit at the heart of a huge mind map that I create to illustrate the information known to me. '99' and an emblem shape reminiscent of my old university emblem, resonate with me a little too much. As I add in details from all the operations I've been on since I arrived in Afghanistan, the mind map starts to resemble a spider's web. The emblem and numbers at the centre of my map have been drawn on what appears to be the shape of a long sleeved sweatshirt or t-shirt. I was 'Class of 99' at university and my old sweatshirt is Elise's favourite night-time comforter.

Whilst the mind map or should I say spider's web is not quite complete, I feel there is a theme connecting them. I allocate a thread from the web to the bright light phenomenon in Turkey. I can't get it out of my mind, and whilst seemingly random amongst all the military operations, it has something in common with them all – me.

Chapter Thirty-Two

Elise

Maximising my De Vere's membership by attending daily is paying dividends, even after five days. I'm far from gym-honed, but on the road to recovery. With one tanning session under my belt and another ten planned over the next five weeks I'm starting to feel more positive. I decide to save my treatment vouchers until two days before my flight to Tampa to maximise their benefit.

The recovery prescription given to me by Amanda for wine to be taken liberally at night has done nothing to prevent my dreams and night-time excursions. In fact, the more I drink, the deeper I sleep, and the longer I dream. The only saving grace is never seeing Joel or the military.

Amanda knows that I can't stop the inevitability of my destination, but I've heeded her advice and kept contact to a minimum, staying high when flying and forcing myself to wake up at the slightest engagement or sighting. Each night provides a fresh perspective; no recurrences and no obvious thoughts of previous encounters. That makes those encounters I've experienced seem even more real. My diary entries for the past few nights are all short, succinct and rather bland.

On Amanda's orders, I arrange a weekend at Mum and Dad's, which is well overdue. Leaving work early and taking a direct train from London to Leamington Spa seems an indulgence. I hop on at Marylebone and feel like a tourist for the one hour and twenty-minute journey. Dad is as punctual as ever and has the car parked only a few metres from the station doors.

He's a man of few words; we embrace, exchange pleasantries as if we're strangers, and then sit in silence for the twenty-minute ride home. I had surprised them both when I called asking to stay, and know exactly what's causing this distance in my father. He's worried something is up with Joel and me, Joel having been away so much and our last family reunion having been Easter. My dad keep's his eyes focussed on the road, and yet I can read his expression, the worry lines on his forehead and the fixed stare which is trying to avoid my eye-line. He's trying to avoid starting a conversation.

It concerns me as we travel along in silence, that if Dad is worried, what will Mum be thinking?

Entering my childhood home, I'm greeted with the wafts of home cooking escaping out into the summer air – the scent of fresh-baked bread, tangy lemon and lavender sponge, and my favourite slow-cooked floral chicken tarragon; all the things that make their home my home. It's warm and welcoming, no matter how long I've been away.

Mum is elbow deep in bubbles, washing pans, when I walk into the kitchen.

'Hi Mum, it's great to see you,' I say whilst embracing her with wide open arms, trying to avoid getting covered in bubbles from her rubber gloves.

'It's lovely to see you too, dear; you look pale,' she replies.

'No change there.'

Mum pulls off her gloves, laying them carefully by the sink, and says, 'Come here and give me a proper hug, none of this air business, you're not in London now.'

Our second embrace is warm, tight and lingering with genuine feeling. My mum is trying to heal all my woes in one big smothering, which leaves me feeling unusually emotional and on edge. My nerves and emotions are on the surface, raw and close to escaping.

'Is everything all right, Elise? I don't like to bombard you the minute you arrive, but your dad and I have been worried, you know, with you suddenly calling and wanting to stay,' says Mum.

'It's all good, Mum, honestly. I just need a change. I've felt lonely with Joel away and, well, a nutritious meal wouldn't go amiss, so where am I going to go that is better than home?' I reply.

'Sure,' says Mum.

'Honestly, I'm fine, but this concern is making me feel sappy, so stop it'. My emotions are bubbling on the surface, my face reddening and giving me away. I need to divert the conversation and draw breath before the commencement of an outpouring which no dam can hold back.

'Cake, Mum, that's what I need, that's what I've come for. I could smell the lavender at the door.'

'It's your favourite. Get some plates, you know where they are, and forks. It's still warm, so it might crumble a bit,' she replies.

My mum is a master cake baker and looks for every opportunity to dazzle taste buds with her creations. Dad and mum follow a sensible diet most of the time, but dad loves it when mum invites friends over as that always signals cake. They both look well on it though.

Pulling open Mum's larder cupboard, which stands proud and tall in the kitchen, I'm reminded of times gone by, with cake always baked, cupboards full of food and an eclectic mix of crockery, all clean and stacked, waiting to be used. Barely two plates or bowls match now, mum having stopped replacing her wedding set years ago. She claims she prefers the rustic mix that is now accumulating. It's far more than two people really need, but plenty in case guests arrive.

The contents of the larder cupboard have not changed one bit. Grabbing three plates and a handful of forks, I join Mum and Dad who sit with anticipation at the kitchen table.

Mum cuts into the cake as Dad and I eagerly watch, wondering who will get the larger slice. As the laden plate is slid towards me, I waste no time and plunge the fork into the deep wedge. My mouth engulfs the moist, delicate sponge, my taste buds awakening to sweet lavender and the sharpness of the lemon icing.

'There's nothing like a slab of cake to cure all ills,' I say.

'You're not ill, are you, Elise?' says Mum.

'No, Mum, it's a turn of phrase, stop fussing. I've missed this, you know, home cooking, and you and Dad of course.'

'That's good to hear. You and Joel are welcome anytime,' says Mum.

'I know. It's been busy, what with his work and my new job.'

'Yes, how's that going? Miss your old one yet?' asks Mum.

'Brilliant, thanks, and yes I miss the people but not the work or the topics. A change was necessary. I've brought a few manuscripts with me, a little light reading for the weekend.'

'Well, you're here to relax, unless you have plans,' says Mum.

'No, no plans. Eat, sleep and read if that's OK.'

'Whatever you want, I made your room up as you like it. Tea is usually about six if that's ok? We don't like to eat late.'

'That sounds fab, Mum, no complaints from me. I may well be in my pyjamas by then, anyway.'

It's so lovely to relax and be catered for. The residual warmth in the air makes sitting outside in the cottage garden a pleasant change and whilst now late afternoon the sunshine still provides benefits. The familiar surroundings, smells and noises are all comforting. For probably the first time in a long while, I truly relax and feel myself, a feeling which has been lost.

Mum and Dad have their routines and I don't see any reason to disrupt them. My stopover is to be short and sweet, so tolerating a string of sitcoms on Gold is a small price to pay for the warmth and comfort showered on me since my arrival.

By seven I'm in my pyjamas curled up on the sofa next to Mum. Dad is team-leader in charge of the remote and an evening of re-runs begins. There's something comforting about watching programmes I've seen ten and twenty years ago. Familiar faces, music, lines, nothing to challenge the grey matter. Having deliberately left my laptop at work and my tablet in my bedroom, my eyes and mind can fully focus and absorb the distraction that the television provides. This is something I've missed since Joel's departure, my nights at home resembling a mixture of internet searching, paper reviewing and channel-hopping, which in hindsight is not at all relaxing.

At ten Dad announces, as if making a statement to all, 'Headlines and bed.'

Mum automatically responds, 'Yes dear.'

I smile a small discreet smile to myself. Their familiarity and contentment is so obvious; after all, they have been married nearly forty years.

Feeling weary from what has been a relaxing, chilled out afternoon, I climb the stairs after my parents and settle into what was once my teenage bedroom. Little has changed in the years since I moved into London and in with Joel. My posters still adorn the walls, my dressing table is still marked with old stickers and my old fluffy pink and white spot dressing gown hangs on the back of the door. The bed is new. Mum and Dad replaced my old single one with a metal-framed double once Joel and I married and the duvet cover is new and freshly laundered in Mum's familiar washing powder.

It's lovely to be home, and in no time I slip off to sleep, buried under the weighted duvet and resting on the two pillows.

*

'Morning, Elise, hope you slept well. Your dad and I are going to the local market soon, do you want to come?' says Mum.

'Morning, Mum. What time is it?' I peer above the mound of duvet and squint to focus in on Mum.

'It's nine thirty, the market starts at ten, so we intend to leave shortly,' she replies.

'Did you say nine thirty?' I ask.

'Yes, sleepyhead, I have fresh bread downstairs if you want some toast and jam,' says Mum.

'Yes please. God, nine thirty, I can't believe it. I cannot remember the last time I slept so well and so late, especially after a dry night.'

'Well, you looked peaky when you arrived; you've already got more colour in you. Come on, I'll boil the kettle,' says Mum.

'Tea please, mint if you have it.'

I stretch out, still buried under the duvet, my head on one pillow, the second to my side scrunched as if cuddled all night. I feel refreshed, and not at all achy. More amazingly, I've no recollection of any dream or dreams. No vivid images or residual memories, nothing. It feels good, but yet a little strange. I cannot remember the last time I did not recall a dream.

I swing my legs over and out and launch myself up, grabbing my fluffy dressing gown and heading downstairs in search of toasted bread.

*

The village market which is held on the church car park is a small affair, with a dozen stalls at most, and a mixture of freshly grown produce, meat, cheese and plants. The local constabulary are also present and marking bikes, so several children are milling around. The weather is pleasantly warm and the air fresh, very fresh compared to London, and the people all friendly. There's no one I recognise, but they smile and greet me as if I'm a local.

It's a million miles from home and a zillion from London, but I can feel the pull to the countryside. It's obvious why Mum and Dad have lived here so long. They belong, they fit into the village and the village into them. I could see myself living further out of London in a more welcoming environment, especially if Joel's work takes him away more often. With Amanda building her own family unit and no longer able to party like the old days, I can feel myself becoming an island; an island marooned in an enormous sea of people, and the only person I want bathing on my beach is Joel, but I haven't quite found the right anchor for him yet.

'Are you OK, dear? You look lost in yourself,' says Mum.

'Yes, fine thanks Mum. You could say I was lost, I was just reflecting on things,' I reply.

'Everything's OK, I hope?' says Mum.

'Yes, Mum … everything's fine. You and Dad have got this retirement lark sussed by the look of things. I know Dad is probably not the best conversationalist for you, but you seem to have got the right balance.'

'You know your dad, never a man of words, always listening and analysing. Rarely does he start a conversation or finish one. It's the way it's always been. He would go to the hospital every day and psychoanalyse patients and then find he couldn't switch off when he came home. He's pre-programed to listen and assess, silently figuring people out, all hours of the day. He seems content. It works for us. The bonus is, I always get the last word.'

'Has he sussed me out yet?' I ask.

'Oh yes, dear, he had you fathomed out from day one when you arrived. Needless to say, he's never wrong.'

'What does that mean?'

'Well, he's talked to me in the past about people's glow, their energy he calls it. A load of psycho-babble,

I thought for many years. But he was an expert at his job and helped so many people. He always believed it was because he could sense them, their inner energy, what made them tick. Well, with you he said you glowed the minute you were born. You were always happy and over the years he would sense before I would when things maybe weren't going to plan for you, or you were stressed. Obvious times like exams and university he felt your glow, your energy fluctuated. When you and Joel got together and got married, it was at its strongest. Then, your father was a very content man seeing his baby girl all grown up and happy. Then at Easter, when you and Joel came to visit, your dad sensed things weren't right. For me there was nothing on the surface which was obvious; as far as I was concerned you and Joel were as happy and strong as ever. But your father was, say, more than a little concerned.'

'At Easter, that was not long after Joel had come back from Turkey. I know he had been away a bit, but we were OK, Mum. We are OK,' I say.

'There's being OK, Elise, and then there's realising, well in your father's words, things are cooling. It's only natural, especially with your careers.'

'No. I swear, Mum, there's nothing wrong with our relationship. Don't get me wrong, I would rather have Joel at home and I worry constantly about him. But he's just following his dream, and I can't be the one to get in his way.'

'Precisely. Well, that's what I said. You two have your careers and they come first.'

'Well, I wouldn't say they come first; they pay the bills, but for me Joel is number one.'

'And for him?' asks Mum.

'I believe Mum, I really do, that he feels the same. He needs to do this. I can't believe Dad thinks we're on the rocks.'

'No, dear, he never said directly your marriage was in trouble. He senses that your glow, this energy thing is fading, and he wants his baby girl to be happy again.'

'Should I speak to him, do you think, to Dad?' I ask.

'No not now; if you feel the need, wait until tomorrow when he takes you back to the station. That way if anything is said which doesn't sit right you will part, but it won't have ruined your weekend,' replies Mum.

'Well, the fact that he's so apparently in tune with my life already somewhat disturbs me,' I say.

'Look, leave it, Elise, but what I will say is your dad is one of those rare men that actually gets it right most of the time. He's sensitive, caring and perceptive. I could go on, and I love him for all of those qualities and he loves you for all of your qualities. Just remember that.'

'I will. I need cake, definitely cake.'

*

By seven, I fall into Mum and Dad's routine. We ate early and now I'm already dressed for bed and the three of us sit cosied up in front of the television for another round of re-runs. Once again I leave my tablet upstairs so as to not be distracted. My phone is in front of me on the coffee table, in case Joel calls.

In some small way, I will my phone to ring so I can spring into action and loudly profess my undying love for my man in front of Dad. One phone call from Joel and my father will be convinced that his little girl is totally, utterly in love, and her husband is the best man in the world.

The problem is that the more I want it to ring, and it remains silent, the more my thoughts turn to reality. The stark reality is that Joel is away, putting his career ahead of our relationship, and that I'm home alone turning into a paranoid 95 per cent certified mad stalker who can't leave her man alone even when she's asleep.

Dad's right, who am I kidding. At Easter I felt fractious after the whole Turkey business and Joel announcing the possibility of working with the military. I was tired and there were tensions between Joel and me. This energy thing that Dad sees also makes sense. Mum may not have got it, although she loves him and respects him enough to believe him, but I understand it.

I know exactly what Dad is seeing. My research has taught me a lot and one thing that I've always remembered is auras, colours and lights, a person's energy. Not everyone can see them, but we all have them and they vary in intensity. Dad is perceptive, but can he read me enough to comprehend what has been going on in my dreams?

Sitting across from Dad who is relaxed into the sofa, the remote perfectly balanced on his right leg, I wonder for a moment what he's thinking right now. Not one word is being spoken between us, yet my mind is far from engaged in the sitcom blaring out from the television. Mum is half-engaged, peering up occasionally above her glasses to view the programme and then returning to her magazine of choice. Dad, though, is a cool customer, outwardly appearing to be fully captivated by the cheesy one liner. Is he really engaged or in fact deploying a psycho-babble sixth sense on me? I always knew that growing up with a shrink in the house could be challenging, but never ever really – until now – thought I was one of his patients, a specimen to be observed and assessed.

As the credits roll and another oldie ends, I stand and offer to make a round of tea and fetch any biscuits or sweet delights that they desire. Simple pleasures on a Saturday night.

By nine, any hope of hearing from Joel has faded. It would already be midnight in Afghanistan so he's either out working operationally or tucked up in bed, either having forgotten to phone or been unable to phone. I hope it's the latter.

*

Amazingly I wake late again having slept immensely well. Two nights without dreaming, without incident. My parent's home is like an oasis for recovery, which sadly I have to leave. Whilst I linger over breakfast, secretly trying to halt time, I know that it's time to leave.

Feeling somewhat warm and emotional I hug Mum tightly, not wanting to let her go. Her slightly rounded form cushions me in all the right places. She has packed me up a picnic of sweet and savoury delights which will feed me for the next day or two, and for which I am very grateful.

Dad gets in the car ahead of me and starts the engine.

'Now look, Elise, it has been lovely seeing you and you look better for getting out of London. I always say it but you know you can come anytime; we would love to see you more often,' says Mum.

'Yes, thanks, Mum, I know,' I reply.

'Now be gentle with your dad, remember he only wants what's best for you.'

'I will; come here give me another hug.' Feeling tears welling up, my eyes smart as I strain to restrain them, I feel genuinely sad to be leaving. My two nights have been a wonderful oasis of calm in my hectic mad life to which I have to return. The little girl in me wants to stay and lock herself in her room forever where she knows she is safe.

Dad was always my knight in shining armour, but that role passed to Joel. The question is, will Joel be saving me or me saving him?

*

The journey takes only twenty minutes; the roads are clear, it being a Sunday. Dad pulls into a vacant spot outside the station and switches off the engine. For a moment we say nothing. Dad's hands remain fixed to the steering wheel, his posture upright.

'Dad. Joel and I, we will be OK won't we? We're not broken?' I ask.

'No, Elise, you're not broken. You're ... maybe a little stretched at the moment, but you're not broken,' says Dad relaxing and turning towards me.

Those wretched tears which have been bubbling under the surface since leaving Mum are knocking on the dam door, forcing their way out, soon to be uncontrollably unleashed.

'Dad, I love you.'

'I know you do, and I you.'

'Dad, I feel we will be OK, Joel and I.'

'You will. I believe that truly, Elise, but both of you need to be reminded of what your love means. You by letting him go truly with your blessing, and him by realising what a marvellous thing he has left behind. You're two souls who are meant to be together, who are just not functioning well apart. Trust me, I know. He may follow his dreams and you may live his dreams, but your collective strength is what will bring you back together.'

'Mum says that you have seen me glow in the past, what does she mean?'

'It's just your energy, Elise. From the minute you were born, I could see you radiating. It was as if white and silver light was shining from within you. I was a new dad, remember, and to me you were my world. The way I would describe it is like when you a get a blurry eye, or oil in water, or a fine mist in the air around you. You have always had it, but occasionally it fades and that's when I've worried, but truly, Elise, all will be well with you and Joel.'

Sniffling and sobbing, I wipe away my tears and smother Dad with a hug, pulling him in tight. For a man of few words he said so much, the meaning of which still eludes, but he has faith and so should I.

Chapter Thirty-Three

Elise

The house is empty and unwelcoming as I enter and place my bag down and turn to secure the door. It's cold and dark, even though the temperature outside is mid-twenties and barely mid-afternoon. Leaving my bag at the door and my keys on the hall table, I wander through to the kitchen, which is a little brighter. The glass lantern ceiling fills it with light emitting from between our house and the terraced roofs to the rear.

With the kettle soon bubbling away and the stereo at a modest volume, the house, our home, comes to life once more. It isn't cosy like my parents'. It doesn't ooze the same warmth that comes with theirs being a proper home, a home that has for many years seen lives grow and expire. The pets we kept were there one day, gone the next, and the changes to the structure and the garden all evolving and improving.

Ours, conversely, feels empty, devoid of warmth, a mere shell in comparison. We had promised to do so much, but in the couple of years since we moved in work and finances always got in the way. It's a perfect bolt-hole for London living, but not a home.

As the sun drops and the evening draws to a close, seated on the sofa in front of the television in full control of the channels for the first time in forty-eight hours, I wish to be back home, back at my parents' cosied up, well fed and warm; warm with love.

As the ten o'clock news starts, I smile to myself and think of my dad. 'Headlines and bed,' and my mum's response, 'Yes dear.'

My dad had said that Joel was following his dreams, and that I was living them. That speech had resonated with me throughout the journey home and all afternoon and evening. *Does he know what I know? How could he? He is perceptive; he's my dad, but he isn't actually psychic.* My over-active imagination is getting the better of me, creating mind-reading conspiracy theories.

My 95 per cent belief in my ability to transcend consciousness, my dreams, is not something I wear on my sleeve or visible in my emotions. Amanda is the only person in the world I've shared it with, and she struggled with the concept I proposed. No, Dad had to be speaking metaphorically, not literally. But then there's my glow. First Mum mentioned it and then

Dad confirmed it; white and silver all around me. It all makes sense.

As I stand up to go to bed now, only just twelve minutes past ten, and the landline rings. Whilst it's late I immediately pick it up.

'Elise, it's me, Joel. Elise, can you hear me?'

'Yes Joel. Hi, god, it's so good to hear from you.'

'I'm sorry, Elise, I wanted to call yesterday but couldn't and I'm sorry for calling so late; it's been hectic.'

'That's OK. I know you would have done if you could and you are now, that's what matters. It must be what, one in the morning for you?'

'Oh, Elise, it has been so busy. It's really ramped up I've got so much material to work on when I get home. I know I can't talk to you about it, but at times it has been awful, but other times just awesome, so what I needed.'

'Great, good.'

'The guys over here are so committed; many on their third tour. You know, when I think about the fact that I'm away for three months and yet these dudes, well, some have barely been home,' continues Joel.

'Great, uh, huh?'

'The food is taking its toll on me, though. Can't wait to get back to my blender. Don't get me wrong, we're all fed well, too well, you know it's just not what I'm used to,' says Joel.

'Uh, huh?' As I continue to climb the stairs, I am waiting for it, but it just doesn't come.

'I spoke to my editor Ben last week, brief but to the point. Both sides of the Atlantic want me to produce back-to-back editorials covering specific operations and an overall perspective of the military role in Afghanistan. I could fill a book just with photos alone without a word being typed.'

'Great, so...'

'Sorry Elise, it's all been about me and my time is nearly up, how's things?'

Sounding as positive as possible I respond, 'Great, fantastic thanks, just back from a weekend with my parents. They're both well and ask after you and—'

'Sorry, I've got someone chomping at the bit to make their call. I'll try to call Saturday. Love you, hun, be good, take care,' says Joel.

Gone just as quickly as he arrived. *'Love you, hun, be good, take care.' Where's the warmth in that? No, 'I'm missing you, cannot wait to see you'. Instead, 'Be good, take care,' a farewell suitable for a child departing for university, not for an absent loving husband to his abandoned, lonely wife.*

Frustration, anger and sadness flood my senses. Those tears from earlier burst through the dam, cascading down the curves of my cheeks. No call on Saturday and then a fleeting one-way update all about him.

Calm yourself, Elise. My mind is trying to rein in my emotions. *Dad said I need to 'let him go with my blessing in order for him to realise what he has left behind.' That conversation was not about me letting him go, it was about me having been left behind.* I know I can either irrationally convert my frustration, anger and sadness into a cauldron of ill feeling towards Joel, or I can take my dad's advice. The advice being to let him go with my blessing, accepting that he called, he's excited, he's following his dream, and I'll be here for him when he returns.

As hard as that is to swallow, I can't shout at him – he's already gone, and that would only cause resentment between us. No, if I follow my dad's advice, as painful as it is, he'll call again and be the same excited puppy dog he's always been about his work, but he'll call and he'll come home.

Settling down into what is a cold bed I pull Joel's pillow into me, hugging it tight, imagining its Joel, warm and soft. A residual tear rolls over my cheek on to my pillow, absorbed by the cotton casing. I close my eyes and softly breathe, my mind clearing as I resign myself to letting him go.

*

The days pass by, and September lives up to expectations and provides some late summer warmth. The shell display on the windowsill continues to grow and starts accumulating dust. It's a daily reminder of Joel's absence and his upcoming return. They're all shapes and sizes, miracles of nature crafted so perfectly.

Work bubbles. With my first book launch looming, I've back-to-back meetings with the author, the illustrator and the marketing manager. I squeeze gym visits in after work, with me twice taking the Late Eight class, a boxercise class which starts at eight p.m. for a full eight minutes' intense workout. Even after only two weeks I'm stronger and firmer in places and the boxercise has really allowed me to vent my frustrations, which I know have built up. My skin glows after two tanning sessions; it's still pale by most standards, but definitely glowing.

The last few nights I've slept well. The pull, the draw that accompanies my usual night-time activities is not as strong. My recollection of my dreams is vague and limited to a few snapshots of snow-capped vistas, but nothing more.

At last I'm starting to relax, rejuvenate and build myself up for my reunion with Joel.

Chapter Thirty-Four

Joel

It sits uncomfortably with me not telling Elise the full story. Firstly, I know the call was being recorded and secondly, it would have only worried her to know the military plan is deviating. Because of several factors, not least the recurring theme of our operations being hijacked, they're relocating our team away from Bagram.

Some distances travelled by the platoon have made us vulnerable. With most of the intelligence focussing on the Hindu Kush and the Nuristan province bordering northern Pakistan, we're moving to Franklin Forward Operating Base, or FOB. Franklin FOB is situated at the foothills of the Hindu Kush. The imposing mountainous backdrop I've enjoyed at Bagram is soon to loom large above me.

The briefing last night was very clear. We had to be on the road by six a.m. and stops between Bagram and Franklin were to be limited. A distance of just over 100 miles doesn't seem a lot, but we cannot drive in a straight line and our speed would average a mere thirty-five miles per hour depending on the terrain. One hundred miles would equate to over five hours in the belly of the beast.

Our departure at five-forty a.m. was met positively by Lieutenant Rogers who is also accompanying us on the last leg of Operation Rattle. Riding up front in the MRAP is Lieutenant Rogers and Sergeant Cox, with Shorty, Jones, Arturo and Williams riding shotgun with me in the back. Two hours in and we stop for a comfort break and a stretch of the legs. We've covered just over forty miles due to the rough unmade roads, potholes and river gorges that our driver has had to carefully navigate.

It's eight a.m. and the warmth from the summer sun is already strong enough to make me sweat. Whilst the men are relieving themselves, I down some water and loosen my body armour to vent some heat. I had put off drinking whilst moving as the jolts and leaning from the endless pits and slopes made me wear more than swallow. My breakfast also threatened on a two occasions to reappear and wreak havoc so instead, I have been shallow breathing and keeping my head down.

The fresh albeit warm air is welcoming, but is short lived as Sergeant Cox signals for us to load and move out.

'You look green, Hamilton,' says Shorty wincing. 'I hope we're not going to be wearing your breakfast for the rest of the day.'

'No, I'm good. If you had asked me that an hour ago my answer would have been different, but I feel OK now.'

'After two months, you should have got used to this,' says Shorty.

'I have. I'm tired, that's all.'

'What kept you awake then?' asks Arturo with a degree of concern.

'My wife.'

The men simultaneously erupt in to a symphony of jeers and guffaws with Shorty saying, 'I'm sure we'd all like to be kept awake by your wife.'

For the past two months, I've not discussed Elise. I didn't want her to be the subject of barrack room banter and because, if I think about her, I miss her, which just makes being here harder.

Arturo gives Shorty two forceful punches on his arm, which is met by 'Come on dude, I'm just pulling his chain,' from Shorty. It's like being at high school and watching a round of birthday beats being dished out as George and Jones join in for good measure.

Once settled, I catch Arturo's eye line and give him a nod.

By the time we arrive at Franklin FOB, the sun is high in the sky and the temperatures peak at ninety-five degrees. The platoon is being accommodated in two vacated pre-fabricated shelters. The base itself is sparse. Whilst there's a military presence at the base, it's limited and the resident troops are ready to pack up and ship out, pulling back towards Bagram. It's all part of the military wind-down in the far more remote and hostile areas. NATO Forces have already withdrawn, and even the night-time operations by the 101st have stopped, the result being the Taliban and smugglers grow over-confident and strengthen in numbers.

The Taliban's superior knowledge of the unforgiving terrain provides them with many vantage points inaccessible by troops on the ground. A network of trails through the Hindu Kush are Taliban controlled, and until the commencement of our operations, the military had not mapped the area.

Our work to date has been on the periphery of the mountain range, but with us advancing forward to

Franklin, we've a whole fresh territory to explore – subject to the right intelligence telling us where to go, that is.

Fresh satellite and drone imagery is now available and the laser marking previously deployed on vehicles is now being utilised on individuals. Whilst it's a gamble to trust the laser data, our commanders are prepared to take the risk. So far it has worked, and an interesting picture of movement is being painted deep within the caverns and valleys of the inhospitable range.

We've not shared our role and purpose with the other military personnel at the FOB. They believe we're yet another platoon serving our time in the tribal area. The Bagram briefing I was present at will not be repeated. Daily orders are now sent to Lieutenant Rogers who will deploy accordingly. Because of the remote nature of the base and the limited ground support available, we're to be shadowed twenty-four seven. The eye in the sky and aerial support will accompany us on all operations.

The first night is reconnaissance without leaving the base. Direct satellite feeds are beamed into an MRAP and Lieutenant Rogers and Sergeant Cox view them and plot target locations. Under the clear diamond-studded sky two of the corporals position functional telescopes fitted with night-vision technology and scan the vast range beyond. A lay observer might think they were just stargazing. To the initiated, those that were present during the briefing, they know that the telescope with night-vision technology is connected to the satellite, the satellite to the drone and the MRAP, and together the most up-to-date three-dimensional picture is being created. This imagery directs each night's activity. Whilst I'm not a lay observer, I still find the environment I'm in surreal. In the broadest sense, my environment is a stark minimalist military base with a vista most travel companies would wish to have on the front cover of their brochures, surrounded by imposing mountains, woodland and wild rivers. All seemingly idyllic, but riddled with smuggling cartels and Taliban fighters, which in turn make it one of the ugliest and most dangerous places I've ever visited.

We have a window of one month. A month for the military to make significant gains. A month for me to collect and finalise my editorial material. A month, by the end of which the troops will all be gone from Franklin.

Night after night thereafter we leave the base via a combination of MRAP and birds. It's a risky strategy. Whilst I signed up to write the story, to get the story, I have to be part of the action. Risk is something I have to accept.

The first three nights are direct action initiatives using small arms fire to take out several Taliban security points. By the third night, the insurgents are spooked as the platoon moves around unseen, picking off patrols. They perhaps accepted the first night was maybe a random attack. With their fighters off guard, the Taliban send reinforcements. They still seem unprepared for the stealthy nature in which the troops deploy, execute and evade them.

On night four and five, we let them rest and regroup. A dubious tactic possibly, but one which brings larger dividends on nights six, seven and eight. The Taliban bolster their security points ready for an open firefight, and whilst they may think they have superior knowledge of the terrain they do not have the technology which supports the platoon. Fitted with prototype night-vision goggles, the soldiers have taken the advantage. These prototypes provide sharp, broad thermal and movement sensors and were flown into Bagram prior to our departure specifically for a trial.

Being part of this ground-breaking mission and exploration of technology is awe-inspiring. My position is firmly cemented as part of the aerial support team. My ability is limited when capturing pictorial evidence of the operations, instead I record my personal experience. My anxieties, fears and shock at the brutal effectiveness of the marines, contrasting with my nervous excitement and adrenalin at having survived a successful mission.

By the end of week one, insurgent activity increases with reserves being called to order. We caught them off guard, having resigned themselves to the military's withdrawal.

The quicker pace of operations is proving fruitful. No reports of suspicious thermal images or vigilantes in the woods. This is spontaneous removal of the Taliban from their own backyard.

Week two – a new strategy. This centres on the aerial bombardment of the range and the trails utilised by the smugglers and Taliban alike. The soldiers using small shoulder-fired missiles seal the already barely passable routes. All carried out under cover of darkness, utilising the laser mapping provided by the drone and our now superior thermal imagery.

By week three, the smugglers and insurgents vacate their strongholds. They scatter and take deep cover within the rugged terrain. This assault on their network is having the desired effect of forcing their operations into the open. With the circuitous trails cut off, those cartels with deals to keep move to open, riskier territory. They believe that moving at night provides them with protection, having learnt nothing from the previous two weeks' attacks.

A combination of human and technological intelligence sets us off on what might be our last operation before bugging out of Franklin, along with the rest of the military.

At eleven a.m. I attend a briefing called by Lieutenant Rogers with the thirty strong platoon. With limited facilities at Franklin for large-scale briefings, the briefing takes place in one of the prefabricated accommodation huts. There are no neat rows of chairs, nor laptop or projector, just the men scattered amongst the bunks all focussed on Lieutenant Rogers and Sergeant Cox who position themselves near the entry door.

'Listen up men, time is critical. I have already briefed the Sergeants and the drivers so there's no need to share aerial photographs and maps today,' says Lieutenant Rogers, whose brow is glistening. The hut is like a sauna, which is full to the brim with overheated bodies and testosterone.

'We are leaving at noon, pack for twenty-four hours, full munitions and supplies. We have a RV point determined and will be joined by our Afghan colleagues. You know the drill. The intelligence provided is clear, a significant gathering is planned to take place tonight between Taliban forces and two main smuggling cartels. The suggestion on the ground being that scores are to be settled as they are each blaming the other for what is in fact our doing,' says Lieutenant Rogers.

The men are getting restless with springs from bunks creaking and magazines being fanned to move the air around.

'Sergeant Cox has the deployment details. We have been given authority to disrupt this gathering and take out a number of high level targets. All eyes will be on us tonight, so watch your backs and let's make sure we bring everyone home,' says Lieutenant Rogers with a slightly graver tone.

'Right, you heard the Lieutenant, grub up boys, I want you ready for your deployment details in forty minutes,' says Sergeant Cox.

With that, the men jump from the bunks and head out like a herd of cattle being called in for milking.

*

Under cover of darkness we veer off-track, heading to a meeting point only identified by coordinates. This operation is fraught with so many dangers, not least driving off-track and possibly through undetected minefields. The men ride with their rifles primed on their laps, there's no banter, and light conversation is not what they want right now.

A bumpy jerky ride ensues as we traverse the rugged terrain before we head up back onto firmer ground that leads to a disused old Soviet outpost. Waiting in a clearing are two trucks of Afghan Special Forces soldiers.

Within minutes of our arrival, the familiar and now comforting hum signals the Chinook descending. I, together with Arturo and two-thirds of the platoon, board the Chinook and quickly ascend to the skies.

The remainder of the men redistribute within the MRAPs, taking on board some Afghan soldiers and then ship out. The Chinook, able to cover ground far quicker, pulls back and allows the ground troops to rejoin the main route, heading now for the target location.

Time to interception twenty-three minutes.

Chapter Thirty-Five

Elise

Catching up with my dream diary on the penultimate Saturday before my reunion with Joel feels a little strange. My dreams in the past couple of weeks have been fleeting and vague, not vivid or lucid. Occasionally I sense a slight pull towards what's now familiar territory for me in Afghanistan. On the whole, though, I've slept well and most mornings have woken with no recollections whatsoever. Bringing my diary up to date takes moments. There are no encounters or sightings to add. No action at all. For me, this means Joel is safe, or at least in no immediate danger. All my worries over the past weeks and months when I've driven myself to distraction by an innate fear of losing him are ebbing away. I'm not losing him, but letting him go.

Only nine more sleeps to go until our reunion. According to my daily diary, Joel bugs out from Afghanistan in six days. His journey to Florida takes him via Germany and into the United States. I know he plans to collect his parents' car first and make his way to Tampa for my arrival. Getting excited, I flick through my diary and map out a schedule for the coming week. Tanning sessions and gym workouts are booked. My treatments are scheduled, and my body is healing. An intense tingling sensation engulfs me. It's the thought of being touched, being seen and being smelt by Joel again for the first time in three months.

Joel not calling is somewhat unusual. Our last few conversations have been very brief, and all he had said was things were escalating, but sounded safe and well. I climb the stairs with my mug of camomile tea and settle into bed. Another early night will bring our reunion ever closer, for which the anticipation and expectation are high. The thought of it makes me feel nineteen again. Flashbacks to our first kiss, his touch, create goosebumps. I feel the warmth of his lips, his scent intense woody and floral. God, he smelt good. Imagining what's coming brings life to parts which have otherwise been numb these past months. A lovely way to fall asleep.

*

The odour of struck matches fills the air. Below, smoke wafts skywards. Cracks and pops leap around, their sound carrying off into the distance without a barrier to contain them. The open terrain with its flat lines lies in a wide bowl and the steep, unforgiving ridges of the Hindu Kush loom large. Dark and isolated, there is no sign of civilisation for miles.

Pandemonium on the ground, sporadic sparks and flashes from many directions. A battle is ensuing.

The pull, the call to be here, is strong. For the first time in three months, I can sense Joel close. Is this the beginning or nearing its end? I don't know. What can I do? Nothing.

A bird in the sky, too big to miss, descends groundwards. Troops are deploying. The pull is stronger. A sensation rises that I'm needed and wanted and that I'm already here; Joel.

Chapter Thirty-Six

Joel

Descending ever closer to the ground, my stomach churns and my jaw locks. Not physically, but mentally I'm attached to Arturo; wherever he goes I do too. Having earnt the trust of the platoon and Lieutenant Rogers, I'm no longer side lined waiting for the "all clear". Tonight, I will be on the ground in the centre of the action, collecting live images of the operation as it unfolds. As the ground looms the dirt and dust spiral into the air creating a fog screen for us to deploy behind. Hitting the ground by my side, Arturo grabs my collar and pulls me behind him for cover.

The engagement is underway. As predicted the cartels will shed blood and the Taliban have decided to join the fight. All lines of communication between the rivals have broken down and the military are here to silence it once and for all.

Scuttling in behind Arturo and crouching down, I hold my helmet with one hand and my video camera with the other. The smugglers are all centrally grouped, having realised that instead of shooting each other they now need to defend themselves from the military and Taliban. The Taliban are harder to spot, having taken a wider arc of ground around the smugglers. The ground troops, having already advanced, are forming a pincer movement, picking off stragglers.

Arturo, falling forward on his elbows, takes up a low level position, steadying his rifle on the ground and taking aim. Falling in behind him and stretching my arms out, I force my video camera forward, hoping to catch as much of the action as possible. The rest of the platoon from the Chinook advance, causing more distraction and disruption.

A whistling crack vibrates through my eardrums as Arturo engages repeatedly. Snaps and crackles wing everywhere. The sulphurous odour of gunpowder hovers in the atmosphere. Between shots, I can hear voices barely audible in front – Pashtun, maybe Dari.

Blindly, I jerk my camera towards gunfire. Arturo has far superior directional ability, aided by the night-vision technology. Pop after pop, he silences another gun.

'Move,' says Arturo.

Scrambling to my feet, my knees bent, my posture hunched, I pursue Arturo as he advances forward.

Dodging and swerving left and right and then hitting the deck once more, I ingest a mouthful of dirt as my face plants into the soft ground. My breathing is fast and furious. Saliva wells in my mouth, washing away the grit. A firm left hand from Arturo is on my shoulder before it takes up position again on the trigger of his gun.

In an instant, the sky is orange, with the piercing whining sound of a rocket having launched and spontaneously exploded. Fifty metres away, the heat radiates outwards towards us.

Jerking me to my feet, Arturo pulls me along with him, weaving left, zigzagging and circling the inferno. With the cover of an MRAP in sight, Arturo signals for me to make haste and take shelter. Running in a straight line to the relative safety of the side of the MRAP, I turn to see Arturo hit the ground once more. On these barren flat plains there's no natural cover, we're all exposed. A cluster comprising Taliban and cartel forms in the centre under pressure from the military, who now occupy all external routes.

Crawling forward, staying low and near to the belly of the beast, I maximise my view. The inferno is now calming, providing enough light. I can see the core of the fighters steadily reducing in numbers. Two more rockets launch and contact vehicles, sending them high in the air. A ping sounds above me as a stray bullet hits the MRAP. The gunfight now slows with sporadic, isolated pops resonating. The enemy is silenced.

Still shaking and gasping, not moving, I just film the last moments. A burst of radio chatter signals the next phase. Strangely disorientated, my ears ring, my shoulders lock and I tense. I ease back, propping myself up against the metal beast for support.

In the distance, the now comforting hum of the Chinook gets louder. Looking skyward through the haze of dust and smoke, I see a light in the sky – a star brighter and lower than the rest. In that instant, all I can think about is Elise.

*

The fire fight seemed to last for only minutes and yet morning starts to break by the time the military have the area under control. Once the dense plumes of smoke clear, the Chinooks land and illuminate the landscape further. A head count of military personnel takes place, and the injured are evacuated. Success has a cost, and not one that comes after a pound or dollar sign. It's the cost of human life, and tonight the price is high.

Two members of Operation Rattle are wounded, a gunshot injury and one from shrapnel. The Afghan Special Forces team reports two minor injuries, but it's the cartels and the Taliban that bear the brunt. A fog of dust hangs in the air, but slowly bodies are recovered and laid to rest. Sixty plus men, some only teenagers, have lost their lives. The injured detainees are afforded medical care, but it's inevitable that several injured will have escaped. They might now lose their lives at the hands of the elements and inhospitable terrain.

At the outset of the firefight, the cartels and Taliban outnumbered the military two to one. The missile attack had the desired effect, though, of taking out swathes of fighters, and the odds swung. Upwards of thirty fighters fled into the foothills of the Kush. The talk amongst the men and the Afghan Forces, is that the number of casualties will impact on the effectiveness of the cartels and Taliban resistance, which means their activities will be curtailed for a while.

I carry on recording the carnage caused by the missile attack, the crater, the twisted metal and the torched shrubbery which provided futile cover. As morning finally breaks the full picture becomes apparent. Dismembered bodies lay strewn, the barren cracked landscape is blood soaked. Those detained are on their knees under the watchful eye of heavily armed Afghan Forces. For the first time in three months I've no thirst to record images, make notes or interview anyone. I know this is war, and I have visualised images in the past of what I imagine conflict to look like, but this is vivid reality. I'm not at home watching TV or hearing a third hand report from a refugee, I'm here breathing in the stench of sweat and excrement and my eyes feel pierced by the sight of limbs detached from torsos, life extinguished by the depression of a finger on a trigger. This is war, it's not pleasant, it is gruesome.

*

The men were silent before the engagement, all part of their mental preparation for the assault. Now, their silence represents something quite different. Having worked alongside them for three months, and observed their interactions and reactions to all manner of situations, I feel their pain. Their tilted heads with blank expressions, closed eyes accompanied by bodily jitters, tell me they're tired, despondent and in shock. With two colleagues injured, the mood is low. There is no celebration, only reflection.

My time is up and I know that in a matter of days I'll leave Afghanistan and return to my day job. Returning to Elise will complete me, but I've a nagging doubt about sharing my experiences with her and what that really means. I have endless material to review and a spider's web of connections between all of the operations which makes little sense.

I haven't discussed Elise with the boys, for obvious reasons, but I'm here because of Elise. On my penultimate night attached to Operation Rattle, I have to ask myself why I'm really here. Why did I feel the need to enter a war zone when I'm not a soldier? I've never articulated a reason for my morbid desire. As I sit alone on my bunk making notes by torchlight, I feel overly emotional. It's an unusual feeling, moisture filling my eyes, a show of weakness maybe. The truth being, a truth I've never admitted, is that I do feel weak. I grew up in a military environment with a father who went to war, who was and is strong both physically and mentally. I never wanted to be a soldier. My passion has always been the written word, and I think for the past ten years I've been trying to win wars with my pen. But after ten years, I've won nothing.

Elise worries about me all the time, I know she loves me, but her worrying makes meal feel as if she doubts me. As if maybe she thinks I need protection. The more she worries, the more I feel I need to prove to her that I'm OK, that I'm strong. After the events of the past three months, I've fulfilled my dream and beyond, but can't help being worried about future nightmares.

Chapter Thirty-Seven

Elise

The train takes under an hour and a half to get to Gatwick. Once I've navigated the departure hall and checked in, I make straight for security, knowing that my trip truly begins once the other side of those barriers.

My passport and boarding card never leave my hand the whole time I walk through security until I place them in a grey plastic tray with my bag. The departure hall throbs with life. Men, women and children are all grabbing at their carry-on cases, shoes and possessions in those trays. My eyes barely leave the sight of mine. Nothing will disrupt my day.

Only an hour remains before departure. The gate number is already displayed on the ceiling-mounted monitors, so I take a moment to breathe and absorb the enormity of what lie ahead. A reunion.

Three months is a long time. Our contact has been limited and strained. My life has been hectic, erratic, challenging and painful but that side of me I'll keep to myself. I'm feeling healthier, my skin is clear, glowing and firm with only three old faint bruises – nothing to raise the alarm.

What will Joel be like, though? He said the food had been a challenge, but I know for sure it would be the combat situations which will have had a greater effect on him. Raw emotions bubble under the surface. A longing to have my Joel back in one complete piece centres in my forehead. It's a dull pressure behind the eyes, a culmination of three months' worth of worry, which I need to suck in and bury and present a strong, happy front.

Downing two headache pills and water, I stand up and make my way to the departure gate. Armed with two magazines, a smorgasbord of sweet treats and my headphones, I embrace the loading of the cattle on to the plane. The next nine and a half hours will hopefully fly by, in more literal way than I am used to.

*

Taxiing towards the terminal, seated as high as possible in an unrealistic attempt to spy Joel, I bite my lip and suddenly a wave of first date nerves washes over me. I don't know whether to beam cheerfully, put on a sad face, or be cool and collected.

Confused by my inability to relax, I feel as if I'm drawing unnecessary attention to myself as I snake through immigration. I feel guilty for no reason but have the eyes of a thousand men staring at me.

My inability to relax, my nervous expectation of my reunion with Joel is making me paranoid. Maybe I have something on my face, food residue or something, but I definitely feel under pressure as I hand my passport over.

'Business or pleasure ma'am?' the officer asks.

'Pleasure, holiday,' I reply.

'Where are you staying whilst on holiday?'

'Sanibel, Sanibel Island. My husband is picking me up.'

'Does your husband live here, ma'am?'

'No, but he is American.'

'Thank you, have a pleasant day.' The words were said in unison with the ink stamp thump on my passport, which is immediately closed and thrust back towards me.

My interrogation over, the last stop before Joel is the baggage hall, an enormous room yet still muggy and smelly, filled to the brim with bodies all having been cooped up for far too long.

The automatic doors leading from the baggage hall to arrivals slide apart and the wonderful warmth of the air hits me. Scanning the waiting crowds, I spy Joel, his tall, muscular physique dominating my eye line. His smile melts me. My fears and anxieties flood away. Flinging my arms around him feels so natural. His embrace is secure and reassuring, and then he loosens his grip and takes hold of my face, lifting it to his, planting his lips firmly on mine. He has taken ownership of me once more. Our lips lock and linger as sensations traverse our very beings, and we are enveloped as one.

My eyes wet, my mascara runs on my cheeks and his gentle thumb wipes away a tear.

'God, I love you Mrs Hamilton,' Joel says as he sweeps me back up in his arms, drawing me in closer and closer to his core.

Digging my fingers into his ribs, forcing him to relinquish his hold, I say, 'Ditto Mr Hamilton.' Our lips lock once more and we forget where we are, being totally absorbed into each other and not our surroundings. Moments, seconds, minutes and lots of people seem to pass us by.

I pull away and wipe my wet nose and face, which I know, regardless of the tanning beds, is now red and flushed. Joel picks up my case, clutches my hand and leads me out of the terminal to the car park.

The journey from Tampa to Sanibel I've planned in my head. Two to three hours in a car with Joel with lots of time to talk. *How will that be?* I still have first date nerves, my heart giddying into a trot and the slightest touch from Joel will cause me to explode. Sitting in a car with him for three hours is going to be a challenge.

'Do you need me to navigate or are you OK with the route?' I ask.

'No, I know where I'm going,' he replies.

'You look well, really well. Someone has been taking in the sun,' I say.

'Hard not to, really, although I wouldn't say I had time to sunbathe,' replies Joel.

'Are you sure you're happy with the route? We missed our turn for the 275.'

'Sure, trust me,' says Joel.

Feeling slightly unsure where we're going, I pull out the map just in case I'm mistaken, but I'm not. The route we usually take is the 275, then Interstate 75. Looking up from the map, the Renaissance Plaza

Hotel comes into view and Joel puts the car indicator on as we pull onto the forecourt.

'What's going on, Joel, where are we going?' I ask.

'You seriously think I can cope for three hours in a car without ripping your clothes off, do you?' says Joel.

Instantly, I flush. I'm longing for him, body and soul. I don't reply, though; I stare at him, eating him up with my eyes, willing the car to self-park and transport us to anywhere vacant and private.

Joel swings into a parking space, flips the boot and hops out. I pause momentarily drawing breath. I check myself over once in the central mirror and then get out. He's already grabbed my case and closed the boot, and takes hold of my hand leading me to reception. His grip is firm and controlling.

'Mr and Mrs Hamilton, we have one night booked,' he says.

'Yes, thank you. Do you have a card to secure the room?' asks the receptionist.

Joel digs out his wallet from his rear jeans pocket, lifting his t-shirt to gain access, affording all around a view of the rear of the year. Even in jeans, it's a tease.

‘Thank you, room 303, take the elevator, third floor and left as you exit. Have a nice stay,’ says the receptionist.

Joel grabs my hand once more, taking control, leading me straight for the elevator. There’s a definite urgency in his manner. The anticipation of what’s coming is overwhelming, I’m tingling, my breasts lifting in response.

As we enter the elevator Joel stands my case up, selects three, and as the doors draw closed he pushes me against the cool metal walls. His mouth is on mine, his hands caressing my tense breasts. My yearning for him is escalating. With a ping, the doors draw open and we step out, turning immediately left and in less than ten paces swipe our room key and fall inside.

*

We don’t stop for breakfast but grab fruit and complimentary cookies before hitting the road a little after eight, towards Sanibel. I can’t wait to walk along the pale golden sand and shell-encrusted beaches, and to swim in the warm sea.

Two-and-a-half hours later we cross the causeway; the sun is glistening in the ripples, and pelicans, cormorants and egrets are all waiting to greet us.

As we arrive at George and Violet's diner lunch time customers are being seated, and despite being hurricane season, it's still busy. The temperature is a very nice, warm eighty-seven degrees, humidity is low, and the beach is beckoning.

'Elise, come here, it's so lovely to see you,' says Violet, embracing me just like Joel had done, firm and tight.

'Violet, I'm so pleased to be here, it's been a while. Is George about?' I ask.

'Yes, he's in the kitchen; he'll be out in a minute. Joel get yourself some drinks, we'll talk once lunch is out of the way,' says Violet.

'Sure,' replies Joel.

I wander out onto the decking and slump down in a chair, feeling like a tourist ready to be waited on by her manservant. Joel appears with two iced teas and, unlike a manservant, slumps in the chair next to me. There we sit, watching the comings and goings of the diner. The air is full with the scents of many wonderful dishes, some of which we will get to taste over the next fourteen days.

Chapter Thirty-Eight

Joel

Glancing over at Elise, taking in her softly tanned features and slim honed physique, with which I've been well and truly reacquainted, I smile. Not a discreet smile, but a broad lustful grin. Elise turns towards me, catching my expression.

'What?' she says.

'Nothing,' I reply.

'No, it's not nothing, you're beaming.'

'Can't a man ogle his wife and feel happy?' I say.

'You can, you have that look about you.'

'What – the look that I want to take you to bed and devour you in every way?' I say.

'Shush, your parents will hear you.'

'We're married, what do you think they think we do?' I reply.

'I don't know, but ...'

'Well, I'll take you somewhere remote and quiet so your only worries will be the wildlife.'

'Promises, promises. Actually, I'll keep you to that. Fancy a stroll?' says Elise.

I stand up, taking her last comment as an invitation. Grabbing hold of Elise's hand, I pull her up from her seat.

'Let me just tell Mum and Dad we're off for a walk,' I say.

'Is that what we're calling it now?' says Elise, her cheekiness arousing me even more.

'Mum, Elise and I are going to check out the beach. Catch you later.'

'Enjoy,' Mum replies. *Little does she know.*

*

The best holidays always end too soon. Our fourteen nights were great. The old Elise is back, and she's made my transition from Afghanistan back to reality so much easier. Our world, now together, is a million miles away from my world back in Bagram. To be properly clean for the first time in three months feels great. A little thing to some, but huge to those who have not felt the power of a proper shower in what feels like a millennium. Wonderful food I've missed too, and Mum and Dad's cooking worked a treat in getting me feeling human again.

I shared with Elise lots of images and footage that I captured, and my copious notes and interviews. I'm still embargoed from publishing until Operation Rattle finally winds up, which, by my calculations, will be any day. Once cleared I'll write as much editorial material as I want, the military having given me only one warning – that I must not discuss feral vigilantes, rogue thermal images or new hardware technology which was trialled.

Elise is nothing but positive about my work, and all the material captured. She has even said she would speak to her agency in case they can represent me if I compile a book. All of that is great, but I've held back a lot from Elise. Something inside me prevents me from talking about the child found in the glade and her description of a woman aiding her escape. I also can't discuss directly with her the rogue thermal images. Those glowing lights in the sky which are unaccounted for, but mostly it's that somewhere in my deep dark Afghan memories I felt her presence, her energy around me. I completed my assignment, I survived combat, I've proven myself to be strong and yet not sharing makes me feel weak still. These feelings, thoughts and experiences will need to be dealt with at the right time but here and now, after such a fantastic two weeks, is not that time. To compound my minor anxieties, for the past fourteen nights Elise has worn my 'Class of 99' sweatshirt in bed.

Chapter Thirty-Nine

Elise

A cool nip in the air greets me as I exit the terminal at Gatwick. Fortunately, I travelled out in a jacket, which has, for the past fourteen days, been languishing in my case, but now is needed more than ever. The train journey and taxi ride home gets me back before lunch, giving me a little over twenty-four hours before Joel returns.

Separating once again at Tampa was painful, especially after what has been a blissful two weeks. Joel's flight home, though, was booked through his editor who insisted he stop over in New York to liaise with the *Globe* before returning.

The time to myself allows me to refresh the house, get the washing done and fill the fridge. Whilst back at work tomorrow, it's mid-week, the weekend is nearing and Amanda and Henry are coming over for supper.

Amanda has only two or three weeks left until the baby literally descends and I'm excited to catch up with her to see how she is blossoming.

*

The air is filled with scents of garlic, cumin and chilli with Joel working his magic and creating a wonderful curry. The steam billows from the wok, momentarily hovering before being sucked up by the fan. Friday evening, how wonderful.

'You're in a jolly mood tonight,' I say.

'What's not to be jolly about? Good wine, good food, good woman,' he replies.

'You can never have too much of a good woman,' I say.

'I may remind you of that later after several glasses, a large plateful of food and you're lying back feeling too stuffed for anything,' he replies.

'Please do.'

Bzz.

'I'll get it,' I say as I leave the kitchen and head for the door.

Snatching open the door allows for Amanda and Henry simultaneously to fall into the hall. The rain has not stopped all day and with no porch, Amanda and Henry bring a flood of water inside with them.

'Bloody miserable night,' says Amanda.

'Here, let me take your coat. Let's take a look at you, lovely lady,' I say, admiring her enormous but very neat up-front bump. We give each other a warm but wet hug, and then Amanda shakes herself down like a wet dog.

'Henry, you well?' I ask.

'Marvellous, Elise, you're looking bronzed. Good hols?' says Henry.

'The best, thanks,' I say as I embrace him. 'Joel's you-know-where.'

'Great, I'll leave you ladies to it,' replies Henry.

'So, you're looking well, a tan suits you,' says Amanda.

'Thank you. I'm feeling well. The holiday was great, just what Doctor Amanda ordered. Shall we get drinks and sit down whilst the boys do their thing? Take a pew. What can I bring you? There's sparkling water, coke and juice, that's all on the soft side.'

'Sparkling water please, that's about as close as I'll get to fizz for some time to come.'

'Fizzy water it is.' I leave Amanda to settle herself in the front room and wander through to the kitchen where the boys are deep in conversation.

'Are you OK for a drink, Henry, I'm just sorting Amanda one?'

'No, I'm sorted thanks, Joel's already done the honours.'

'Great.' I wander back to the front room and join Amanda who's now beached, stretched across the sofa.

'I hope you don't mind bringing my dinner in here tonight, I'm not sure I can get back up. Your sofa has swallowed me.'

'Be assured, we have two strong men who can lift you if necessary. You look well though. Are you feeling OK?'

'Not bad, I'm not sure what I should feel like though. I don't think I'll be a very intuitive mum.' Amanda gently caresses her taught swollen tummy, holding it protectively.

'Every first time mum has doubts, but I'm sure you'll be great, and there's bound to be plenty of advice on offer. I think you'll be a natural though. A mother-in-waiting if there ever was one.'

'Maybe. I'm glad I've stopped working now, my mind is all fuzzy, like candyfloss. I'm not sure I can add up two plus two, so I definitely should not be let loose with millions. I'll be glad when it arrives though.'

'How long now, two weeks-ish?'

'Well, two weeks or so – my dates were never 100 per cent so it could be tonight, here and now, or Christmas if you want over-cooked.'

'Now that would push it. I need it out by Christmas so I can go shopping, I can't wait.'

'What about you then, does my bulging bump make you feel broody at all?'

'No, not really. I can't wait to hold your baby and be involved, but I'd like to put this year to bed before the idea of extending our family is really considered.'

'How was it, how was Florida?'

'Fab, just great, Amanda, it truly was. I'd been so worried, but it was like a second honeymoon.'

'Ooh, say no more.'

'Quite right, say no more, but it was wonderful, truly great, things are good.'

'What about your other nocturnal activities? The ones which give you bruises?' asks Amanda.

'A lot less intense. I really have worked hard at avoiding dreaming, and if my dreams are unavoidable, then I've worked hard at avoiding contact and conflict. Joel would be none the wiser. By the time I reached Florida, my bruises were virtually invisible. Whilst there we were so wrapped up in each other that we barely talked about what I got up to whilst he was away.'

'So, do you think it's over, finished, no more flying and fighting?'

'Amanda, I'm really not sure but all I can say is that for now it's not a problem. Joel is home and I believe whilst he's home my soul has no reason to fly.' Hearing myself explain it like that to Amanda, makes sense.

'OK, all very bizarre, but OK. Actually I'm not as shocked as I first was. This pregnancy lark means my fuddled mind is very accepting of what you say. The crucial thing is you guys are happy and you do not get yourself hurt anymore.'

'We're great, Amanda. The absence brought us closer together. I'm not kidding myself, I know he'll have to travel again; it's after all part and parcel of his job, but all being well, not into danger.'

'Ladies, dinner's served,' Joel hollers from the kitchen.

'Can you get up or would you like a forklift?' I ask Amanda.

'Cheeky. Actually, you wouldn't mind pulling me up, would you?'

I pull Amanda to her feet and escort her through to the kitchen where we join the boys and enjoy an evening of Green Thai Curry and Lamb Rogan Josh.

Amanda and Henry leave in a taxi just after eleven, and Joel and I head up to bed not long thereafter. Joel was right in his assessment of me – I'm stuffed, tiddly and fall straight asleep with no inclination towards sex whatsoever.

*

The call from Henry comes at just after eight in the morning. Amanda has safely delivered a baby girl weighing six pounds twelve ounces. Henry sounds exhausted but confirms the ward Amanda is on and what the visiting times are. He finishes the call by saying, 'Tell Hamilton his curry did the trick, he'll understand what I mean.'

'Who was that calling this early?' asks Joel.

'Well, it was Henry – and you'll never guess what. They're proud parents to a baby girl, woo hoo!'

'Fantastic, coming back to bed?'

'Didn't you hear me? Our friends have just had their baby within hours of leaving our house; I'm too excited to come back to bed.'

'Well, you don't have to sleep, but we could always…'

'And what's this about the curry doing the trick?'

'Oh, really. Well, Henry said Amanda wanted it to be over and it's an old wives' tale, but sometimes spicy food can help it along. So, the Rogan Josh might have had a little extra chilli in it last night.'

'You're rotten. I thought it was a little hotter than usual. I take it Henry knew you had added more chilli?'

'Oh yes, it was his idea.'

I pick up my pillow and throw it across towards Joel. 'That was naughty, you know.'

'Well, it worked, didn't it?'

'Yes, but…'

'No buts, come here,' says Joel.

Joel pulls me back into bed and under the duvet where we get lost together till after nine.

*

With Christmas fast approaching, Joel and I have lunch with Amanda, Henry and new arrival Grace, booked for midday. A swanky bistro off of Regent Street within steps of the lights and attractions makes for a lovely Saturday excursion.

'Well the lights won't be truly effective till after five,' I say as we exit the bistro out into the frosty dry air.

'You do realise Elise, that grace is unlikely to be wowed by them, I think her vision is limited to black and white shapes at the moment,' says Amanda as she smothers Grace in layers of blankets and zips up the front of the pram as if she was hiding something hideous.

'Experts can be wrong Amanda, and for all you know, Grace may well be a genius and advanced for her age.'

'Yes, child prodigy aged five weeks, I think not,' replies Amanda.

'Look you two, let's wander before we all freeze. I've never known you Elise to want to hang around in the cold. Hey is that Philip over their by Liberties?' says Joel.

'Oh my lord, yes it is. That must be Mark, well I hope its Mark. Look, I'm just going to pop over say

"Hi" and then we can continue. Won't be a minute.' With that I power walk through the shoppers and without warning throw my arms around Philip.

'Why hello, darling. It's so lovely to see you,' says Philip all full of smiles.

'God, it's been so long, you look so well and …' I pause looking at Philip and then glancing towards the slightly younger man smartly dressed in a long overcoat who I assume is Mark.

'Sorry darling, of course you have not met Mark have you. Mark, this is Elise, you probably don't remember her, although you should because she's fabulous, but Elise was with me the first time I came looking for you in the salad bar,' says Philip.

'Hi Mark, lovely to meet you.'

'So, I have you to thank then, for bringing Philip in to my life and rocking my world,' says Mark.

'Yes, I suppose you do. Look I would love to stop and have a real catch up, we must do lunch in the New Year. I'm out with Joel and friends and they will be getting cold.'

'Joel, where is he, let me wave at least,' says Philip scanning the crowds.

'He's over there.' I point across the road, catch Joel's eye, wave, smile and Philip does the same.

'Still as gorgeous as ever I see,' says Philip.

'You're wicked, reign him in Mark. Look, New Year we will do lunch. Have a great Christmas both of you and send my love to Jo. I gave Philip and Mark both a warm embrace, already feeling the love for them both and then swiftly returned to my luncheon party.

Christmas is perfectly timed. As we all continue to wander down Oxford Street and take in the splendour of the decorations and the lights, I feel 2012 is going to be rounded off perfectly and can already feel the anticipation of what 2013 will bring. My dreams, the action, conflict and pain seem a distant memory for the time being. Whilst they remain my secret, maybe they will become my past.

Chapter Forty

Joel

Since returning from Florida and from Afghanistan, time for me has evaporated. Grace's arrival has brought excitement into our lives. Not excitement born out of a thrill, but excitement and the sheer delight and amazement of the creation of life. Grace is adorable. There are fresh places to visit and see and new things to talk about with the oldest of friends. Elise is on top form and has been equally thrilled with the early arrival of Grace. Elise is glowing with contentment.

Whilst being held hostage to Elise's flirtations, I agree to spend Christmas in Warwickshire with her parents. She gushed about the wonderful food her mum cooks and how spoilt we'll be.

I haven't discussed my work with Elise for a while. I'm busy covering routine assignments and, when time allows, pulling together the editorial material from Afghanistan. Ben, has arranged for me to spend two weeks in the New York office of the *Globe* in January, when the stories will run daily. Coverage includes many of the operations I'd personally been involved in. It'll be a great exclusive for the papers and positive propaganda for the military. I've written all my stories favourably, about the soldiers, the guys I bunked with for three months, had saved my life and had my back on so many occasions.

I've still not broached the more sensitive material and aspects of my tour with Elise, nor Ben. The rogue thermal images and feral vigilante aspects are all embargoed. Whilst I'm OK with that, regarding the paper, I can't shake the guilt of not being frank with Elise.

Whilst the past few weeks have been wedded bliss, I still have this unusual nagging feeling about the entire 'Class of 99' sweatshirt issue. It's probably nothing, but if that's the case, why haven't I felt comfortable enough to discuss it with the one person in my life who would understand most?

I need to break the news about my impending travels to Elise without it ruining Christmas, and as food is to Elise what gold is to men, I know how to win her over – with a meal fit for a queen. I just need my mum's old recipe book, which is no longer in the kitchen where I left it. Before I can craft I need to plan, so the hunt begins.

*

'You're home early,' I say as Elise bursts into the house, letting a breeze of icy air into the hallway.

'Yes, wrapped up sooner than planned today. Next week will just be lunches with clients and then the office party; everything's winding down, no new releases till the New Year. What's for tea?' asks Elise.

'Just pasta tonight, but I'm looking for my mum's recipe book, the one with her handwritten meal plans. I want to cook us something different tomorrow. Do you know where it is?'

'No, not recently. It's not something I class as bedtime reading. If it's not in the kitchen, there's a pile of books and magazines on the coffee table in the front room. Maybe it got mixed up amongst those,' replies Elise.

'Thanks.' Elise unshackles herself from her bulky winter coat and boots and heads straight upstairs.

Right, coffee table. Great. No, no, not the dream diary, no.

‘I think we could open up a paper shop with all these magazines,’ I shout upwards, not realistically expecting Elise to respond, and keep shuffling.

No, nothing, so where are you?

I put the slippery pile of glossy mags back on the coffee table, separating out Elise’s dream diary to balance the pile. Curiosity getting the better of me, I open the first page of the diary expecting to see dates and times, but instead it’s a lined notebook. Page after page filled with scribblings and drawings and then paragraphs of writing. Date and time tags are added in the margin, but it’s all very random, not even chronological.

> *Snow-capped peaks, deep gullies and ridges. Rugged inhospitable terrain. Dusty sandy tracks, roads traversing the landscape with huge unyielding boulders for verges. Potholes and craggy edges.*

I keep turning and reading.

Utility vehicles with mounted weapons. Men all tied up. Burning vehicles.

Swallowing the hook, I carry on. This book, this private diary, which I've resisted nosing in for the past decade, captures my attention.

Afghanistan, mountains, glade and 3 vehicles.
Brown resin in bags (possibly drugs).
A girl, young, olive-skinned. Scared and crying. What happened to the girl?
A girl on the back of a truck, tied, hands bound. Men, 6 men, guns and knives in the truck. A man punching and swinging.
A man punching and swinging
Swinging punches, I block to defend and grab his throat, squeezing and overpowering him, and then there's the knife, my leg.
The knife. I took it from the cab of a vehicle. I had the knife; I

lunged at the man but dropped it.
The girl.
I hid the girl in the trees and bushes. The military, a helicopter arrived and then nothing.
The man stabs my leg and is still holding the knife, prepped to lunge again when I grab him and throttle him until he loses consciousness. Blood oozing down my shin and calf, I make it to the trees with the girl, and then nothing.

Snapping the book shut, I throw it back on the coffee table and then move it so it's now hidden between the magazines, sending them off balance. Standing sharply I return to the kitchen and immediately take two pans out of the cupboard, one for mince, one for pasta. Grabbing all the ingredients I need from the fridge, I throw them on the work surface as if speed is of the essence.

My mind is racing; I can't ignore it, what I've read and the meaning of it. A meaning which makes absolutely no sense. Chopping frantically at the onion, garlic and peppers, I throw them into the pan and then the mince all together, one big pot, and turn on the heat. The cooking is no distraction. My mind will not let go of the words on the page and the drawings and scribblings. But how? I need answers, yet what questions do I ask?

So absorbed am I by the enormity of my discovery, I don't hear Elise come down the stairs and into the kitchen.

'Did you find it?' she asks.

'Find what?'

'Your mum's recipe book, you know, duh.'

'No, no, I didn't. Did you hear me shout up to you about the magazines? You could open a paper shop.'

'No, I didn't, but you caught me bang to rights.'

'What?' My mind is confused, unable to proffer sensible responses.

'I'm guilty, I've spent a small fortune on magazines whilst you were away. You're right, I could open a corner shop, but I'll put them in recycling tomorrow if you want them cleared,' says Elise.

'No, no. No, I don't want you to throw them away, there are just so many,' I reply.

'No sign of the book though?' says Elise.

'Book?'

'Book, duh, recipe book, what's gotten into you tonight?'

Elise, unaware of my discovery, pulls open the fridge door and grabs a bottle of white wine, unscrewing it before grabbing glasses.

'Glass of wine Joel, I think you need one.'

'Yes, sure. I think I do too.'

Chapter Forty-One

Elise

'Shout when it's ready. If it's OK, I want to check out those magazines.'

Taking a sip of wine as I leave the kitchen and wander through to the front room, I try to fathom Joel's behaviour, his lack of self. Placing the glass on the coffee table, I grab at the first glossy mag on the pile and slump onto the sofa. Flicking through a now familiar edition of *Home Style*, I cast it to one side and grab another. Dislodged and unbalanced, the pile of magazines slide onto the carpet and my dream diary onto the top of the coffee table.

Having not written in my diary for a while, I had wondered where it had got to. Somehow it seems to have lodged itself amongst the magazines, the same magazines that Joel was looking through.

No, he wouldn't, that's the unwritten rule. Never in ten years; and yet …

An ache grows inside. I realise that Joel not being himself, his lack of focus, memory loss and edginess could just be because of the diary.

Grabbing it off the table, I flick through. There's nothing obvious. Nothing to suggest he's read it, but what mark would he leave behind? No physical mark but the one thing he has already exhibited – shock.

Taking a gulp of wine I stand up, placing the diary on the table, and walk through to the kitchen. If my feelings, my intuition, are on point then I need to act normal and see what he says. My scribblings and rantings might mean nothing to him, in which case he'll probably think I'm slightly cuckoo, or if he's connected the dots, this evening could get interesting.

'I've changed my mind, you know regarding the magazines, would you like a hand?'

'That's a first, what's come over you?' asks Joel.

'Nothing, you're right – I'm not interested really, but it seems wrong relaxing whilst you're cooking, so tell me how your day was?'

'Busy, usual snippets to follow up on, almost routine really,' he says.

'How are the Afghan editorials coming along? Is Ben happy with them?'

'Good. Ben's impressed; better than he hoped. He intends to give me plenty of coverage, but not until the New Year.'

'That's great. Are you able to give him full access to your work over there, or are there still matters which are embargoed?'

'There are operations which the military won't let me write about; Ben knows that.'

'And you still accept not being able to write about those operations?' I ask, knowing full well I'm crossing into dangerous territory, which isn't the first time.

'I accept it, but that doesn't mean I don't think about them, but I'd rather not discuss work which is going nowhere.'

'OK.'

'Let's eat,' says Joel.

Joel is holding back, that much is obvious. *Why haven't I questioned him before?* Something he knows or has read tonight has changed him, distanced him.

'What shall we do this weekend? Do you fancy seeing if Amanda and Henry are up for something? We'll be at my parents' next weekend, so…'

'Sure. Look, Elise, I was going to tell you tomorrow but…'

'What?'

'Ben wants me to go to New York in January. Just for two weeks, to sort the editorials and to be there when they run the stories.'

'OK, and you were going to tell me tomorrow. Why now, why do you feel the need to blurt it out?'

'Look, I don't want to go if truth be told. Things are just not right when I'm away. 2012 has also been a mixed year for us with me being away so much, so I was hoping to break it over a meal fit for a queen, but...'

'But tonight over pasta instead feels right. I ask too many questions. When I get close either to you or to something you've been involved in, it's as if you need to escape, I get it.'

'No Elise, you don't. I don't want to go but I have to go, and actually once done, I'll put the Afghanistan experience to bed and move on, I want to move on.'

'Sometimes you make no sense.' I put my fork on the plate and push it to one side, my appetite lost. 'One minute you cannot wait to get up close and personal to a war zone, and in a flash you've had enough.'

'I thought you would be happy with me saying that I don't want to go, but instead…'

'Instead, what Joel? I've given you so much support this past year. I've been left at home alone and literally longed for your return, but you feeling obliged to stay at home or sacrificing what you want to do, makes me feel shitty.' Tears and gloop are flooding my face, my overly emotional response oozing out. Nine months of worry, anxieties and pain pour on the table.

'This, this here, Elise, is why I don't want to go away. See what me being away has done to you?'

'You've no idea what it's done to me.'

'What, what do you mean?' asks Joel.

'Nothing, nothing. Sorry for being a wreck. Go to New York, with my blessing, but do not feel you must give everything up for me. I'll only ever be happy if you're doing what you love and what you do best. Staying at home and filling yourself full of resentment for the life and experiences you miss out on has the potential to eat away at you and us.'

'Where's this come from Elise?'

'You earlier, all distant, edgy, scared. You're fearful of something, Joel, and my mind is racing with a million possibilities of what it could be and...'

'Your diary. Your dream diary. I read it,' says Joel.

'You read it? Read what precisely?'

'Look I don't understand how it works whether those notes in your diary were made whilst I was away or since I returned. If after I returned that might explain them, but…'

'But?'

'Elise, some of those notes and scribblings mirror operations.'

'Go on.'

'There are things I've not shared, operations which didn't go to plan, the outcomes of which for an unknown reason are detailed in your diary. Yet they're the very stories that are embargoed. It makes no sense. How would you know those things?'

'They're my dreams. I'm not sure how to explain it or where to begin. That was then, and this is now. I can't explain it, you'll think me mad. I shouldn't have pressed regarding the embargoed operations, but I've been going mad trying to make sense of it all. I suspected you were holding back. Look Joel, I wouldn't know how to explain. Some things are best left unsaid. None of this made sense to me, and I'm sure your head feels like mine did a couple of months ago when those notes were made. Don't let this, whatever it is, stop you from following your dreams.'

Joel is kneeling, his head in my lap. Both of us are crying like silly children, blubbering with unspoken emotion. Taking hold of my face gently, Joel looks into my eyes.

'Elise, I love you far too much to hurt you. My head, god it's throbbing, but through all of my confused thoughts one thing is clear, you must never sacrifice yourself for me, do you understand? We're equal: equal in love, in life, in everything, and I love and respect all of what you do. The truth is I don't want to go away, but it is part of what I started by going to Afghanistan. I've not been honest with you about the real driving force behind me wanting to get involved with the military.'

'Go on.'

'I could only admit it to myself at the end of my tour. It's you Elise, I feel I need to somehow prove myself to you, to be a strong military man like my father.'

'I've never asked you to prove yourself, and I hope I haven't made you feel as if you need to.'

'No, you haven't, it's more about me really. You worry so much, and I have interpreted that worry as you doubting me. The more you worry, I feel the more you doubt and somewhere along the way I've tried to escape, just to prove to you that I will return.'

'My dad told me I had to let you go in order for you to return. He was so right. Strength doesn't come from muscles, testosterone and fighting, strength comes from love. The love that you and I have is strong. You have nothing to prove to me. I want you to do what you need to do. My diary is inconsequential to all of it. Forget it – I cannot explain it. I'm with you wherever you go, remember that, with you in here.' I place my palm on his chest, feeling his pulsating heart racing under his skin. Our lips softly touch and collectively we glow.

Chapter Forty-Two

Elise

Christmas at my parents' house is a welcome break from our frosty home. Regardless of the number of loving embraces we share, I can still feel a tension between us, as if something is still going unsaid. Rather than tensions dissipating, the nearer we get to Joel's departure to New York the more they escalate.

Two weeks, hopefully only fourteen nights, and no war zones, and he'll be home. Whatever is happening to me, to us, I need it to end one way or another.

Flying to New York, Joel is stepping back in time. Five hours, to be precise. Time reversed is an unfamiliar experience for me. Joel's travels in the past twelve months have always been to countries where the time zone is ahead of London, but not now. Now whenever I go to bed, he'll be five hours behind and I've no idea how the nights will unfold.

Joel phones and FaceTime's daily, sometimes twice a day, and on one occasion three times. He's buzzing with the release of his editorials and has even been offered a deal with a publishing house. He sounds more relaxed.

My work is frenetic too. January fever is upon us and tons of books are being shortlisted for the 'best of' categories, and that includes two that I worked on. I too feel as if 2013 has potential. My night-time excursions have been limited, bordering on non-existent. I'm sleeping well and feeling great, and those Christmas blues are fading.

At eight p.m., seated in front of the television surrounded by several newly purchased magazines, my tablet buzzes. Pressing the green button to connect, Joel instantly appears in front of me.

'Hi hun. Can you see me OK?' says Joel.

'Yes, you caught me in my pyjamas channel-hopping,' I reply.

'No change there then. How was your day?'

'Amazing, really good; one of my books, one of the first ones I edited, has been shortlisted for a newcomer prize, which is so exciting.'

'That's great, well done. You look gorgeous.'

'Thanks, you like my new fleece pyjamas?'

'You wouldn't need them to keep you warm if I were there.'

'No, that's for sure, but they're a wonderful substitute. How are things going? I've been reading some online reviews and they're very positive.'

'Great actually. One more round of releases tomorrow and then work starts to wind up here.'

'When are you likely to fly home, Thursday or Friday?'

'Well, that's the thing. The *Globe* has asked if I will cover a story in Miami that's unfolding.'

'OK.'

'They had a reporter attached to the Drugs Enforcement Administration (DEA) in south-west Florida for the past month and their operation should wind up any day. Unfortunately, the reporter has landed himself in hospital with a burst appendix so they need someone to step in see it through to fruition.'

'And they asked you?'

'Well, they asked, but I did sort of volunteer. I overheard them talking about it this morning. I'm here, after all, and it would only be another couple of days just to shadow the final showdown.'

'It sounds like everything is already worked out.'

'Not really, but I head to Miami tomorrow evening and need to get myself up to speed with the reporter's work. Elise, it should only be a couple more days. They're convinced the lid is about to be blown on the operation and just need me to cover the finale so they get their exclusive. Once done I'm home, promise.'

'It sounds great Joel, fantastic opportunity, go for it. Work's going to keep me busy here, but I'm a little jealous of you getting to go to Florida again. Do you think you will have time to pop and see your mum and dad?'

'Possibly, I don't know. I have to admit I'm looking forward to thawing out. It's minus five here most of the time, whereas Miami is a very pleasant twenty-two degrees. I'm not dressed for it though, the closest thing I have to sun wear is my khaki gilet and a vest but, hey, I'm not complaining.'

'You can pull anything off, even a string vest.'

The power of technology allows us to FaceTime for nearly an hour and is only curtailed because Joel's phone rings. Miami and working with the Drug Enforcement Administration is different; a door which has only been levered open because of his work in Afghanistan. Miami has some challenging areas but is not a war zone. How my subconscious self, deals with it is another matter, one yet to play out.

*

The following two nights Joel phones instead of using FaceTime. He's in Miami staying at a budget motel and is cramming on notes and recordings made by his predecessor. He's met with the officer in charge of the operation and has been briefed about his role.

Sitting at home alone on the Friday evening when Joel should have originally returned from America feels slightly odd. I'm relaxed, though. I know where he is and what he's doing, although my mind can't help but drift to thoughts of him here with me keeping me warm. He's coming home soon, and I need to remind myself of that.

At eight p.m. on the dot my tablet buzzes, I press connect, and Joel is there beaming through the screen as he adjusts the angle so the camera is not so close.

'You're looking sunny today,' I say.

'Yes, what do you think of my re-worked attire?' he asks, giving me a twirl and modelling his white short-sleeved vest top and khaki gilet.

'Very fetching with your trousers and boots, I'm sure.'

'It's moving on at a pace here and if all goes to plan, they plan to execute the operation in the next couple of hours. We're making a move soon, so with any luck I'll complete the story tomorrow and, all being well, be home by Tuesday.'

'Tuesday, great. Things are wrapping up there then?'

'Well, Tuesday is best case. The strike teams have been briefed, as have I. Really, I'm just along for the ride on this occasion. The culmination of six months' work should hopefully be rewarded.'

'I feel sorry for the reporter who did all the groundwork.'

'Yes, I spoke to him yesterday, he's been invaluable even from his hospital bed. Most of the undercover work has been in and around Miami itself, but the strike is further south towards the Keys. Apparently, this crew from Cuba have been importing drugs for years, but the intelligence is only now good enough to act on. They have also kept themselves off the radar by using old warehouses concealed by the Everglades around the national park boundary. I think from what I have read, it's the Ramos family, small fry in Cuba, but obviously they are now trying to get a foothold on US soil.'

'Wow, that's amazing. Are you sure you should be telling me all this, I mean…?'

'No, it's OK. Phone's not being monitored, and who are you going to tell? Anyway, tonight it should all be over, so no harm done.'

'No, quite.'

'Well, intelligence suggests that a boatload of drugs has just been brought in via Manatee Bay at the mouth of the Keys. They moved it to the warehouses for processing and packaging and then tomorrow it's being shipped out nationwide, hence our strike tonight.'

'You're going to be careful?'

'Sure. The DEA seems to have all angles covered. Should be straight in and out. Look, I'll call you tomorrow with the news. Must go, we're hitting the road shortly.'

'OK, take care, love you.'

'Love you too.'

I hear his last words as the screen freezes and then reverts to my contacts list. Never has Joel shared so much about an impending operation. I think of all those occasions I was literally in the dark in Afghanistan, and yet here tonight I've just been given my very first briefing.

My heart starts a familiar trot as my anxieties rise. I know I have told myself and Joel that I am "letting him go", but I feel drawn to him. I'm not even asleep, and yet somehow I feel ready to fly.

Armed with these snippets of intelligence, I set to work. Firing up my laptop for ease, I start with Google Earth, scanning the Everglades next to Interstate 1 – seeing buildings, compounds and water inlets all randomly dispersed. There are no obvious signs of the target premises, nothing to build on the limited details I have. Then the Ramos family. They're Cuban-based, who according to the newspapers are linked to an escalation of violence between gangs. One paper suggests that the Ramos family might try to take over from the Pavlos Cartel as they increasingly use violence to cement their position on the streets.

The Cuban newspapers and the images accompanying the stories make for uncomfortable reading. Concern for Joel and concern for the DEA operatives stirs inside. *Have they planned it properly, do they know enough, are they prepared?* All these are questions flashing through my mind. I fear it's not going to be as plain sailing as Joel makes out. Not because he's trying to protect me, but because it's Joel that needs protection.

Doing the maths, it's now eight minutes past five Miami time and eight minutes past ten my time. The sun will set in less than an hour in Miami. I doubt it will have started yet, but in truth I've no idea. There'll be travel time; Joel said he would be 'hitting the road,' so that would take them a while. Also, depending on numbers they'll look very obvious all driving down Interstate 1, so maybe they've officers on the ground already, or are using helicopters – unless Joel is already there in the strike zone, in which case my timings will be wrong. Either way, I need to get to sleep and see where my dreams take me.

With my mind racing, sleep will not come naturally. Popping a pill combo of pain relief, sleeping pills and antihistamine washed down with an enormous glass of wine, I go upstairs to bed. I pull on my favourite night-time sweatshirt and climb in, snuggling under the depth of the duvet, hoping that I'll warm quickly and drift off into a slumber. Part of me just wants to sleep and part of me wants to fly.

*

I'm there in an instant, thrust into the melee, the scene in front of me. Light is fading, the sun yet to set. My timing is off. I'm not flying; I've no recollection of travelling to where I am now, I'm just here, pulled into the fight.

Three old wooden barns to the rear of the land mass are illuminated and surrounded by trucks. Men are running in different directions, some still loading pallets, and gun shots are being fired to the front.

Sprinting towards a more modern warehouse, large and imposing and made of breeze block construction, I zigzag and dodge behind abandoned old vehicles and machinery until I reach the cool side wall. Skirting the length of the side, moving forwards, I come towards the entrance to the land now filled with trucks, vans and cars, all illuminated. Their blue lights are flashing and headlights on full beam. Police are out, dispersed amongst their own vehicles, using them for cover as a firefight is ongoing between them and several armed men.

This is it. Something has brought me here and I need to remain focussed to stay. Scanning the scene, I can see a few local police officers. They're taking cover behind the doors of their vehicles and are armed, quite lightly in the circumstances, with personal handguns – nothing to rival the semi-automatic weapons being deployed against them. Joel is not amongst them. He'll be with the DEA, wherever they are.

Two transit vehicles swing in off the highway through the entrance and steam past the ongoing firefight. Maintaining cover, I watch as a dozen heavier armed officers deploy and join in, equalling the odds.

Where's Joel? Running back the way I'd come down the side of the warehouse, I stop at the corner and peek to see if it's clear before making for open ground towards the barns and the trucks still being loaded.

The gunfire is sporadic. Random shots – no proper direction, more for effect – are being let off. Approaching the rear of one truck I hear a holler, 'Stop. You back off.' Those words, directed at me, bring me to a halt instantly. I stop dead. Unarmed, I instinctively raise my hands. A young man, twenties, holds a handgun, waving it at me, indicating for me to move away from the vehicle.

'I'm not police, don't shoot.' I hear my words in my head. Focus.

'Back away, what are you doing? Get down,' he says, waving the gun towards the ground wanting me to kneel.

The uncontrollable sensation welling up inside me is now controlled. I cannot fly.

I'm on my knees, my hands now on my head; the man moves closer and two more behind him approach. Gunshots are firing wildly. I can feel the police, I can feel Joel.

'Shoot her, we have to go get on with it,' says a male voice.

'No,' I scream. I flinch, my ears ringing and my eyes stinging; the man drops to the ground. In my peripheral vision, a police officer advances. Standing quickly, my hands no longer subservient, I run forward towards the derelict barns, away from the police and away from the trucks. Looking back quickly, I see him – there behind the door of a police vehicle, crouching low to the ground – Joel. At last. The police are pinned down, no longer advancing. A stalemate ensues.

Creeping inside the barn, I see a frenzied scene of men with paper masks speedily packaging powder. Armed men are standing guard, pressuring them to work faster and faster. The melee, the fighting outside, are all carrying on in a parallel world. There's a crate of guns, rifles and semi-automatics; Pandora's box is being pillaged and directed towards the police, towards Joel.

'You, what are you doing?' an armed man shouts in my direction.

Jerking my head behind me, I see a man, armed and angry, waving his gun. In slow motion, I lift my hands again only slightly; Pandora's box is within my grasp. Grabbing a gun, any gun, I leap forward towards a table for cover. A shot pings past me, splintering wood near my legs as I crawl along the floor, distancing myself from the advancing aggressor.

'Stop, not in here, you idiot,' a voice shouts out.

Crawling faster now along the line of tables towards the back of the barn, I hear a crack shatter a barrel in front of me, halting me in my tracks. The contents of the barrel are now discharging on to the ground.

'Here, down here.'

My gun, the gun I'm dragging with me, is light and compact. It's plastic, almost fake, like a toy. I'm pinned down at the rear of the barn with men now advancing closer and closer; my heart is racing, almost bursting out of my chest. The force, the pressure, throws me to my feet; my arms thrust forward and my finger presses instinctively on the trigger, firing wildly in an arc towards the bad guys. I cannot hear a thing, lost in the moment as glass fragments shatter, bodies drop and bags of white powder explode.

There's silence for a second, maybe two. I drop to the ground, my back now up against a wall, a door within my reach, and then I hear thuds on the ground and raised voices in the air. Jumping up, pressing the trigger again once, twice, three times, and turning, I throw myself out of the door and on to densely matted undergrowth.

Scrambling to my feet, I sprint towards the front of the barn with no escape behind, back into the path of the firefight, into the void.

The police are static, their position held. Intermittent shots ring out. Sliding to a stop now in full view of the participants in this show, I'm surrounded. Neither a good guy nor a bad guy.

Emerging from the barn a sole gunman, a sacrificial lamb, exposes himself by storming towards the police. Armed with a pump-action shotgun, discharging as he advances, he makes directly for Joel – for where he is sheltering behind the door of a vehicle. Lead ricochets, hitting two officers now down on the ground. He's not stopping.

My gun raised, my finger poised, I press a continuous stream of fire; the lamb hits the deck.

A sledgehammer hits my back, once, twice, three times. I fall forward; nothing breaks my fall, my face planting itself in the dirt. Choking on blood in my mouth, spread-eagled, I lie paralysed, unable to move. I sense black shadows above me. Wet and warm, my chest has exploded under the pressure of the gunshots. My eyes close, no longer able to focus. A distant cry of 'Elise' is the last thing I hear.

Chapter Forty-Three

Joel

'Elise!' Standing immediately, I raise my head above the parapet – the doors of the vehicle. I'm snatched back to the ground by the heavy hand of a police officer pulling on my flak jacket.

'Get down, what the fuck do you think you're doing?' the officer says.

'Elise,' I respond.

'Who's Elise?'

'Elise, my wife, there.' I point to the lifeless body lying on the ground several metres in front of me. Shot before my eyes.

'You're losing it, man. Hold here, don't move,' the officer says.

Cracks continue to whistle out, some pinging past my head. My head explodes at the thought of Elise there, dead in front of me. I can see her. I can feel her. I have led her to her death. I grip my hair, my forehead, unable to focus, unable to move, seated in the dirt behind the door, my cover. I no longer want to be here. I want to be home. I want Elise back.

*

'All clear,' shouts one officer.

It isn't silent; voices holler all around. It's carnage. The operation has gone well off plan. The DEA has totally underestimated the drug dealer's response to our raid and the casualties are now being counted.

I ease to my feet, my hands dropping to my side, and stare forward to where I'd seen Elise fall. Stepping from behind the cover of the vehicle, I run the distance to where her body had previously lain. The ground is bloodstained, and yet there's no body, no Elise. I definitely saw her. Saw her wearing my 'Class of 99' top. It was her. But where is she?

*

The sun having set, it's now dark and the only illumination is coming from the vehicles and the lights in the barns. Dozens of men are detained, many of them looking as scared as I. Bodies lay strewn all over the compound. It was an urban war zone and casualties mount on both sides.

I move in between the officers, looking for Elise. If her body isn't here, maybe she's just injured, not dead. Nothing makes sense, how could she have been here? But as time ticks on and the last of the casualties are counted, I start to lose hope.

Fear grabs me round the throat and starts strangling me. I can't breathe, I need to escape. I need to go home.

'Chief, I need to go, I can't follow this through, I need to go home now,' I say to Chief Anderson. He would never understand, how could he; I don't understand. He's a man in his fifty's, with a broadening girth whose used to hard nose intelligence and facts, not ghostly sightings and night-time meanderings. No he would never understand.

'What are you on about, now's not the time,' the chief responds.

'It is. I have to go now. I'm sorry. You don't need me anyway, you have this shitload to sort out and I cannot imagine your director wanting a word published in relation to it.'

'Fuck you Hamilton, you saw what happened,' the chief replies.

'Yes, yes I did. Someone fucked up. You were unprepared for this. I need to go now.'

'Well, you must make your own way back, you're on your own now.'

'Fine, I'll sort it.'

I storm away from the barns, past the warehouse and the waiting police transport and out onto the highway. Traffic has stopped yards away from the entrance, nothing is moving, but I'll get home. I walk in the only direction I know, north towards Miami. Sticking my arm out with my thumb raised, I'll walk and will wait and will eventually get a lift. I know hitchhiking is dangerous, but right now nothing could be worse than losing Elise.

A trickle of cars pass me, several blowing their horns, others overly swerving to avoid me as if I'm the size of a truck. The dark, barely lit road could become my graveyard if I do not get picked up soon.

A mile, possibly a mile and a half along, an articulated lorry ploughs past and then its rear brake lights shine brightly as the vehicle slows to a stop. I run to its passenger door, stepping onto the footplate and pulling it open.

'Any chance of Miami near the airport?' I ask.

'Sure, hop in. Are you mad or something on these roads this time of night?' says the driver.

'Something,' I reply.

*

The drive back into central Miami and to the airport takes over an hour and a half. I try calling Elise on both the home phone and her mobile, but the signal is intermittent and there's no reply. The driver, Ken, talks non-stop and yet I can't remember one word he's said. I thank him, slipping him fifty bucks and run into the terminal.

Scanning the boards I look for a flight to London Heathrow or Gatwick, it doesn't matter – just home. The nine p.m. Finnair flight to Heathrow has already boarded; the nine forty p.m. Delta to Heathrow has its gate listed but there's still time.

I run over to the Delta desk and thrust my passport towards the counter assistant. 'London Heathrow, please. Can I buy a ticket?'

She looks at me, her eyes scanning me for luggage and clues, her expression one of concern that a person so late in the hour, in an obvious hurry, wants to buy a ticket to London. She opens my American passport and flicks to the photo page, and then her eyes back to me again.

'One-way or return, sir?'

'One-way, please.'

'Just a moment,' she says. Tapping random data into her computer, she looks back up towards me. 'It's a busy flight, sir, I have Premium Economy available, and you will be travelling with our partner Virgin.'

'Great, yes, I'll take it,' I reply.

'Any luggage to check in?' she asks, stretching herself from her seat to scan the area around my feet.

'No. No luggage, just me and my rucksack.' I hand over my credit card, willing the transaction to be swift.

'There we go, sir, seat 10A. They're boarding shortly, so please make your way through security and to the gate. Have a pleasant trip.'

'Thank you, I will,' I reply as I start walking away at once towards security and departures. The security screening hall is quiet. I remove my shoes and place my wallet, phone and passport in the grey security tray. I try once again to call Elise. If she's home, she'll be all right. I grab my phone from the tray and speed dial Elise's mobile. It rings. 'Come on, Elise, answer.'

'Sir, you cannot make calls in the security hall. I must ask you to turn your phone off and place it in the tray. Now, sir,' says a female security guard.

I hold it one moment longer. It keeps ringing, but Elise does not answer.

'Sir. Now, the phone.'

'Sure, sorry,' I reply placing the phone together with my other belongings as they disappear into the scanner.

Once clear of security I make for the gate, eager to board. I repeatedly dial Elise's mobile and the landline, neither of which she answers. I leave message after message, hoping she responds. *She must be at home, she must be asleep, and she must be alive.*

As the last cabin check is completed, and the captain issues the order for flight crew to take their seats for take-off, I pray for Elise. I'm not religious, but just like the Syrian refugees, I need hope and faith.

*

The dimmed lights on the red eye do little to make me relax and sleep. My mind is a blur with what I saw – Elise there in the middle of the firefight, and then shot. I have innumerable questions and not one answer.

As the plane taxies into Heathrow I switch on my phone, wait for a signal and then check it for messages – none. I dial both the home and Elise's mobile numbers but still nothing, just the constant ringing and voicemail recordings. I leave a stream of messages on both devices in what now feels like a vain hope that Elise will call and be OK. The prospect of me really having witnessed her death is becoming more and more likely.

With no bags to collect, I breeze through security and depart Heathrow into the crisp January air. Heading straight for the taxi rank, I want the quickest transfer home. With any luck, I'll be with Elise in forty-five minutes and will know for sure her fate.

*

As the cab pulls up outside our terraced house I lean forward and post cash through to the driver. Springing out of the semi-moving vehicle, I head straight to the front door. None of my calls have been answered. My worst fears are front and centre in my mind.

Turning the key in the lock, I long for Elise to be smiling and waiting on the other side of the door. As I push the door open, there's no one.

Nervously I close the door behind me, pause and place my keys on the hall table. Drawing in a deep engulfing breath, I slowly walk through the downstairs of the house. My haste is now replaced by calm, cold fear of what I might find.

Nothing downstairs. I climb the stairs, heading for our bedroom first. The door is ajar and, being late morning, the room is illuminated, although slightly shadowed. On entering, I can see that the curtains are still closed.

There, face down on the bed, is Elise. Leaping to her side, I grab her and start shaking her. 'Elise, Elise, wake up, wake up, please be alive.'

Elise's face is warm and clammy and her hair damp. Scooping her up in my arms, I gently turn her face towards mine. There on the pillow below – blood.

'Elise, come on hun, wake up,' I say as I rock her gently back and forth, the moisture from my tears falling onto her porcelain skin.

'Joel.'

'Elise. My god, Elise, you're OK, thank god.'

'Joel, I'm sorry.'

'Elise, I'm sorry. I thought you were dead.'

'I don't feel great, Joel.'

'You look great, hun, you're alive. I've been calling and calling and I'm home and never going away again.' Elise finally opens her eyes, squinting and unpeeling her face as if she had been lost in a sleep forever. I rock her and hold her tight, never wanting to let her go.

'Joel,' Elise says, 'I don't…'

Elise stops then coughs a weak tickling cough, pulling her hand up to cover her mouth. She tries to speak again, but I can see her lips are now a deep red. Grabbing her hand, I can see blood.

'Elise, Elise, stay with me, Elise. You're not well. I need to get you to a hospital. Stay with me, Elise,' I plead.

'What will you tell them?' murmurs Elise.

'That you saved my life.'

Chapter Forty-Four

Elise

As I started this, it's only right that I end it. Telling the Accident and Emergency staff the truth doesn't seem like the best idea. Instead, I recall how I had awoken after falling down the stairs following an episode of sleepwalking. Joel, having been away in America, was none the wiser until he found me back in bed at home unwell. Keeping the lie simple makes for fewer questions being asked.

After five and a half hours I'm released, having had a scan and an x-ray. The diagnosis is three cracked ribs and minor pulmonary contusion. The prescription given by the hospital is for rest and occasional pain relief.

Telling Joel the truth is a must, it's just a matter of the delivery which requires thought.

Three broken ribs and bruised lungs have a way of focussing the mind. Whilst my physical being is bruised and sore, my mind is sound and clearer than it's ever been. It's taken me over twenty years and an intense twelve months of dreaming to work out what my dreams are all about. What they have been leading up to.

Regardless of the love I felt growing up and when I met Joel, it's taken one subconscious transcendental experience to teach me that to truly love is to sacrifice. It was the one thing that Joel told me not to do, and yet until I made the ultimate sacrifice for him I believe I'd only been playing at being in love.

My dream world allowed my soul to evolve and join with Joel's. In the words of a wise man, Aristotle, 'Love is composed of a single soul inhabiting two bodies.' Joel and I are now one.

*

The first few hours at home with Joel are oddly calm. We tiptoe around the events of the previous twenty-four hours, neither one of us knowing how to start the conversation that we need to have.

Taking a leap of faith, armed with two mugs of tea and a caddy full of biscuits, I slowly explain.

Explaining my diary, my research and new-found knowledge takes time. Etched on Joel's face the same confused expression that Amanda had some five months earlier. The bruises and the injuries which to me confirmed my new reality are to Joel shocking. His once tanned complexion is now pale and hollow. Whilst we both struggle with the concept, neither of us can deny the last twenty-four hours.

'And then Miami, Joel. Once you'd shared the operational details with me I had no choice. I know I said I would let you go, but I felt compelled to be with you.'

'So if I hadn't told you what was happening, and where, you would have been safe, you wouldn't have come.'

'No, that's just it. All of it has led to this last encounter. It was meant to be. For the first time in nearly twelve months, I knew exactly where I wanted to go and what I needed to do. The other occasions were me testing my new theory and my soul practising for the actual event.'

'You mean—'

'I mean, somehow in the deepest darkest crevices of my inner subconscious my soul knew it would need to save you. It was just a matter of when. I'd had this recurring nightmare of losing you, which fuelled my anxieties, but also channelled my energy. When you left for New York I sensed somehow that the end, whatever that meant, was near.'

'But you could have died, Elise.'

'Yes, possibly. In previous dreams maybe, but as I said with my research, physical laws do not apply. Yes, I'm injured, but I didn't die, I wouldn't have died.'

'When I saw you get shot, you were there, really there. Your body fell. I saw my sweatshirt, 'Class of 99', it was so real, and I'm sure others saw you too. The men that shot you must have seen you.'

'I know, it has taken me a couple of decades to make sense of it. It's been quite a revelation this past year, but it was my soul, not me.'

'I couldn't live through that again, Elise. We argued before Christmas about me going away and you thought I would resent you if I stayed. Well, I've had my fill of wars and fights and injuries. I never want to leave you, Elise, not because of what might happen if I go away but because missing out on living every single day with you would be a life not worth living. I understand, Elise. My heart and eyes are open and I can feel it. Your soul, our soul.'

'A spikey old lady once told me that the eyes were a portal to the soul. We're one, Joel. We were always meant to be.'

There's nothing more to say. We spent hours rationalising the irrational. All we can do now is hold each other. I cling to Joel as tight as I dare without causing myself discomfort. His warmth is comforting to my bruised and battered body. Long into the night we stay conjoined as one on the sitting room sofa, silent apart from our breathing, which is in total synchronicity.

Epilogue

'Be careful, bending down like that, you've all the time in the world to collect shells,' says Joel.

'Well, in my mind you can never have too many, and today might be the day I find an elusive Junonia shell. Anyway, stop fussing, I'm not ill,' I reply as I straighten and massage my lower back.

'Come on, let's head back, I fancy some of Mom's salsa,' says Joel, turning and taking hold of my hand, his bronzed features showcased by the subdued light from the oncoming sunset.

'Now that's a hook, salsa dip. I would race you back, but I'd hate to drop any of my treasure.' I hold up my net of shells, jingling them for effect and dislodging the smallest which escapes back onto the golden wet sand ready to be tumbled by the waves once more.

Some twelve months on from our post-Afghanistan reunion, we're back on Sanibel Island savouring the heady warmth of the American fall. It's been five weeks to the day since we left our London lives. Longer than a holiday, but not long enough to call the island home, just yet.

George and Violet have welcomed us into their home and their lives. Whilst temporary, their home gives us time to decide where our roots are to be nurtured, whether on the island or elsewhere.

As we reach the decking outside George and Violet's diner, Violet steps out to greet us, phone in hand.

'You just missed your mom Elise, she has news on the house. It's all completed, the keys were handed over today,' says Violet.

'That's great. Wow, we've done it,' I reply as I slump into a low slung wooden beach chair taking care to position my treasure from the sea away from the cracks in the sun bleached decking. 'I'll call her later, I'm sure she'll have lots to fill me in on. Thanks, Violet.'

'So, Mrs Hamilton, what's next for us then?' says Joel.

'Well, in the not too distant past, I might have said shopping with that kind of bank balance, but I think you know where my heart is,' I reply whilst entwining my fingers through Joel's and pulling him down towards the wooden recliner next to mine. It's just after five, the sun is setting for the day and the whoosh of the waves provides a gentle reminder of the rawness of the island alongside the beauty it beholds.

With Joel loosely holding my hand, our atoms freely flow between us, the prickles of the residual energy flow tickling my palm. As Joel lets go of my hand and places it on my ever-bulging belly, I know I have all I could ever want in the world. A new life is growing inside me; my soul, our soul, is now aligned to the baby within, and – for the time being anyway – gives me no reason to fly.

'There is no great genius without a mixture of madness.' – Aristotle.

Acknowledgements

This book first started taking shape in 2017. As a lifelong dreamer, the story unfolded easily, but how naïve was I about actually writing a novel. I imagined, that once I had completed the manuscript, the hard work was done. For me, writing the bones of the story was the easy part, turning those bones into a novel which others may want to read was the hard part.

I left my project to gather dust for a while, and would occasionally reread it and make a few amendments, still ignorant of many of my errors. Finally, this year, I dusted it down and engaged my mother-in-law on the case. As an avid reader, Liz knows a thing about books and having read it through put me straight on hundreds of silly errors. I then started working with a professional editor Judith Leask, who has helped me bring it up to publishing standard. So, I have Liz and Judith to thank for making me pull my socks up and produce a polished piece of work.

As a debut author, who has 'gone it alone', I don't have a team around me advising me constantly and picking up the slack when I want an evening off. Instead, I have my family – all of them. Everyone has believed in me, but especially Martin, Luke and Maddie for tolerating hearing about the endless formatting issues, my procrastination over book covers and my eagerness to move on to my next novel before completing this one. Writing a book is a truly herculean effort by everyone concerned, so thank you.

Printed in Great Britain
by Amazon

53489098R00244